Delta Redemption

SEAL TEAM PHANTOM
Book 6

By Elle Boon
elleboon@yahoo.com

Delta Redemption, SEAL Team Phantom 6
Copyright © 2017 Elle Boon
First E-book Publication: 2017
Cover design by Valerie Tibbs of Tibbs Design
Edited by Tracy Roelle

Dedication

I'd like to give a big huge thank you to all my family and friends. Y'all have been such an amazing group who have kept me grounded through all the ups and downs. Without you, I'd have probably gone crazy this past year. Well, crazier anyhow.

Thank you to all who've read my stories and wanted more. I hope you enjoy Jase's journey as it's a doozy. I know that the road to a happily ever after isn't always smooth and hope I gave y'all one hell of a ride with his story.

In this story you're going to see some real issues people face. There are real life tragedies that many of us have had to deal with, and one of those I touch on in this story. Suicide affects many of us, and for me and my family, it hit home a little over six years ago. A beautiful young man, took his own life at the young age of nineteen.

They say suicide is the cowards' way out, but all I know is that we are now left with a huge hole from the loss of our loved one. The statistics for suicide are crazy with 121 in every 100,000. I truly do believe in helping where we can, so if you know of someone who is suicidal, or if you are, please reach out to someone for help. There are people who care and would be there. With such a large number of suicides across our nation a day on average, the thought that a simple call or letter could help to prevent one, seems little in the grand scheme of things.

You can now talk to someone at the National Suicide Protection Helpline or even text. Here's the link to their site if you know of anyone in need. https://suicidepreventionlifeline.org/

Love y'all so hard,
Elle

Other Books by Elle Boon

Erotic Ménage
Ravens of War
Selena's Men
Two For Tamara
Jaklyn's Saviors
Kira's Warriors
Shifters Romance
Mystic Wolves
Accidentally Wolf & His Perfect Wolf
Jett's Wild Wolf
Bronx's Wicked Wolf
Paranormal Romance
SmokeJumpers
FireStarter
Berserker's Rage
A SmokeJumpers Christmas
Mind Bender, Coming Soon
MC Shifters Erotic
Iron Wolves MC
Lyric's Accidental Mate
Xan's Feisty Mate
Kellen's Tempting Mate
Slater's Enchanted Mate
Dark Lovers
Bodhi's Synful Mate
Turo's Fated Mate
Contemporary Romance
Miami Nights
Miami Inferno

Rescuing Miami, Dallas Fire & Rescue
Standalone
Wild and Dirty, Wild Irish Series
SEAL Team Phantom Series
Delta Salvation
Delta Recon
Delta Rogue
Mission Saving Shayna, Omega Team
Protecting Teagan, Special Forces
Delta Redemption

Chapter One

"It's a shame to have lost him like that. He was a great man."

Jase grunted as he shoveled dirt on another grave. Damn shame when you lose a loved one, but the only sympathy he felt was for the people left behind. Not the man himself. The sun beat down on him while he and Greg worked side-by-side, putting the final mound of dirt over another fresh grave. Greg, clearly a devoted employee of the cemetery, also was up on who was who in the town. "It's a shame to lose a good soldier," Jase said instead of agreeing. The older man leaned on the shovel, squinting at the gathering in the distance, nodding at Jase's words.

The wig and prosthetics Jase wore itched, but he wanted to see the bastard being put in the ground; six feet under wasn't deep enough to hide his sins.

His eyes strayed to the front row of mourners, stopping on the woman who'd held his heart longer than any other. Hell, she still held it. Wind whipped in from the north, making the hat her mother had on fly off. Brooke Frazee reached up, grabbing it before it could fly away. His first instinct was to go to her and offer his help, but he held it in check. Years as a SEAL and then the last two of being on the outside looking in, kept him in place, knowing anyone could be watching, waiting to take him out with a single, well-placed shot. Shit, he spent six months in a federal prison for crimes he didn't commit. In that time, it only hardened him, making him into what he was today.

He turned away as the minister continued his sermon, extolling the virtues of the man who was deceased. Admiral Frazee, the man he'd once trusted, a man he'd looked up to and wanted to be like. Jase looked around the graveyard, a prickle of awareness had him searching the shadows. Jase had become good at hiding, blending into those dark areas where nobody could see. Hell, he was forced to become a shadow; a ghost, if his old team were to see him. At first it had burned like acid in his gut knowing that's what they'd think if they were to see him, since they thought he was dead, or they'd want to kill him, either option wasn't appealing.

His mind went back to the last day he'd been close enough to hug his brothers in arms. No, they were more than that. They were his family. He'd done everything to keep them safe and was still doing what he could, only they had no clue.

The main goal had been working to figure out who'd been infiltrating the US Government and selling top secret information on missions. He had been close when he'd discovered the Smirnov's were not only alive and well but had a daughter. That female child was now a young woman who'd been placed in foster care and had been hard to track down, but with the help of his new partner Erik, they'd found her. Her parents had been spies, willing to trade their own lives to find her, and Jase, having the information they needed to reconnect with her, was on the verge of making that final discovery of who was the real mole in the government. He hadn't counted on Kai Swift falling for their daughter, Alexa, and his old SEAL team being the one to protect not only her, but the Smirnov's in the end.

Luckily for him, the bastards he'd been working undercover for at the time had a man who looked enough like him. The explosion Jase had set was one that ensured everything in its vicinity would be toast. He'd watched, timing it perfectly as his old SEAL team had arrived to see the other man in the vehicle. Everyone assumed it was Jase. With the level of heat and the amount of time the fire had burned before they'd been able to put it out, there was nothing left of the child rapist bastard for DNA analysis. Hell, he'd gone to Federal Prison for his country. What's being blown up and buried and letting others think he was dead in the grand scheme of things?

*****

Brooke wiped a stray tear as she watched her mother adjust her hat. The men and women dressed in their white Navy uniforms stood out amongst the rest of the mourners, but they were remarkable to see. However, for her, she just wanted to go home and pretend this day was over. Once the chaplain finished speaking, the soldiers began removing the flag, holding it up and over the bright silver coffin. She flinched as the first shot rang out. The twenty-one gun salute, signaling the end to a life. For her father, his time on earth had ended, now the time for her...them, to go on without him would begin. The truth of that last bit hit her square in the chest, nearly doubling her over with the pain.

"It's not fair," she whispered.

Her mother squeezed her fingers tightly. "Ssh, we must be strong. We're Frazee's, girl."

She was so sick of hearing that. Like the woman knew what it meant to be a real Frazee. Hell, she was a socialite who'd done nothing but bemoan the fact she was married to a military man. The only reason her mother was showing any remorse was because she was in public, and it was the right thing to do. Hello, it would be crass for her to not cry. Out of the corner of her eye, she watched as her mother did the whole dab dab beneath her own eyes again as if she was truly shedding a tear for her deceased husband.

When the soldiers began folding the flag from her father's coffin, she bit her lip so hard the taste of copper filled her mouth. The soldiers made their way to her and her mother, she knew they were going to present it to the widow, knew it was tradition, but Brooke also knew her mother would toss it into the closet, or even worse the trash when they got home.

Holding her arms out as they neared, she dared her mother to intervene. There was a moment of hesitation before the young man tasked with presenting the flag knelt down on one knee, his face shadowed with sadness. Emotion clogged her throat while he whispered words of condolences, words she was sure they said each time they had to present a flag. Hating herself for thinking so poorly when he was being so kind. "Thank you for doing this for him. He would have been honored," her voice cracked on the last words.

He gave a brief nod of his head, the signal he was done she assumed, then her father's flag was laid in her arms, its weight insignificant in the grand scheme of things. She pressed it to her chest, trying her damnedest to hold the grief inside. Her father, the man who'd taught her how to tie her shoes, to ride a bike, to hit a ball and to rebuild the 351 Windsor engine in her beloved 1974 Bricklin SV-1. Mark Frazee was more than just a soldier; he was her hero, beloved father. Now he was dead. Tears fell unheeded at all the things he'd never get to do with her, like walk her down the aisle, and teach her son how to play football. All the things he'd taught her to do. She looked up at the clear blue sky and made a silent promise to him and herself. She'd do everything for Jack that her dad did for her, everything his own father couldn't do.

A funeral wasn't the place for a little boy. Hell, a funeral wasn't the place for anyone, but especially a little boy. Yet, looking over her shoulder she found her son sitting with her best friend and her husband, sleeping soundly. His dark hair reminded her of the one man she wished she could forget. Her one regret, but the one man who gave her her greatest love.

"That was truly uncalled for, but I guess you're good at doing things like that," her mother whispered.

Brooke met dark eyes with so much hate in them. "Maybe so, but we both know you don't deserve this or want it. Don't make a scene, mother," Brooke said in a tone too low for anyone other than her mom to hear. God, she hated the woman who birthed her with a passion that reminded her...nope she wasn't going there today.

Her father had been a career Navy man, going through the ranks from SEAL to Vice Admiral. She had no doubt he'd one day make it to the very top, except his best friend held that position. Her eyes shifted to the Chief of Naval Operations, her godfather. He made a striking figure in his Navy uniform. Even in his late fifties, he was handsome and clearly very fit with his salt and pepper hair. His dark blue eyes met hers. For a moment, Brooke thought she saw a hardened gleam in them as if he disliked her, but then, they softened as they always had.

She turned back to face the casket. God, this couldn't be happening to her. She thought back to the day a week ago. How a call could rock the very foundation of her world seemed impossible, until they'd explained her father had been killed in a car accident, a fact that was hard to deny no matter how much she wished it wasn't true. It still didn't seem real. They'd had their customary weekly dinner the night before. In hindsight her father had been a little distracted, but like always, he'd brushed her questions aside and focused on her and Jack. Now, she wished she'd pushed him for more time, that's what survivors do, wish for more. Supposedly, he'd driven into the lane of an oncoming diesel truck. Of course, it had been late and there were no witnesses. The truck driver had told the cops the car came out of nowhere without any lights. However, none of that explained why his car had exploded; the fire getting hotter than a normal one, destroying all but the metal of the vehicle. What they had to bury was literally ashes. The medical examiner believed her father hadn't suffered before his death. That small bit of information was the only thing that gave her comfort.

"Lord, it's hot," her mother muttered.

Brooke shot the woman who birthed her a quelling glance. "I'm sure it wouldn't look odd if you were to get up and go back to the limo. Everyone would assume you were too upset to continue sitting through the rest of the service." To those looking in, her parents had a perfect relationship, but Brooke knew better. Her mother was a righteous bitch. She'd given Mark two children, and he gave her a life of luxury. The Frazee's were not only wealthy but connected. Brooke could remember a time when their family was happy. When they were complete. Before her brother died. That day, her entire world was ripped in half, making her parents almost enemies. Her mother blamed her father and even Brooke to an extent. How an eleven year old could be blamed for her eighteen year old brother's suicide, she had no clue. Grief did strange things to people.

Her father was wonderful and had been a good-looking man. Rumors swirled in their small community of infidelity on both sides. Brooke didn't want to admit it now or then. Heck, at eleven the only thing she'd cared about was unicorns and rainbows.

"I think I'll do just that. Do try to hurry...after," Nancy Frazee said, getting to her feet.

The Chief of Naval Operations, her father's best friend, stood up with grace. A look of concern on his face. They both nodded as he helped her mother make her way to the car.

Brooke fingered the folded flag in her lap, knowing where she'd put it in her home. A small sob escaped. One of the soldiers standing offered her a white cloth. God, these men were offering her more comfort than her mother. The empty chair next to her was a startling reminder that her life was forever going to have another huge hole.

Her grandmother reached across the chairs; her fingers squeezed gently. They'd lost their son too. Brooke brought the cloth to her eyes and wiped at the fresh tears. Her father had always said it was okay to cry if you had a reason. Well, today was a damn good reason.

Taking a deep breath, she straightened her spine. She would make her father proud. At twenty-four, she was a single mom to a great kid. She had a job she loved and friends. Yes, there was another hole in her heart and soul from this loss, but like before, she'd plug it and learn to move forward. One breath at a time. One step and then another until before too long, a year will have passed, and the pain won't be so bad. God, she couldn't wait until that day.

*****

Jase watched the emotions flash over Brooke's beautiful features. She'd matured in the years since he'd seen her last. Fuck! The younger version of her had been a stunner at twenty-one, too young for his old ass of thirty. It was almost illegal the things he'd felt for her. It had been a losing battle to keep the feelings at bay for the daughter of the man who had been his idol. Even though the Admiral was the reason the Navy had called to him, from the moment he set eyes on Brooke Frazee, Jase forgot all about why she was off limits and why staying away was wise. When a visit to see the admiral for the first time in years brought him face to face with a gorgeous blonde in a bikini top and daisy dukes, he'd been shocked speechless. His mouth had dried up while his eyes had thankfully been hidden behind his sunglasses. 'Love at first sight' was a phrase that was used in movies and romance novels, but for him, what happened in that moment was something far different. Lust at first sight with a little more. She'd placed a small hand on her chest, right above one small, perfectly formed breast and smiled at him. Jase was sure the sun had shone down on her right then and there. For two years, he'd stayed away. Somebody give him a fucking medal, 'cause sure as shit, if a man deserved one, it was him for being able to avoid contacting her.

He shook the memory away, focusing on the vision in front of him. She'd been having her eighteenth birthday party the first time he'd met her. Now, six years later, she was still the sexiest woman, even with grief etching her face.

"Come on, man, we're done here. I'll show you what we do next."

It took Jase a moment to realize he'd been daydreaming, his body had been moving, doing the job at hand while his mind had wandered. Shit! Way to go Tyler. If he didn't get his head on straight, the next one they'd be burying for real would be him, only he was pretty sure it would be in an unmarked grave. No flag draped casket for him. Why hadn't Admiral Frazee been buried at Arlington Cemetery? Jase shrugged, then picked up the tools they'd been using.

With one last glance toward the crowd gathered under the tent set up for a soldier who didn't deserve the love and respect being shown him, he sighed. Jase had held the Admiral to a high standard, only to find Mark Frazee had sold out his country. His fists clenched in renewed anger at the deception and lives that were destroyed because of the admiral. His eyes sought Brooke one last time, stopping on the sight of her walking back toward the line of limos, holding a small child. Next to her, he saw a couple, their arms around each other as they stayed near Brooke and the kid, ready to stop anyone from getting close. Jase wanted to snort at the absurd notion. If he wanted to get close, he could without breaking a sweat.

He waited 'til she and the others filed into the car, frowning when she didn't get into the lead one with her mother. Instead, she and the child, along with the other couple piled into the second car. Although he still had feelings for Brooke, he couldn't allow them to sway him from his course of action. He'd come to watch his old admiral be buried, not get involved with the one woman who held his attention and heart. Nope, Jase Tyler was dead. In his shoes was Tyler Jackson. The irony wasn't lost on him, but in the new world he was now ensconced in, they made the rules. He just broke them occasionally.

Chapter Two

Brooke buckled her son into his car seat before settling in next to him. Her best friend Brenda and her husband Brian sat across from them. She and Brenda were both hair stylists, while Brian owned a garage. They were so different from the type of people her mother thought she should be friends with, but Brooke didn't listen to Nancy Frazee. They didn't see eye-to-eye on many things, especially the type of people she should associate with. Now, sitting next to her son, she glanced across at the pair who were closer to her than family, giving thanks for not listening to her mother. "Thank you for being here today. I don't think I could've made it through that without knowing you were there for me and Jack."

Brenda reached across the aisle, her long fingers with their hot pink nail polish that matched the tips of her hair made Brooke smile. "You don't have to thank us. I wish the need hadn't been there, but you know Brian and I will always be here for you. Do you want us to take Jack back to your place or ours for the night?"

She thought of allowing her friends to take her son home with them. There, he'd have another child to play with and not a crying mother, because as sure as the sun sets each night, Brooke knew she'd be a mess when she got home, but she wasn't going to take advantage of her friends. Taking a deep breath, she shook her head. "No...I know you both have to work early tomorrow. Besides, Carly isn't feeling well, and your parents...well, I know you'd like to have her with you tonight." The funeral would be followed by a small reception at her parents' home. When Brooke had offered to help her mother with the preparations, Nancy had coldly informed her she was having it handled by a professional organizer.

"Your dad was a good man," Brian said breaking into her thoughts.

She reached for the bag that had been left in the car, pulling out a tissue and wiping her eyes. "Yes he was," she agreed.

The next couple hours were going to be some of the hardest as she would have to listen to men and women tell her how sorry they were for her loss. God, why did he have to...no, she couldn't allow herself to ask questions as to why things happen.

"If you two don't want to come in, you can take Jack and go either to my place or yours. I'll give you a key to my apartment so you can..."

Brenda placed her hand over Brooke's. "I've got this. If you don't need us, we'll take him and head out. We'll go to your place, since it's got all his stuff there."

Brooke looked at her family home, seeing the vehicles already beginning to fill the street and driveway. "This is no place for a two year old." She opened her mouth to say thank you, but a glance at Brenda's face let her know it wasn't needed.

"Thankfully, I parked on the road this morning," Brian muttered as he motioned to the cars blocking the driveway.

Brooke looked down at her sleeping baby. He was getting so big. He'd lost his father and now his grandfather. Heck, before he was ever conceived, before she was old enough to think of sex, his uncle had committed suicide. Was every man in her life doomed? There was no way in hell she'd allow anything or anyone to harm one hair on his dark head; she silently swore, running the back of her fingers over one plump cheek. "If you need me for any reason, call me. I don't care what time or how small, you holler. He's my everything." She kissed Jack's cheek then unbuckled him before passing him to Brenda.

"You know I will. We'll take him to your place where all his things are and let him go crazy," Brenda promised.

Brian got out first, holding the door open for Brenda and Jack, waiting until Brooke got out then shutting it. "Do you need anything before we leave?" he asked, his bright blue eyes looking around the yard.

She shook her head, leaned up on her toes and kissed her sleeping boy. "You can let him climb the walls if you want, just take care of him. I'll call you when I get ready to head home. Thanks for being here you two."

Her friends left, taking all the happiness with them. Lord, now she had to go inside the house that no longer felt welcoming. Straightening her shoulders, she took a deep breath. Her father had always told her that believing in oneself was half the battle. He'd talked about going into meetings, or battles, not knowing what the outcome would be exactly but told her to always believe you'd be the victor and you would be. That belief he said had kept him alive on more than one occasion. Why she felt like she was going into battle she had no clue, but anytime she faced her mother without her father as a buffer, it seemed that way. "She's your mother, not a...well, she's sort of like the evil queen, but she's still your mother," she muttered as she made her way to the front door.

The sense that she'd entered someone else's home slammed into her. Whereas before, the living room was filled with her father's memorabilia, now, it looked as if it had been overhauled by someone with a black and white canvas. She couldn't stop the gasp of shock as she searched for the family photos that used to adorn the fireplace mantel. "Mother, what have you done?" The whispered words escaped from a throat gone dry.

"Pardon me, ma'am, are you okay?" A voice asked from beside her.

Brooke looked at the woman, wondering who the hell she was.

"I'm Helen, the housekeeper. Can I get you a drink of water perhaps?" The thin, grey haired woman asked.

She took a moment to collect herself, taking in the changes her mother had made in the last week since her father had been killed. For crying out loud, Nancy Frazee hadn't wasted a moment to make sure her father was erased from more than just the earth.

"Where is my mother?" she asked the housekeeper.

The woman's eyes widened. "My apologies. I didn't...I will escort you to her quarters."

"This is my home I think I know where my mother's bedroom is, thank you." Brooke nearly growled. Hell, she may have if the woman's step back was anything to go by.

"If you need anything, I'll be in the kitchen."

Brooke felt sorry for being so harsh and made a mental note to find the woman and apologize. It wasn't her fault that the lady of the house hadn't told her she had a grown daughter. God, what else had her mother changed. A knot formed in her stomach. Her brother's room had sat like a shrine since the last day he'd been alive. Nothing was allowed to be moved with the exception of what her mother took, and that was only for cleaning purposes, to Brooke's knowledge. However, Brooke's old room was now a guest room. None of her old stuff was allowed to linger after she'd moved out, except a few tubs and boxes in the basement.

She stopped at the double doors that led to her parent's bedroom. Taking a deep breath, again she squared her shoulders, feeling like she was getting ready to face a den of lions. Her mother wasn't a sweet woman, but she hadn't been an...ogre. Well, she was, but Brooke wasn't going to allow that to stop her from confronting the woman who birthed her. Nancy Frazee had another think coming if she thought it was okay to toss her father's things out.

Brooke raised her hand and knocked. "Mother," she said while giving the door two hard knocks. At first, she didn't think her mother was going to answer, and then, the door was opened by a man she'd known her entire life. "Admiral Davis, what are you doing in my father's bedroom?" Brooke looked past him, pain lashing at her when she didn't recognize anything of her father inside.

"Hello, Brooke. How are you holding up, dear?" The admiral's hands gripped her bare arms, giving them a gentle squeeze before he pulled her in for a hug.

Brooke's eyes narrowed as he carefully sidestepped her question. The stern man had always made it hard for her to accept any form of affection from him. There was always an aloofness to him that her father had said came with the position he held. Now, as she stepped away from his embrace, the feeling that the older man just didn't like her made her rub her arms. "I'm fine, Sir. I'd like a moment alone with my mother please."

The sight of the slightly rumpled bed had Brooke's eyes narrowing on the couple.

"Not now, Brooke. I have guests I need to greet." Nancy stood, smoothing down her black Dior dress.

The memory of the last time Nancy had worn the dress flashed into her mind. It was when Mark Junior was laid to rest. That day would forever be burned in Brooke's brain as Nancy had tossed the dress off after raging at Brooke's dad in the hallway. At eleven, Brooke had picked it up and hung it in her mom's closet, only to have gotten slapped across the face for daring to touch her mother's things. Of course, the incident had been brushed away by her mom like every other such time, because she'd been drunk like many other occasions. Yes, her mother was an ogre.

"Yes now, mother. I'm pretty sure you don't want me asking you in front of your guests where the hell my father's things are, do you?" Brooke moved around the admiral who seemed to have become her mom's bodyguard.

Nancy's blue eyes narrowed. "You don't speak to me that way, young lady. Not in my home."

Her mother's voice became calmer the angrier she got. The fact her tone was level let Brooke know Nancy was seething. "This was my father's home; the house he built and paid for. His body isn't even cold and buried, yet, look around, you've almost erased him from the place." She was shaking as she took in the master bedroom and how different it was from her last visit just over a month ago. "What the hell did you do, have renovators on standby, just in case?"

"That's enough," the admiral said, gripping Brooke's arm. "Your father wouldn't want you and your mother arguing. Grief does different things to different people. I'm sure your mother has your father's things in a safe place." He looked over his shoulder.

Nancy nodded. "I just couldn't look around everywhere and know he was never c...coming back to me. Everything I touched reminded me of him, so I called and had it changed," she cried.

Brooke stared at her mother, thinking she was putting on a good show for the admiral. She could always tell when her mom was faking it to get her way. Just like she was attempting to now. "What about his study? Did you get rid of him there as well?"

Her mother sniffed. "No, that room hasn't been touched. Yet. Listen, darling, I don't want to fight with you. This has been a stressful week. Let's get through the rest of this circus, and then, when the will is read, we'll sit down, and you can have whatever you want of your father's."

The finality of the reading of a will had tears welling. "When? Do you know when that is?" Please don't let it be today.

"The lawyers are supposed to call me. I'm assuming in the next couple days. Now, if you don't mind, I need to go out and play hostess."

Her mother stood tall and regal as always, no sign of the fake tears showed, reminding her of the master manipulator Nancy Frazee was.

"Mother, a word of warning. Don't let me find out you've gotten rid of one thing of my father's," Brooke warned her mom.

Nancy stopped and looked Brooke in the eye. They were both blonde and stood about the same height of five feet seven inches tall. While Brooke wore a pair of two-inch wedges, her mother had on a pair of stiletto's giving her an extra inch or two in height. Her mother was also thin like Brooke, but there was where their similarities ended. She had tattoos and several piercings, while her mother abhorred anything that wasn't classy and in her mother's words, posh darling. The scent of Chanel No. 5 wafted through the air as Nancy exited, stopping outside. "You coming?"

She took a deep breath then wished she hadn't. Her mother's perfume was one she would always hate as it reminded her of the woman. Gah, get over it, Brooke.

Like a good soldier, she took one last look around her parent's...no, it was her mother's room now, then followed at a slow pace. Lord, she hoped there weren't going to be any more surprises today.

By the time they entered the large family room, it was filled with friends and coworkers of her father's. Brooke's face hurt from smiling or attempting to at least. She didn't want to listen to the stories of how such and such met her father or how great of a man he was. Her father was the greatest, and she didn't need anyone else telling her things she already knew.

Knowing she couldn't stay a moment longer, Brooke looked around for her mother, finding her leaning against the admiral. The image seemed too cozy for Brooke, but again, he was like a member of their family. She took a shuddering breath and eased out one of the french doors that led to the backyard. The summer sun had gone down while she'd been inside, leaving the lawn in shadows. Small lights lit up around the pool, along with twinkling ones along pathways so people could see where they were going. Brooke didn't need any lights to be able to navigate to the treehouse she and Mark had used. As she stood under it, her thoughts of one day watching Jack play inside were evaporating. After Mark had died, Brooke and her mother's relationship became even more strained. Her older brother was the one their mom had doted on, the beloved one, and when he was gone, it was as if a light had died inside Nancy, too. Death did strange things to people, and for Nancy Frazee, it made her a cold-hearted bitch.

Brooke thought back to when Mark had died. The pain of losing her best friend and older brother still hurt as if it were only yesterday.

Mark was so vibrant and fun, until his senior year of high school. She wasn't sure what had happened, only knew he'd come home from school with a black eye and several cuts and bruises. When she'd asked him what had happened, Mark had shoved her out of his room and told her to mind her own business.

"*Mark, can I come up there?*" Brooke called up to her brother from below their treehouse. It was really hers now, but for some reason, her big brother was inside.

The sound of breaking glass had her stepping back. "*Jesus Christ, Brookey, can't you just leave me the fuck alone?*"

She bit her lip. Her brother was Brooke's champion, always looking out for her, never raised his voice, let alone cursed at her. "*I'm sorry...I just thought,*" she whispered.

Her brother's bruised face looked over the edge. "*Come on up, peanut.*"

Swiping at the tears on her cheeks, she secured her backpack on before climbing up the ladder. Once inside, she saw whatever Mark broke had been cleaned up, but the scent of alcohol hit her. "*Are you okay?*" The backpack gave her a reason to look away from his tall gangly form.

He let out a sigh. "*Growing up is hard to do, peanut.*"

"*I brought you something to eat since you missed lunch and dinner.*" Brooke showed him what she'd smuggled out of the house, making him laugh. She loved to hear him laugh. He was always so serious that it didn't happen often.

"*Thank you for this.*" He bit into the peanut butter and jelly sandwich. They ate in silence. She handed him a soda when he finished off his second PB&J. "*I'm sorry for yelling at you. You know you'll always be my best friend right?*"

Brooke smiled around the bite in her mouth. "*I'm the peanut to your jelly,*" she agreed.

Mark nodded, but looked away, a strange look on his face.

Brooke wished she knew that would've been the last time anyone saw her brother alive. The last dinner they'd ever eat together. "God Mark, why'd you leave me alone. You said you'd always protect me, but where are you now? I'm all alone now that daddy's gone, too. It's not fair," she whispered brokenly, slapping her hand against the sturdy oak that held so many memories.

*****

Jase watched as Brooke cried out, wishing he could go to her, her pain eating at him. If things were different, he'd be there holding her in his arms, promising that everything would be alright. It would be a lie, but he'd have done his best to ensure she was safe. He waited until she went up to the house, surprised when she didn't go back inside where all the people were. It was no secret there was tension between her and Mrs. Frazee, but surely, in times like these, they'd lean on each other? Keeping to the shadows, he followed Brooke until she got into her neon green Bricklin. He still couldn't believe her father had helped her rebuild such a fast car, let alone allowed her to drive it. The engine roared to life without a hitch, reminding him of the fact she was more than just a gorgeous girl. A tomboy. That was how she'd described herself, but to him, she'd always been all woman.

He ran a hand down his face as she maneuvered the muscle car out of a tight spot with ease then headed away from the house that was no longer her home. Jogging to his rental, he quickly jumped in and followed at a safe distance. His curiosity piqued as the couple who'd been with her at the funeral left her apartment above the salon she owned, without the child, shortly after she arrived home.

With a sigh, he sat back and waited to see what she was up to. More than likely the couple had taken the child to a family member or something, he reasoned. "Fuck, this is the shittiest part of an assignment," he muttered.

Jase didn't mind sitting around in the middle of a desert or even on some frozen countryside watching an enemy camp for days on end. Hell, having done it more than once, it was almost second nature. However, sitting in a rented SUV outside his ex's place hadn't ever been on his list of things to do. The last time he'd left her place, dreams of a future with the stunning beauty were filling his head. Admiral Frazee put a huge gaping hole in those plans, and his heart, that night. Hell, they all knew he wasn't good enough for Brooke when she'd been twenty-one to his thirty, but age didn't seem to matter to them. Looking back, he could see why her father thought differently. He was a SEAL who put his life on the line, while she was...everything he wasn't. Of course, Mark Frazee was a fucking traitor who had risked all their lives and sent him to prison by setting him up. Yeah, he didn't shed any tears for the bastard when the news of the car accident spread.

He tapped his fingers on the steering wheel, wondering why someone had been sent to watch over Brooke. Ever since he'd been freed from Fort Leavenworth, although freed was not really the word most would use since he had been officially a wanted man until he'd faked his death. Jase had been working on the outside trying to find how far up the chain of command the dirt went, but it was slower than he'd hoped. The phone buzzed next to him, it's caller ID showing him it was his contact within the military. "Tyler here," he said in a clipped tone.

"Have you made contact with the admiral's daughter?" The distorted voice asked.

The light from the huge window overlooking the street went out. "That wasn't my mission," he answered.

A sigh came over the line. "How are you supposed to protect the target if you don't make contact?"

His teeth ached as he ground his jaw together. "I wasn't informed that was the mission." Fuck, he didn't think he could be in close proximity to Brooke without wanting to make love to her. Shit, she'd probably smack him upside the head and call him ten thousand names, ones he was sure would blister his ears, and he was a SEAL. When the time came for him to break things off with her, she'd had tears in her eyes, but with her teeth gritted and a dismissive nod, she turned around and walked off. To this day, he hated himself for breaking her heart. Her father was a lying, cheating bastard who had an agenda all his own. How the man could've looked Jase in the eye and told him he loved his daughter and couldn't stand the thought of her being hurt, when all the while he was selling out his country, giving terrorist information that cost hundreds of thousands of lives was still a mystery. Up until then, Jase had thought he was good at reading people, but he'd bought the admiral's story and was sure Brooke hadn't cared for him the way he had her. His mind wandered back to the last night they'd had together.

Chapter Three

Three years ago...

Jase checked the cooler, making sure everything had survived the bumpy road on the way to the secluded spot. He wanted to make tonight special for Brooke and him. He checked his watch then glanced at the door to her parent's house. At twenty-one, he was shocked she still lived at home, but hearing about her brother's suicide and how her mother was still shaken from the loss, he understood. He whipped his head back to the house, the breath nearly freezing in his lungs. "*Holy shit, you look amazing.*" He wasn't sure what surprised him more. The sight of her in a flirty little blue and white polka dot dress or her shy smile. His Brooke was always sexy, but she usually wore jeans or shorts.

"*Why thank you, kind sir. You look mighty fine yourself.*" She did a little curtsey as she said the words, making his dick hard.

He looked back toward the house, wondering if he should go say hi to the admiral. His eyes must've given him away as Brooke leaned up and kissed his cheek. "*My father isn't home. Let's get going,*" she said in a husky whisper.

Damn, everything she did and or said had him harder than he'd ever been, even way back in the days of his youth as a pre-teen with a dirty magazine in his hands. "*In you go.*" He opened the driver's door of his pickup and helped her in, getting a glimpse of her blue panties.

He headed back toward the area he'd set up earlier, hoping she liked the place as much as he did.

"*You gonna tell me where we're going, or do I have to guess?*" She sat next to him on the bench seat, her hand holding his.

"*You'll see.*" He gave her fingers a little squeeze.

The trip took a little over twenty minutes. Jase had never truly enjoyed listening to a woman chatter, but with Brooke, he found he loved it. Her dreams weren't crazy. Attainable would be the word he used.

"*I love the salon I work in now, but I want to own a place that is uniquely mine.*" She let go of his hand and gestured with her hands.

Jase grinned as he watched her move. "*Everything about you is unique.*" And it was, down to the cute little dimples in her cheeks.

A blush bloomed on her face and neck. He wondered just how far south the becoming color went then cursed himself as his cock twitched behind his shorts.

"*You, Jase Tyler, are most definitely a charmer. I like it. What did you pack for us to eat?*" She glanced through the back window at the cooler.

He grinned but didn't answer her as they made their way toward the little slice of paradise. Oh he was sure lots of people had been where he was taking her, but for tonight, it was theirs. Her little gasp of delight had him reaching for her hand again. "*What do you think?*"

"*It's wonderful. I've never been back here before.*" Her gaze took in the large pond with the gazebo on the far side.

"*We can fish, swim, take a little boat ride around the pond. Whatever you want to do. From here we can see the fireworks from the ball game without the crowd.*" He turned the truck off and rolled the windows down to allow the cool breeze to blow through.

"*Did you bring fishing poles and live bait?*" Brooke turned in the seat with one leg on the bench, her eyes shining with happiness.

He snorted. "*Of course, what kind of fisherman would I be if I didn't come prepared.*" His mind went to other things he'd come prepared for, but he pushed those thoughts to the back of his mind.

"*Well, let's go, then. I bet I catch more than you,*" she teased.

As they fished, her face shone with happiness. Of course, she'd caught more than him, since he kept having to rebait her hook, giving her the chance to put her line back in more often. He didn't mind in the least, since his reward was a kiss, which usually led to him losing his own bait. "*You're speaking to the fish, aren't you?*" he teased.

By the time they were done fishing, they were both hungry. Their dinner was packed full of her favorite food from a local café, bought solely because he wanted to please her. "*Come on, let's go eat.*" He led her to the gazebo after grabbing the cooler out of the back of the truck, her tiny hand enclosed in his.

She squealed in delight as they entered. The place was clean and looked nice since knowing they were coming there Jase made sure to set it up earlier, wanting to make it special for her. "*Jase, what did you do? This is beautiful.*"

He shrugged, feeling a little stirring of something, he wasn't sure what to call it, flutter in his heart. Pushing aside the odd sensation, he guided her to the table that was set up in the center. After carefully taking out the food, he sat down opposite her. "*I wanted to take you somewhere special where everyone didn't constantly stare at us. Somewhere we could relax and have fun, just the two of us.*" The farmer had nearly been robbed by some kids trying to steal his wallet, but Jase had saved him, albeit without expecting anything in return. When the old man had recognized him as the young feller who was taking young Brookey around, he'd offered to let him court her out at his old farm. It had been pure coincidence, or fate, for him to help the man out on the same day he was trying to find a place special to take Brooke.

"*Thank you. This has been the best day of my life.*" She ducked her head and started eating.

Jase reached across the table and lifted her chin with his hand. "*Mine, too,*" he said with honesty.

They ate in silence as the sun dropped in the sky, and as they finished dessert, he led her to the grassy embankment that faced the north where the fireworks would go off. "*Tell me your biggest dreams, Brooke. Something you've never told anyone else.*"

"*I wanted to be a singer,*" she said with a laugh.

"*Not a fantasy but your dream for the future. What do you see yourself doing, or what do you want, that you've never told anyone?*" The sound of insects chirping could be heard as silence descended. He didn't think she was going to answer, and that was okay. Not everyone wanted to share their inner most dreams.

"I want to get married and have children. I want to have my own salon where people make appointments, because I'm in demand. And I want my mother to love me," she whispered the last.

He rolled over on his side. Her dreams started an ache in his heart. A family. She wanted a family, something he wanted as well. He placed his hand on her stomach, thinking of her as his. Then, his brow furrowed. *"Your mother loves you."* Having only met Mrs. Frazee once, and while she was sort of cold, he didn't think she disliked her daughter.

Brooke sat up, dislodging his hand. *"No, she doesn't. My mother doesn't love anyone but herself."* She wiped her fingers under her eyes. *"I'm sorry, I don't want to ruin this magical night with thoughts of my mother."* She turned sparkling eyes toward him. *"Make love to me under the stars, Jase."*

His heart raced at her words. Common sense told him to slow down, that she wasn't in the right place emotionally. Then, she leaned over and kissed him and rational thought left him. The feel of her slender body leaning into him snapped his control like a twig, and there, beneath the stars, he lost his heart and soul to Brooke Frazee.

Jesus, he'd fallen so hard for her. They'd made love under the stars, and again while the fireworks had gone off, making their own explosion together.

When he drove her home, she'd never looked more beautiful to him. She'd brushed her hair and put her flirty little dress back on. *"I'm keeping these,"* he said holding onto the little blue panties.

"You are such a bad man," she giggled and smacked his arm.

They pulled up to her house, and he cut the engine. *"Come on, I'll walk you to the door."*

"Thank you for making tonight...magical." She ducked her head.

Jase tugged her against him. "This is only the beginning. I plan to have many more nights like tonight with you." He rubbed his cheek against the top of her head.

At the back of the house, he gave her a long kiss goodnight, hating to part with her, waiting until she was inside, and he heard the door lock before he went back around to where his truck sat. He pulled up short as he saw the admiral leaning against the side, anger pouring off the older man.

"Did you have a good time fucking my daughter, soldier?"

Jase's body tightened. *"Don't talk about her like that, Sir."*

"That's my baby girl. Whatever happened between you two is over. Do you understand me? Over!" The admiral stepped forward, his finger stabbing into Jase's chest.

It took all of Jase's willpower not to break the older man's finger as he glared into his eyes. The man's anger was felt in every prod of his finger as he jabbed him right above the heart. *"I believe it's up to the both of us, whether it's over or not, Sir. And with due respect, I care very deeply for your daughter,"* he gritted out when all he wanted to do was tell the man to go fuck himself.

The admiral laughed. *"Boy, you think she cares about you?"* His eyes narrowed. *"Oh, you thought she was single, well she is, but that's only because her and Darron have had a little spat. He'll be back in a few weeks, and they'll be back like they've always been. Your best bet is to pack up tonight and move on, or I promise I will make your military career a living nightmare."* The honesty in the other man's words hit Jase harder than a sledgehammer.

He struggled to keep his temper in check. The thought of Brooke playing him for a fool while her boyfriend was out of town had him clenching his jaw. *"If what you say is true, I'd like to hear it from Brooke."*

"If you want to continue moving up in the Navy, son, I suggest you climb up in that truck and head back to where you came from. My daugh-

ter doesn't need to get mixed up with a soldier boy. Not even one I admired."

Jase didn't miss the fact the admiral spoke in past tense. It was as if he'd already dismissed everything that Jase had accomplished because he'd made the decision to fall for his daughter. *Fuck!* He looked back at the house knowing Brooke was inside and would probably think he screwed her and then left without a backward glance.

"Don't worry about her. Just as soon as Darron gets back, she'll forget all about you and this little thing you two had. I'll make sure she thinks you were called out on a mission so you don't look like a total asshole. She's my little girl. The light of my life. I only want what's best for her." The admiral took a step back, his hands clasped behind his back like the decision had already been made.

"And if I don't agree?" Jase asked.

The admiral's eyes hardened. *"You do have aspirations to be more than what you are now, don't you? Captain, Lieutenant, or even higher?"* The admiral waited a beat, looked up at the sky before staring back into Jase's eyes. *"Believe me, I do have that kind of pull. Don't test me, son."* He reached his hand out to touch Jase's shoulder.

Jase moved out of the way. *"Don't call me son. As of tonight, don't call me anything other than Tyler."* It was a designation a lot of senior officers called those below them, only addressing them by their last names. Jase would never look at Brooke's dad as Mark Frazee, father of Brooke again. No, he was the fucker who took his heart and stomped it into the ground. He jerked the door to his truck open, climbed inside and left without causing a scene.

He jerked awake two days later as he was getting ready to ship out. The feel of a three day old beard was rough against the palms of his hands. He looked around the room, wondering what had pulled him from sleep when he heard the banging on the door. It took him a couple seconds to pull a pair of jeans on over his nakedness, hopping over to the front door in his hurry to see who was there. A peek out the small window made him swear internally and his fist clenched at the vision that met his eyes. Brooke Frazee in all her gorgeous glory stood on the other side of the door, looking as if she'd been crying.

Jase exhaled and opened the door. "*Hey, what's going on?*"

Brooke blinked up at him. "*Why haven't you returned my calls? Why are you ignoring me? Did I do something wrong?*"

He heard the catch in her throat and hated her father and himself even more. "*Babe, you were great. It's just...I'm shipping out tonight as a matter of fact. Didn't your father tell you?*" Jase wanted to kick the asshole in the nuts for lying to him.

She wiped her hands on her legs. "*No. He left the day after our...he left a couple days ago. Just because you're leaving doesn't mean we couldn't have spent more time together. Or even after you left, it doesn't mean we have to,*" she waved her hand between them, "*stop being together.*"

"Yeah, it does. *Long distance relationships don't work, Brooke. I figured it would be better to just break it off. I spoke to your dad.*" He had to look away when he mentioned her dad, or the rage he felt couldn't be hidden. Just looking at her made him want to pull her into his arms and promise to keep her safe, yet knowing her father would rain hell down on him and her kept him on his side of the door.

"*So, you're saying you used me for what? A good time? A wham bam thank you—*"

Jase couldn't let her continue thinking he thought that way. It was one thing to leave and for her to think he was shipped out, but another to have her think he thought less of her. He covered her mouth with his, pulling her body into his. The instant connection had her softening against him, moaning into his mouth. God, he wanted to spin on his heels and take her to bed, take her far away and not have to answer to the admiral. However, reality reared its head with an incessant ringing from Brooke's purse, breaking the moment.

She gasped and shoved against his chest, struggling to find her phone. Her eyes squeezed shut then opened. "*It's my mom.*"

He nodded, waiting for her to answer. The distraction allowed him to refocus and look across the street to see a black sedan with tinted windows. His eyes narrowed as he watched the car move forward, the very fact the vehicle had the fine hairs on his neck standing up made him reach for Brooke.

"*I'll be right home, mother,*" she said in an agitated tone.

Jase dropped his arm. She wasn't his to protect. Hell, more than likely the car was following Brooke on the admiral's orders. "*I assume you're leaving?*" He couldn't hide his displeasure of her father from his tone.

"*My mom has...issues and needs me to stop and get her prescription. When do you leave, Jase?*" Her eyes lifted to his bare chest.

"*This afternoon,*" he answered. "*Listen, Brooke. You deserve better than I can give. Go home to your mother and your fancy house. When your boyfriend Darren, what's his name, returns you can lie and pretend I never existed. Pretend this thing between us never happened. The most I'd be able to give you is a life of uncertainty, fear and a good time in the sack. Is that what you want, another round with me, only this time on a bed?*" Taking a deep breath, he put his hand on her arm. "*I'm sorry, that was uncalled for. You deserve better.*"

"*So, this is goodbye then?*" She inhaled deeply and took a step back.

He could see the hope in her eyes that his answer would be no. Hell, maybe that was his own hope reflected back at him. His throat clogged up, unable to form words, he nodded once. His teeth ached from gritting them to keep from begging her to wait for him. No, her father wouldn't allow them to find any peace or happy ever after together. It was better to let her go now before either of them got in too deep.

She didn't say goodbye, which he could tell cost her, the same pain sliced through him. Instead, she turned on her wedges and walked away. Jase shut the door, unable to watch her walk out of his life. In that moment, he wished with all his being that Admiral Mark Frazee would go straight to hell. After five minutes passed, he made his way to the bedroom and packed his stuff, knowing he couldn't be in the same town as Brooke and not see her, not go crazy with wanting to be with her.

Once he had his things in his duffle, he walked out the door. "*There you go, admiral. Go fuck yourself,*" he muttered as he took the steps two at a time down to his truck. His hometown was no longer going to be a place of solace. He'd made a huge error when falling for the admiral's daughter, thinking he was good enough for her. Jase hardened his resolve as he drove away, knowing his heart was forever going to be left with a blonde haired beauty with hazel eyes.

*****

Jase scrubbed his hand over his face, wishing he could forget the pain in Brooke's eyes. Pain that he'd caused, especially with everything he knew now. Her father had been playing a deadly game at the time and didn't want Jase anywhere around where he would overhear something he shouldn't. "Bastard was a traitor." Jase pinched the bridge of his nose and looked in the mirror. With the prosthetics on, he hardly recognized himself. He tugged until the pieces of fake skin came off, looking through the console he pulled out a wet wipe and cleansed the glue from his face.

A year after walking away, he'd been in the middle of Kuwait when his team met up with another. Jase still couldn't believe the proof that had landed in his hands from the team leader just before the man had died. He fingered the leather cuff on his wrist, a constant reminder of their sacrifice, the titan symbol burned into both sides reminded him of where he'd come from and those who lost their lives that night, including him.

To have been close to exposing Frazee as the man behind the other teams' slaughter, only to be blamed himself was like a shot through the heart. His own team thought it was he who'd turned on them. A mirthless laugh escaped as he thought of Kai and the rest of his team. Of course, they believed the evidence stacked against him. The men who'd created it were good and had the technology to create unmistakable proof. The only thing they didn't have was a confession from Jase, and they never would. The golden ticket came in the form of a breakout of prison scheme, along with a chance to prove his innocence with help from the government. "Fucker had to go and get killed before I could get my redemption, jackhole." Jase stared out the windshield, watching as the lights went out at the apartment above the salon and day spa. "I wonder what mommy dearest thinks of you waiting on customers?" The few times he'd met Nancy Frazee the woman had given him the cold shoulder. The woman didn't like to rub elbows with those below her in status and made it clear to all those in their town.

He settled down to rest his eyes. Tomorrow, he'd watch and see who would approach Brooke. Somehow, he'd have to figure out a way into her parents' house and knew it wouldn't be by trying to be nice to the woman he still cared for since by all accounts he was dead, and she wasn't going to trust just anyone. Mark Frazee may be dead, but the man wasn't working alone, and until he knew she wasn't a target, watching over her would be his job. His phone buzzed in his pocket. As he glanced at the encrypted message, he grimaced. "I swear to fucking all that's holy, I will smash your head in," he swore as an image of Brooke at the funeral came across the phone from an unknown number.

Jase forwarded the image to his tech guy, the one who'd gotten him out of a federal maximum security prison as if he was just taking a stroll around the park. Yeah, Erik was a genius, but he was also a crazy shit who scared most people on his good days.

His phone lit up with an incoming call. "What's up, Erik?"

Erik grunted. "You watching that pretty little blonde like a lost puppy?"

Jase switched the phone to his other hand so he could look around the dark neighborhood. "You got cameras on me?" An image of the big, tatted up, battle scarred man, sleuthing around the dark putting up hidden cameras, made him laugh.

"Man, I told you. If there's video surveillance anywhere in the vicinity, I can tap into it." Satisfaction rolled through the air.

"Yeah and what did I tell you. You can tap wires, I can tap ass." Jase tried to find where Erik was watching from.

Erik's deep chuckle had him glaring at the phone. "Sure and I'm Prince Charming. Hell, you're probably the next thing to a born-again virgin. If women can say they've regrown a hymen, what can men who ain't had no action in a few years claim?"

He raised his middle finger in the air, even though Erik couldn't see him. "Fuck off and fuck off again, Erik. I had more action in my thirty plus years of life than you'll ever see in your entire life."

"You keep telling yourself that. Alrighty, on to more important things. It seems the elder Frazee mama has gotten rid of most of the stuff in the house in the past few days, except the admiral's office. Now, here's the interesting part. It looks as if his old buddy is spending an awful lot of time there consoling the widow, if you know what I mean," Erik growled the last. Neither of them cared for cheaters.

"See if you can find out if they were an item before his death. Be careful, I don't trust him."

He could picture Erik glaring daggers at him through the line. "You didn't just question my abilities. Do I say to you '*Oh, Ty, be careful out there, those men are so big and bad?*' No, so don't question my abilities."

Jase laughed as Erik's voice pitched to the level of Erik's version of a woman then back to normal at the end. "I apologize. Now go do your thing and let me get some rest."

"Watch your six, man. You went to prison and lost everything over that woman there."

"No, I went to prison and lost everything because her father was a fucking traitor who pinned it on me. This goes a lot higher and deeper than him. I aim to find out just how high and get my name back." He rubbed the cuff again.

"Hooyah, brother. Remember, failure isn't an option. It's the opportunity to begin again more intelligently." Erik Branson's deep timber settled his raging emotions. The SEALs familiar saying had him smiling as the other man tacked on the additional bit at the end.

"You're a smart man. One day, you'll make someone a fine husband." Jase jerked his head up to the upper floor of Brooke's apartment as a light came on.

"Don't even joke about that shit. Listen, your girl's moving around, and there's movement behind her place. Looks like a couple shadows in the shape of men." Erik's teasing tone had been replaced with the one Jase recognized as all business.

Sliding out of his vehicle silent as a ghost, he made sure he had his weapons in place before switching on his communications device to his ear. "Where are they now?"

"One is looking upward as if he's thinking of scaling the brick wall. She has two entries and exit points. The one in the front and one in the back. Her back door looks to be solid and has a gate in front of it that's proving to be an issue for them. Shit! They're moving to the side of the building between the alleyway. I don't have camera access there."

Jase cursed quietly as he headed for the building. "Did they both go that way or split up?" His need to protect Brooke had him sweating.

"Looks like they went together, but I have no visual," Erik cursed.

He mentally went through scenarios on what were his options. "I'm going in the front and getting to Brooke first. Have everything I'll need for them ready in two hours. I'll check back with you when we're settled in one of the safe houses."

"Already on it. I think they're either working to get to her floor via the side or are already on their way up. When I scouted the area earlier, there wasn't an easy access there. They'd have to have climbing tools, which I didn't see on them."

He wasn't taking chances. The men clearly thought she had something they wanted, or they were going to use her for their own purposes. He'd be damned before he allowed one hair on her head to be harmed. "You got access to the front?" He paused at the security lock to the salon entrance.

A few beeps later and the red light turned green. "Not too secure," he muttered.

"Actually, it was pretty good. I'm just better." The sound of tapping let him know Erik was working away at his computers. "There's another door leading to the stairs inside. I'm assuming that's the way up to her apartment. Shit! It looks like she's got a keycode entry but also a physical one. When's the last time you did a little B&E?"

Jase didn't answer him as he crept through the salon to the back entrance that led to the apartment upstairs. Even though she had a separation from her home and clients, he still didn't like the fact she was exposed. Hell, a truly determined criminal wouldn't be deterred by a few locks. "I can't believe her father allowed her to live here," he growled as he reached the back.

"She's a twenty-four year old woman. Pretty sure the days of her father telling her where she could live ended a long time ago." Erik's tone sounded distracted.

He didn't bother correcting his friend. If the admiral had any say in the matter, Brooke would live where he allowed and do what he said for the rest of her life. However, now that the old man is dead, she no doubt would be making up her own mind. He had to wonder what she planned to do. The woman he'd met and fallen for had been young but headstrong to a point. Not many twenty-one year old men or women lived at home if they didn't have to, and from what he knew, she'd had the means to move out at the time. He shook off the memories of the past, focusing on the deadbolt.

Pulling a small kit out of the inner pocket of his jacket, he took his time as he worked the picks into the lock. "Are the alarms disengaged?" he asked.

A grunt was his answer as the lock slid open. When no blaring noise sounded he pulled the door shut behind him, locking it in case the men somehow found their way inside. No reason to make it easy for them.

"Movement by the front. I only see one man, though."

Jase could picture Erik with his long hair unkempt as he sat in front of several computers. His body was as big as a tank, but he could work magic on a keyboard. Most would look at him and assume he was one thing, with his tattoos and muscular build, but the man was one of the smartest individuals Jase had ever known. Heck, even up against Taylor Rouland, the computer expert from SEAL Team Phantom, Erik could probably teach him a thing or two. The thought of his old team, the men who believed he was a traitor, brought a slight ache to his chest. Once he found who was selling out their government, setting things right with his team would be a priority. The constant cloak and dagger was a fine line to walk, and he was getting tired. When the CIA pulled him into the mission, having nothing to lose, it was a no-brainer. Facing a life in USDB at Fort Leavenworth for crimes he hadn't committed, Jase couldn't sign on the dotted line fast enough. His only stipulation had been his team, Kai and the rest of his friends were not to be brought in. No way in hell was he going to sacrifice his life if they weren't safe.

The sound of a woman's voice singing a lullaby had him slowing his steps. He cocked his head to the side, listening for any other noise.

"She must be watching the kid for her friends," Erik said.

Jase had already figured that out, thank you very fucking much. He refigured his plans on getting her and the kid out safely. First, get them to a safe spot in the apartment then eliminate the immediate threat. As he approached the room with the light trickling out where the singing was coming from, he made no sound, but his body was responding to hearing the woman who'd starred in his dreams, singsong voice. Telling his unruly dick to ignore something it had wanted for the past three years was like telling a moth to stay away from a flame. Impossible. Shit, being celibate for the last three years had been easy until he was within touching distance of the woman who held his soul.

He eased around the door frame, needing to check out the rest of the apartment before he faced the one he let go. The living room opened up to the kitchen, with a small eating nook tucked into the corner. The only thing that separated the rooms into different spaces was a large counter that had barstools for extra seating as well. He checked out the hall bathroom, noticing kids toys and accessories neatly stacked on the shelves with the glow from a nightlight. Across the hall was another bedroom. His curiosity had him pushing the door open slightly, the creak the old door made had him stilling his movements. A quick look inside the space showed him it was the master bedroom, done up in soft peaches and baby blue. The very feminine room made his lips twitch. No way was a dude spending too much time in the ultra girlie room. He traced his eyes over the large bed in the center of the room. Picturing Brooke laying there had him moving toward the bathroom before his imagination went nuts and he ended up going over and sniffing the bed, or some other stalker ass shit.

"Looks like our guy out front is playing look out. Have you heard or seen movement inside, well, other than the lovely singing?" Erik's amused tone had Jase narrowing his eyes. He didn't like the thought of the other man hearing Brooke. Damn, he was losing his ever-loving mind.

Knowing he was somewhat safe and that he could still hear Brooke, he glanced around the master bedroom and then went to the window overlooking the side. "Nothing so far." From where he stood, the vantage point gave him a view of the wrong side of the building. Which meant the guy could possibly be scaling the wall leading to the room across the hall. "I'm going for Brooke and the kid. If he's making his way up, it'll be on the opposite side." The large closet would work for a place to stash them.

Jase opened the door, coming to a hard stop at the image of Brooke holding a gun aimed at his midsection. He raised his hands, wondering where the kid was. "Hello, Brooke."

She gasped. "Jase?"

He tilted his head to the side, looked behind her as he pictured the guy making his way into the room. Her head turned to see what he was looking at, giving him the opportunity to move forward. In seconds, he had her shoved against the wall, her arm with the gun raised above her head while he pinned her body with his. "I'm not here to hurt you, but there's someone outside who is. I need you to trust me," he whispered close to her ear.

"I'm supposed to trust a man who betrayed his country?" she bit out, struggling against him.

The familiar anger burned in his veins at the accusation. "That's a discussion for another time. Right now, I need you to believe me that you're in danger. There are two men trying to break in, and they sure as fuck wouldn't be holding you against the wall talking to you."

"Oh, and you're different because you happened to already break in. And, let's not forget, you're holding me, quite firmly I might add, against a wall. I'd say you're not much better than those so called men," she spat, wriggling against him. "Really," she gasped as her pelvis came into contact with his.

Jase shrugged. "Sorry, it's a natural reaction whenever I'm around you...oh for fuck's sake, stop it. I'm not going to hurt you. Listen, time is ticking, and if you left the kid in that room alone, he could be in harms way as we stand here arguing." He nodded his head toward the room with light spilling out.

Chapter Four

Brooke froze as the ring of truth fell from Jase Tyler's lips. "Oh, god! Jack. Let me go," she demanded.

"Give me the gun." Jase stared down at her.

She wanted to tell him to go fuck himself, but her baby's life was more important than hating on Jase. "Take it and move away."

The ease with which he did so made her eyes burn with unshed tears, but she battled them back, refusing to allow him to see her hurt.

"Let me make sure it's safe," he ordered.

She rolled her eyes as he released her, watching him tuck her Ruger into the back of his black cargo pants. While he turned to step toward Jack's room, she ducked under his arm, rushing into the room first. Her son would be afraid if Jase's hulking form appeared first, especially with him dressed in all black, like he was some special ops soldier or something. Her heart beat frantically as she knelt down on the colorful rug where Jack was playing with blocks. He looked up, smiling happily as he saw her. "Mama, who's that?" he asked pointing at Jase.

"Come here, big boy." She scooped him into her arms, turning to face Jase with their son against her chest. She waited for recognition to hit him.

"He's yours?"

She watched the Adam's apple in his throat bob as he swallowed. God, the thought of this first meeting had run through her mind a million times, but never had it been when some crazed men were supposedly trying to break in. The need to fill the silence had her opening her mouth then closing it as he raised his hand. "I need you to take your son into your closet and stay there until I eliminate the threat."

Anger poured off him in waves. Brooke wanted to soothe him, but Jack reached his hand out, handing the block to Jase. "Block," Jack said, smiling up at Jase.

Jase blinked down at Jack. "Thank you, little man." He looked up at Brooke. "Go on," he said in a toneless whisper.

Her father had been in the military her entire life. She'd been around enough to know when to obey an order and when not to. The absolute fear for her son had her stepping around him, grabbing Jack's blanket on the way out. Her son loved many things but was truly only attached to the blue thermal blanket with ships on it, which had a silky edge and a teddy bear. Jack's little chubby hands pulled the blanket against his chest as she made for her closet. Why she was listening to Jase, the man who'd left her heartbroken and pregnant, she had no idea. The only thing she was sure of was that Jase was back, and he looked harder. Deadlier. The man in the other room wasn't the same guy from years ago, who made her fall in love with him without even trying. "No matter. We're Frazee's, and we face our battles head on," she whispered as she rubbed her forehead against Jack's.

"We battle, mama?" Jack asked rubbing his eyes.

She stared at the best thing in her life and kissed his nose. "No, little man."

Inside her closet, she put Jack down as far away from the door as she could and pulled out the lockbox. Jase may have taken one of her guns, but she had a spare. She pulled the Sig Sauer P320 out, double checking it was loaded and the safety was on. Her hands shook slightly as she waited for Jase to come or heaven forbid, the other men.

She bundled up a blanket and placed it around the bottom of the door, hoping it kept the light from showing into her bedroom. A glance at her cell phone she pulled from her back pocket showed they'd been in the closet for a little over seven minutes and counting. How long did it take to...eliminate the threat? God, did that mean he was going to kill the men, or was he calling the police? Shit! Should she call 911? Her finger hovered over the screen and stopped. If Jase had told her to call, she would've. Something had her trusting him, even though he'd devastated her. "Cause I'm a fool," she muttered.

One of the old wood floorboards creaked outside in her room. She stepped back, moving the safety off as she held the gun up.

"Brooke, it's okay, it's just me. I'm opening the door," Jase said loudly.

She pushed the safety back on, but kept the gun at her side. "What happened?" she asked as he opened the door, keeping her body between him and Jack.

Jase tilted his head as if knowing what she was doing. "I figured you had another weapon in here," he said instead of answering.

A wet spot on his shirt had her moving toward him. "You're hurt." Her finger stretched toward his side, but he moved out of her reach.

"I'll be fine, just a scratch. Come on, we can't stay here. You need to pack a bag for you and your son. Enough for a few days. Does he need diapers or formula? Crap! How old is he, anyway?"

"He just turned two," she said. "He's potty trained, except at night and I only put trainers on just in case. As for formula," she narrowed her eyes at him. "I breast fed him, so no there wouldn't have been any need for that, but he's two. He doesn't nurse or take a bottle anymore. Do you, big guy?" She swept Jack up as he ambled over to hug her legs. Why she was rambling and telling him things that were none of his business, Brooke didn't know. She turned away from his penetrating gaze.

*****

Jase was struggling with the knowledge that Brooke had not only moved on, but clearly done it so soon after they'd broken up. Hell, the kid was probably Daryl or Darron what's his name's.

He nodded. "That'll make it easier. I'll get you both to a safe house and figure out what's going on."

Brooke took a deep breath. "We need to talk, Jase."

"Yeah, we do, but not here and not now. Those two are...no longer going to bother you, but they could have a backup team waiting for them. We need to move and move quick." He stepped out of her closet, the feeling of being too close to a flame and being burned washed over him, only his flame was a petite blonde with hazel eyes that saw too much. His side throbbed from the knife wound. "I'm going to stand out in the hall and listen for traffic. If you need any help, holler."

She bit her lip. "I'll be quick."

In a time of crisis, the woman did just that. She sat her son on a large faux fur rug, whispering to him as she tickled his stomach. Jase clenched his teeth so hard he worried his next dentist visit would be to replace his back molars. He walked back down the hall, pausing outside the kid's room. He grimaced at the broken window from where the intruder had tried to come in. If little Jack had been in the room, flying shards of glass could have hit him. Whoever sent the hitmen didn't care if there were casualties. Brooke and her son needed to get gone quickly. "Erik, I'm gonna need a clean up here."

"I figured as much. That means it's personal. How much bleach we talking?" His friend sighed loudly.

Jase thought of the two men lying the kitchen. "Roll around back and pick up your delivery. A few gallons will do you."

"Fuuuck, man. Why I always gotta do the dirty work?" Erik groused good naturedly.

Jase stepped back into the hall as Brooke came out of her room with a duffel bag. "I already packed some of Jack's clothes from the laundry I hadn't put away. Let me grab a few of his favorite toys and we can go." She indicated he should step out of the way.

He shook his head. "There's a lot of glass all over the room. I'm not sure if any of it got on his toys or not."

She inhaled loudly. "He's got some in the living room. I'll grab a few from there, and before you veto that, let me tell you a child likes his things. Familiar things keep them happy. You do not want a small child to be unhappy. I promise you that."

His gaze zeroed in on the sturdy little guy staring up at him from his mom's arms. "You're the expert. Let me take your bag."

Jack held his hands out. "Hi, I'm Jack."

He froze, unsure what to do as the boy held his arms out.

"Jack, you want to help mommy pick out some toys to go bye bye with us?"

"No, Jack want him." Jack pointed at Jase.

Brooke's eyes met his. "Can you hold him? It's past his bedtime, and seriously, he's getting heavy. This is the time when things can go two ways. Cranky, or quiet. From previous experience, it's not gonna be the latter."

He watched her bounce her hip with Jack still holding his arms out. Stubborn kid. Holding his arms out, he plucked the boy from Brooke, careful to keep him away from his injured side. "You're gonna be a holy terror when you grow up, aren't you?" Dark eyes stared back at him. If he was a betting man, he'd have bet his last dollar the boy was sizing him up. Ridiculous since the kid was only two.

"You tell stories?" Jack asked.

Jase froze, wondering if all two year old's could talk, and do it well. "Um, not right now. How about we go see what your mom is getting for you. Do you like trains?"

At the mention of trains Jack started making choochoo noises and squirming to get down. Jase couldn't allow him to do that, not unless he had a way of blocking the kitchen access, which he didn't. "Hey, is that your train?" Jase asked trying to distract the wriggling mass of boy in his arms. He looked over to see Brooke with a grin on her face.

"He's a lot tougher than he looks. Come here, Jack. Help me put your toys in the bag." Brooke looked behind the counter, letting Jase know she was aware what was behind it.

Moving so his body was blocking the space, should Jack decide to make a run for the kitchen area, he looked at his watch, gauging the time. "We need to move, Brooke."

"I'm ready," she said, holding onto Jack's hand.

"We'll go out the front. Do you have a car seat for him?" Jase had come prepared for Brooke, not her and a child. He ran his eyes over the pair, feeling as if he'd missed out on an entire life.

"In my salon, I keep an extra one for...well, emergencies it would seem." She walked past him, only to come up short as he put his hand on her arm.

"I go first. Stay behind me, and do as I say," he ordered.

Her eyes widened then narrowed. "I'm not going to put my son's life in danger any more than it already is, Jase. Clearly, this is your area of expertise, but know this, once we're some place safe, you and I are going to have a talk. Now, lead the way, soldier."

He couldn't control the grin that quirked his lips. Although he did keep himself from bending and covering her saucy lips with his own. Barely.

After double checking the street was clear, he led the way back to his vehicle, cursing the entire way inside his head. His plan had been to make sure she was safe then figure out a way into her father's office. The old man wasn't stupid enough to keep any records in his office at work where the good people of the United States Government would have access, so that left his home. Why did he think this mission was going to be easy?

At his vehicle, he held his hand up. If anyone had been around the SUV while he'd been inside with Brooke, Erik would've alerted him, but it was still second nature for him to double check. He did a quick scan of the car's exterior, looked underneath before opening the back door and placing the car seat inside for Jack. The kid stared at him over his mom's shoulder. Dark eyes pinning him in place as if the kid was daring him to hurt him or his mother. Jase shook off the absurd notion, and indicated it was safe for them to get in.

"I'll ride in back with Jack." Brooke didn't look at him as she fastened her son in.

Jase stopped scanning the streets at her words. "We need to talk, and it'll be a lot easier if I'm not having to look over my shoulder." He'd been doing just that for the past several years and didn't want to have to do it in the vehicle if he didn't have to.

Brooke let out a puff of air, drawing his gaze to her chest. When they'd been together, she'd been tall and slender. Not much had changed except her body had filled out a little more. His fingers itched to trace the curves of her body that didn't appear the same. He'd loved her tomboy ways, but this version was stunning.

"You're staring, Tyler."

Her use of his new identity had him freezing until he realized she was calling him by his last name, something that was common in military families. "You've changed," he answered, holding the passenger door open for her.

"Yo, you might want to get your asses out of there, Romeo," Erik grumbled. "I'm coming in on your left and really don't want your girl to see me pulling in with the cleaning crew, if you know what I mean."

Jase shut Brooke's door before he reached around and buckled her in, chastising himself on the short jog around to his side. He could see the nondescript van at the stop sign a block away. With a quick twist of his wrist, he had the engine on and was buckling up as he put the vehicle in gear. "I'm assuming he doesn't require anything special to eat or drink, right?" A primal urge to punch the bastard who'd knocked Brooke up had him spitting the words out.

"His name is Jack, and no, he doesn't require anything special that you or I don't eat or drink as long as it's healthy. I don't feed him junk or sugary things. I like to make sure he has a well-balanced diet and tries everything on his plate. He has a fondness for the strangest things, so

I let him indulge every once in a while." She crossed her arms over her chest and looked out the window.

Her defensive posture and mama bear attitude made him wish for things he couldn't have. "What do you mean, strange?"

She shrugged, but didn't answer right away. Jase was beginning to think she wasn't going to until he heard her sigh. "He likes peanut butter sandwiches with banana slices on them. It's the strangest thing, 'cause one day I'd made him a sandwich and I had a banana. The little monkey held his hand out and said *nana*. I gave it to him, thinking he wanted my banana. He opened up his sandwich and squished them together. He made a huge mess, but watching him eat it was like watching someone win the lottery. You'd have thought he'd died and gone to heaven. I have it on video."

Jase stilled at her words. His favorite snack was a peanut butter sandwich with banana slices. Of course, lots of people liked it he was sure. "Kids got great tastes," he said.

"I'll admit I tried it, and it's not bad. So, where are we going? Obviously anywhere I know of won't be safe." Her hazel eyes met his. He could see uncertainty written on her face.

"I've a safe house about an hour from here. We'll go there tonight, and I'll explain what I can. There are things I need to ask you, and I'm sure you have questions. Some things I can answer, others I can't." He put his hand on her leg, halting the nervous bounce that had started.

Brooke bit her lip. "There's definitely some things we need to discuss. I can't promise not to get upset, though."

"Fair enough." Jase kept looking in the rearview mirror as he got on the highway. When he was confident they didn't have a tail, he took the next exit and hopped back onto the highway, heading the opposite direction.

"Um, you realize you just did a circle?" She twisted in her seat to check on Jack and looked out the windows.

"I wanted to make sure we weren't being followed before I went toward our destination." He glanced back at Jack, watching the boy as his eyelids started drooping. "He'll be out in no time."

"Yeah, when he was a baby he always fell asleep in the car, which sometimes was a blessing and a curse. If he slept while I drove, he was rearing to go when I was ready to drop after a trip." Affection laced her words.

"Where's his father?" Jase's fingers gripped the steering wheel, hating the unknown man.

"Are you kidding me?" Brooke asked, her words came out in a low hiss.

His jaw ached from grinding it together. "Why would I joke about something like that?" The woman was confusing the hell out of him.

Brooke turned in her seat, lifting her leg up so it was bent and crossed the other over her foot. Her arms folded in front of her as she glared daggers at him. "Jase Tyler, I can't believe you can sit beside me and question who his father is. I mean look at your mini me back there. Anyone would think it was obvious you were his biological dad," she whispered.

Everything seemed to freeze in that moment. The dark eyes that reminded him of the ones that stared back at him every time he looked in the mirror. The too serious face of a little boy who he'd seen in pictures, only they'd been his pictures, not the little boy in the backseat. Hell, she was right. Looking at Jack was like looking at a miniature version of himself. Only, they'd used protection. "How?" he choked out.

She looked back checking on Jack, making sure he was sleeping before she continued. "I don't know. I...was on the pill, but I guess the low dose didn't work with your super SEAL sperm or something. I'd never missed a pill, not once. I told the doctor that, too. She said it happens. That's why it's not a hundred percent effective. I wasn't on the pill for birth control, but for my," she looked away before continuing, "anyway,

I wasn't on it for that specific purpose, therefore I was on a lower dose. Clearly, it was too low for...that."

Chapter Five

Brooke was utterly mortified to be having this conversation with Jase. Not the fact he was Jack's dad. Heck, he should've known from the beginning he was a father. If things had worked out differently, she'd have loved to of had him be a part of her son's life. When he'd up and left, telling her dad to explain to her, it had been worse than had he just disappeared. She could've handled that a lot better than having her father pat her on the shoulder with a look that to this day still mortified her. Somehow, knowing your parents were aware you'd had sex and presuming it were two very different things. Her growing stomach had been a glaring reminder she and Jase had done a lot more than held hands three years ago. Seeing the look of torment on her dad's face made her wish things were different, while her mother had actually been excited once it was known Brooke was having a little boy. Of course, Nancy wanted her to name Jack after her brother, but she couldn't do that. No amount of crying or cajoling could get her to do that to her child. No, Jack would have his own identity, although his name was similar to his father's. He was his own person.

"Why didn't you tell me?" Jase's harsh words pulled her from her memories.

She let her hands fall into her lap. "At first, I admit I was being a selfish bitch. You just left me. I thought you cared, but after you left, my dad gave me your message. I was," she turned to stare out the window of the SUV, giving herself a second to gather her thoughts. "I was wrong. I should've told you when I found out, or at least when I had Jack. However, I'd heard about your...well, you know. And then, I had a baby to raise and protect. I'm not saying what I did in the beginning was the right thing, but after...well, Jase, I'm sorry, but you went to prison for crimes against our country. Crap, I just don't know what to say. I did what I thought was best for Jack."

Jase sighed loudly, the sound of him adjusting himself in the leather seat had her chancing a glance at his profile. His jaw was throbbing visibly, and his fingers were gripping the wheel with one hand while he rested the other on his thigh, making her wish things had been different.

"What did your dad tell you exactly?" he gritted out, finally.

"Does it really matter, Jase?" Thinking back to the night her dad had come into her room and explained that Jase was leaving and didn't want her contacting him had nearly killed her. If she hadn't had a little baby growing inside her, she would have crumbled into a heap right then and there. Instead, she'd nodded and shut the door on her dad's face.

"Yes, it fucking matters. He stole two years of my child's life from me. I could've been there for his birth, even before that. I could've watched him growing inside you. I could've done things differently." Both hands gripped the wheel now. His words came out so low and tortured she wanted to offer him comfort but didn't think words would help.

"We can't change the past." Her fingers trembled as she reached toward his arm.

"Don't. Just don't," he said without looking her way.

The heartache from everything she'd lost seemed to swell as she felt his words like a punch to the stomach all over again. "You owe me answers. You think it was easy for me?" she gasped then stopped. "I'm not sorry for Jack. You can think and feel however you want but know this. I was told his father, the man I loved, didn't want to have anything more to do with me. I was too young and that he...you were going overseas and didn't want me to call you again. So, I moved forward with my life. I became a mother, and I've done a damn good job. Jack's smart and happy. When I'd heard you'd died, 'cause yes, my father told me that, I swear a little piece of me died, too. Now, all of a sudden on one of the worst days of my life, you appear out of nowhere with this crazy story that some men are trying to...whatever the hell they are. God, I am sorry I didn't hunt you down and tell you about Jack. I'm sorry I didn't go to USDB in Fort Leavenworth and show you your son. And I'm sorry I didn't take him to your funeral," she sobbed.

The SUV rocked as they came to a stop on the side of the road. "Damn, I'm sorry, Brookey. So damn sorry. Come here," Jase murmured, unbuckling her seatbelt and pulling her across the console.

For a few moments, she allowed herself the comfort of his embrace, to soak in the warmth that was Jase Tyler. The sound of her son moving had her squirming and realizing it wasn't quite comfortable draped across the console. "Where are we?" Darkness surrounded them along the stretch of highway they were on.

"About fifteen minutes from a safe house. I'm sorry for being a dick. It's just...damn." He bent and kissed her forehead. "Let's put a pin in this conversation until we get to the cabin."

The small show of affection made her stomach flip. "Okay. I'm thinking you need me to move."

Pressing his forehead against hers, he laughed. "It would probably be easier." Jase helped her maneuver back into her seat, waited until she was safely buckled, before he pulled back onto the highway. They both sat in silence. Brooke wondered what secrets he would divulge and how they'd move forward after tonight. She knew without a doubt that Jase Tyler wouldn't be willing to walk away without wanting to be a part of his son's life. Her problem was she wanted him to be a part of her life as well.

*****

Jase could see the emotions flittering across Brooke's gorgeous face. If her father had still been alive, tracking him down and beating the shit out of him for the years he'd missed out on in Jack's life, would be the least of what he'd do to him. The little boy slept peacefully for now, but had he been five or ten minutes later and the men who'd been sent to take them out reached the apartment above the salon first, his son could have been taken from him before he'd ever gotten a chance to know of his existence.

A beep in his ear let him know Erik was back on line. Hell, the other man may have overheard everything that he and Brooke had discussed. Not that Jase gave a damn as he continued to drive to their destination. Erik was one of the few men he still trusted. An image of Kai and the rest of his team formed in his mind.

"*Yo, Jase. Operation Cleanup is finished. I'm glad you're not a messy eater. Thanks for putting the dishes away before you left. You'll have to replace a few glasses, but other than that, everything sparkles.*" Erik's running commentary through their earpiece would've been comical had the situation not been dire.

"Thank you. I'll have to make sure I give you a good review on the web." Jase signaled when he spotted their turn off. As he looked in the rearview, he was relieved to see there were no other cars on the highway, making his decision to continue on with their exit easy.

"Who're you talking to?" Brooke asked, blinking over at him.

He pointed to his ear. "My partner. He was taking care of things at your apartment. You probably should shut the salon down for a few days."

Brooke nodded. "I already did on account of my dad." Sadness filled her voice.

He reached out with his right hand and brushed a lock of hair behind her ear. "I'm sorry for your loss." No matter how angry he was at the admiral for his lies and the role he played in Jase's screwed up life, he knew Brooke loved her father.

She swallowed audibly. "Thank you. He was a great dad and truly loved Jack. It's gonna be hard to adjust, ya know?" Her eyes stared out the window as she said the words, the anguish evident.

Jase didn't know what to say or how to alleviate her pain. He took the hill up toward the cabin. The switchbacks would be a bitch in the winter, but right now, they were manageable, however he'd rather face an icy terrain than a crying Brooke.

"I bought some provisions, and there should be some at the cabin as well. If we need more, I'll run into town and get some tomorrow." He could see the road between the trees that led to the cabin. Most would've missed it, unless you'd been there before. It was safe enough for him, but figuring in Brooke and their son, plans needed to be changed. The big SUV rumbled down the dirt drive, and within moments the headlights lit up the small log house.

"Oh," Brooke said. "Is this like a hunting cabin or something?"

He looked over at her and smiled. "Or something. Come on, let's get you two inside." He shifted the car into park and shut off the engine.

"I'll grab Jack," she agreed, opening her door.

Jase put his hand on her arm. "Wait here. Let me make sure everything is okay first."

Brooke pulled her door shut. "Do you think whoever was at my apartment knows about this place?" She looked out the side window and back toward him.

He shook his head. "It's better to be safe than sorry. We've set up some safety protocols and parameters around this place that I just want to make sure are still intact. Erik, how's it looking on your end?"

"*Everything looks quiet and as it should,*" Erik reassured him.

Even hearing the other man's words, Jase needed to make sure himself before he allowed Brooke and Jack out of the relative safety of the vehicle. "Brooke, I need you to listen to me. If I'm not back in three minutes, I want you to climb into the driver's seat and go back down the mountain. My partner Erik will find you if you head East. They'll expect you to go back toward home, but you need to go in a direction that makes no sense to anyone but me and someone I trust."

She shook her head. "Don't go. If you think it's too dangerous then let's just continue driving." Touching the ear piece, he silenced it so he could talk to Brooke without Erik overhearing.

He put his hand on the back of her head. "I don't anticipate anything going wrong. I just said if. It's always good to have a backup plan. Trust me, Brooke."

Watching her internal war with doing just that, had him leaning over and kissing her on the lips. Just like all the times before, that small connection had tingles shooting straight to his heart. Shit, he'd never felt an instant attraction to another woman like he had with Brooke Frazee.

"I do trust you, but damn it, I'm scared," she said on an exhale.

He fisted his hand in the back of her hair. "Good. I'd rather you be scared than think it's nothing. I'll be right back, cause I've got some explaining to do, right?"

A laugh bubbled out of her. "Damn right you do, mister."

Another quick peck, and then he was pulling away and sliding out of the vehicle. He tapped the window, pointing at the lock. When she immediately hit the button, he gave her a thumbs up and walked away, pushing thoughts of her and Jack to the back of his mind.

The tour around the cabin showed no signs of an intruder. The trip wires he'd set up, along with those that he knew Erik had in place, were all still exactly as they'd left them. He double checked the doors and windows, making sure they were still secure. "Fuck, I have a son," he muttered as he rounded the side of the cabin, raking his hand through his hair. Through the darkness, he could make out Brooke in the front of the SUV holding Jack. He picked up his steps until he was next to the passenger door and tapping lightly on the window. She jerked as if he'd scared the crap out of her.

"Sorry," he said as she unlocked and opened the door. "I thought if I tapped lightly it wouldn't startle you."

She held a sleeping Jack closer. "I think I'd have freaked even if you sent a text and smoke signals. Everything okay?"

He nodded. "Did he wake up?"

"Yeah but fell right back to sleep once I put him in my lap. He's not used to this much activity." She ran her finger down his chubby cheek.

Jase reached out and followed the same path she'd traced. "He's perfect. You did a good job."

Tears shimmered in her eyes. "He really is, isn't he?"

For a moment, they both stared down at Jack. Jase wanted to wrap them both in his arms and lock the world away, but he knew that was fairy tales and make believe. He lived in the real world, and the real world was hunting the mother of his child, and he planned to find out why.

"Come on, let's get him inside." He helped her down, then grabbed the bags out of the back. The wound on his side throbbed, but he knew it was just a flesh wound. When he got Brooke and Jack settled, he'd clean it up and put a bandage on it.

He punched in the keycode for the lock and waited for it to disengage, stepping inside ahead of Brooke and Jack. The hall light was the first thing he turned on, illuminating the long entryway, casting out the shadows. "There's two bedrooms. You and Jack can have the master, and I'll take the other one. Let's go settle him on the bed and then I'll show you around."

The small five room cabin wasn't large, but it was clean and nice. What he liked most was that it was stocked with all the necessities, had a generator that worked, and was ready to go in case of an emergency.

"He looks so tiny in that big bed," Brooke said as she placed Jack in the center.

Jase nodded. "Should you put pillows around him so he doesn't roll off?"

She smiled. "No, he's old enough he should be fine, besides I'll be with him in a little bit. Come on, let's take a look at that side now."

To say she'd shocked him would be a major understatement as he allowed himself to be maneuvered into the large ensuite. "Listen, I'm fine."

Brooke rolled her eyes and pushed his hands out of the way. "I'm sure you are, but why don't you just let me see." Her hands pushed the tactical vest off his shoulders, laying it on the floor with care before she eased the black fabric up.

Jase hissed in a breath as the fabric tore away from the wound. "Sheot," he grumbled.

"Oh god, I'm sorry. Maybe we should wet it down or something. I think it dried with your sweater to it."

He gritted his teeth and pulled the material away from the wound and dropped it to the floor. Brooke's intake of breath had him glancing down to see what she was looking at. The scratch wasn't bad, just needed a little cleaning and a bandage. "It's fine. I've had worse." He tried to reassure her.

"When did you get these?" She traced the tattoos on his chest and on his arm. He'd had the skull and designs along with the flag over his shoulder and down his arm done when he'd gotten out of Fort Leavenworth, a symbol of his old life dying and his new life starting. "They're so detailed."

"A couple years ago." He couldn't look at her when he said that. Staring at the sink, he took a step away. "Can you get me the first aid kit?"

"Oh, yeah. Where is it?" She licked her lips. Her hands dropped to the sides fidgeting with the seam of her pants.

"In the mudroom, off of the kitchen." He'd seen it there when he brought up groceries the other day.

While she hurried out of the bathroom, he looked at himself, trying to picture what she was seeing. He was thirty-three to her twenty-four. He had dark hair and hadn't seen any grey in it yet, but the way his life was going he was sure to be seeing some soon. His tattoos were covering his right arm and chest and all across his back. He wondered what she would say when she saw them. His little Brooke had been sweet and almost innocent, too innocent and young for him, but he couldn't resist her then any more than he could now.

"Here you go," she said, coming to a halt in the doorway. "Oh, that's magnificent. So, lifelike."

Totally stunned, he met her eyes through the mirror. "Thank you," he said. "I'll take that." He nodded toward the kit in her hands.

She shook her head. "Have a seat and I'll clean it up. I don't think it's deep now that it's stopped bleeding. Oh," she gasped. "Is that why you wear black, so nobody can see blood on you?"

"Brooke, I'm not the bad guy here," he reminded her.

He sat on the seat of the toilet and let Brooke clean his wound. She grabbed a towel and tossed it on the floor next to his feet then knelt down, giving him all kinds of dirty thoughts. His thoughts shut down as he watched her deftly clean and apply a cream to the small wound, keeping the curse inside and then helped her apply a bandage.

"I know you're not the bad guy," she finally said as she was throwing away the wrappers they'd used.

Jase grabbed one of her hands and pulled her in front of him. From where he sat, she was almost at eye level with him. Or rather, her chest was, putting him in a lower position. Usually he didn't like to be in such a place, but with her, he allowed it, knowing she needed the feeling of power. "Tell me what you think you know, Brooke."

She glanced back toward the bedroom and then toward him. "Not in here."

He nodded; with his hands on her hips, he gave her a little nudge back, giving him room to stand. "Let me grab a clean shirt, and I'll meet you in the living room."

No matter what, he knew the day of reckoning was there. He'd tell Brooke everything, leaving nothing out, even things the CIA had told him he couldn't. She had his son, and he was sure the alphabet fuckers knew about Jack. They'd allowed him to go for two years, almost be killed dozens of times, all while his son was being brought up without him, without a father. He looked up at the ceiling and flipped up the middle finger on both hands. "Fuck you, motherfuckers. That's my kid. Fuck with me and my life, fine. Not my son."

A new resolve straightened his spine. He didn't worry that he could keep himself and Brooke safe, but he would need backup. A team he trusted above all others. One that thought he had betrayed them. "Fuck, I hope Tay still has the same number," he muttered as he exited the bathroom and went to the bed, staring down at the smallest angel on earth. "I may not have been here for the past two years, but I'll do everything in my power to be here for the rest of my life." He laid his hand over Jack's tiny chest, feeling the beating of his heart. Emotion choking him, he felt the sting of tears and let himself have it for a moment. Let the first tear drop fall, followed by the next. He took a shaky breath, unable to believe he was looking at his son. Bending, he kissed Jack's cheek, amazed at the downy softness. "I'll protect you until there's no breath left in my body, and even then, I'll make sure you're safe," he swore then stepped away. If he didn't leave the room then, he knew he'd curl up next to the boy and stay there until his son woke or someone made him.

Chapter Six

Brooke slipped back down the hall, tears streaming down her face. Oh god, her heart was breaking at the real heartache Jase was showing as he stood next to the bed and talked to their sleeping son. She thought back to the day he'd told her he was leaving and when her dad had given her a similar message from Jase. She didn't understand why at the time they'd both been so cruel in the way they'd ended things with her. Sure, she'd been falling head over heels for Jase. Maybe she'd been building dreams of the two of them together, but she wasn't a young naïve teenager bent on ruining her life. Well, some would say getting pregnant may have been a bad decision, but she would never regret having Jack.

She got out two bottles of water from the fridge. A bundle of bananas had her smiling as she pictured Jack wanting his favorite treat when he woke up.

"What's that smile for?" Jase asked as he entered the room with a clean black shirt.

"I was just thinking Jack would enjoy a peanut butter and banana sandwich tomorrow." She held out one of the bottles for him. He took it and unscrewed the lid, taking a long pull before he looked at her again.

"Good thing I've got the best peanut butter." He grinned. "Let's go into the living room and have a seat."

Nodding, she followed him. Finally, she'd have answers. His easy grin and acceptance of their son as his own lifted a weight off her shoulders.

Jase motioned to the couch while he paced by the fireplace. "It'll be easier if you sit down. I'm not sure where to begin."

"How about the beginning," she said helpfully. "Tell me why you left the way you did. I thought we...that you and I were starting something. Instead, you made me feel like just another notch." She had to take a deep breath to keep the anger from her tone.

He shook his head. "You were anything but a notch, Brooke. Your dad was waiting by my truck, when I came back from walking you to your door. Basically, he told me if I didn't leave you alone, he'd make sure I regretted it. He was powerful and could ruin my career. I could see the truth in his eyes when he threatened me. If I continued to see you, he'd make sure I had nothing. Hell, he had the power to have me court martialed on a trumped-up charge." He turned away. "I ended up getting exactly that and doing time. I bet your dad laughed his ass off over that. To this day, I don't know why he hated me. I only know that he must've been worried I'd figure out what he was."

She sat up straight as his words. "What do you mean, what he was?"

"He's your father, Brooke. Or was. No matter what anyone says, my duty has always been to serve my county. I'm not a traitor. I've been working to discover just who the fucker in our ranks was that's been selling out top secret information. Information that has gotten men, friends of mine, killed in the line of duty. Only someone with high clearance would have intel like that. Someone in a position like an admiral." He let his words hang in the quiet of the room, waiting.

"Are you accusing my father of being a traitor?" She jumped up from the couch, no longer able to sit and listen as the man she loved accuse her dad of such a crime.

Jase turned with his arms crossed over his chest. "All lines point back to your father. I've been gathering intel, working my way slowly up the chain of command from the outside in. Everyone thinks I'm a traitor so I hear lots of things. My handlers are the only ones who know the truth, and even they're a little on the fence as to which side I'm on.

You see, when you have nothing to lose, people tend to be wary around you."

With her lip between her teeth, she looked at Jase. "Because you'd lost your place in the Navy and had no family?"

He gave an affirmative jerk of his head. "Yes. Brooke, the last thing I want is for your father to have been behind the leaks, but from where I'm standing," he trailed off.

"It doesn't make sense. He's always been all about the safety of our great county. I mean, he literally bled red, white, and blue." Growing up, she was so proud of her dad and what he did. The thought he'd been doing what Jase was accusing made her ill. "I can't believe it. I know you say you have evidence, but until I see it, feel it, I can't believe it."

"That's sort of my next issue. I need to get into his office." He held up his hand. "No, listen to me. If your dad has information that he has or hasn't sold, it would be there. We've been inside his office at the base but uncovered nothing. The last mission I was on, I was...blown up. Jase Tyler is supposedly dead. If I can get into your dad's office and find out what he was or wasn't working on, I would be able to reclaim my identity, my life." Jase took a breath. "Hell, maybe you're right, and it wasn't your dad, but without searching through his files, I won't know for sure."

"Okay, back up to the part of you being blown up. You look pretty good for a dead guy, so explain."

*****

Jase twisted his head from side to side. Shit! He hated having to explain about his undercover work, but Brooke deserved the truth, even if he wasn't supposed to divulge that information to anyone. "My last mission had me as part of a group that was seriously unhinged. Suffice it to say, they're better off dead than alive. I ended up on the opposite side of my old SEAL team." He took a breath. Even saying his old team brought an emptiness to him. "The team leader Kai, had a stake in the target we had secured at a cabin. Luckily, when they extracted the woman from my boss at the time, I was out on patrol. Of course, they came to our secondary location wanting to kick ass and take names. I always have a backup plan. Everyone had already left by then, or so I'd thought. I didn't realize one of the fuckers was still in the cabin I had rigged to blow. I may be a lot of things, but a merciless killer isn't one of them. Anyway, I was far enough away and saw the teams moving in. When I knew they were close enough, I had my finger on the button and ready. The bomb blew up as intended, only the cabin, which did have my heat signature thanks to technology, had a real body to go along with the explosion. The man looked enough like me that Kai Swift, the leader of the SEAL team, positively identified him as me, even though there was nothing left of him after the explosion."

"Oh my god. You could've died. Like, they could've killed you." Her voice trembled.

He looked across the room to where she sat, her eyes as big as saucers. "Sweetheart, that was probably one of the tamest jobs I've done since leaving the Navy." Instant regret hit him as she sucked in a breath and lost what little color she'd had to her face. "Everything I did, I did for the betterment of our country."

She jumped to her feet, slashing her hand in an arc. "Bullshit. Don't even say that. Your life is not expendable. You have a son, Jase."

He rocked back on his feet. Her words hitting him harder than a sledgehammer being swung by the mighty Thor. "I didn't know that at the time. My only thought was to protect and serve our country."

"What about now? What about that little boy in there? Do you plan on being around for him as he grows up, or are you going to continue to put your life on the line like that?" Tears swam in her gorgeous hazel eyes, making them appear more emerald.

He inhaled deeply. "I need to finish this. I'm this close to finding out who the mole is. Please understand. It's not just a matter of quitting my job but finding out who killed my friends. Who's responsible for killing dozens of soldiers and hundreds of others. This person did it for personal gain, all while posing as an upstanding citizen. My team and I were there. We were ambushed and couldn't get to the other team. We watched as the night lit up with gunfire, and by the time we got to them, they were already dead. Some of them were married with children at home, others were like me, wanting to settle down, but that opportunity was taken from them. Knowing I'm this close," he held his thumb and forefinger together before continuing, "and not doing everything I can to right the wrongs done to them, would be like their lives were nothing."

"Why you?" Her hand came to rest on his chest.

Jase lifted one shoulder. "I don't know. Maybe because I was the team leader. For whatever reason, I was singled out and went to Fort Leavenworth. I was there for six months when I got a visitor telling me I had a chance to get out and clear my name."

"Wait? Clear your name?" She fisted her hand in his shirt. "What do you mean?"

He gave a mirthless chuckle. "Oh, you didn't hear? I was tried and convicted as the one who gave away the other team's location. Somehow, I was supposedly able to sneak off and meet with the leaders of the warring nation and gave them the intel on where the other soldiers were setting up camp. I was charged with the killings of all those men." Anger pulsed through his veins at the memories of his team looking at him as if he were a monster. None of them had believed him when he'd claimed his innocence.

"What about your team? I mean...aren't you all like brothers? Why didn't they stick up for you?"

He dragged a deep breath into his lungs. "The evidence was pretty convincing. There was video, although grainy, that looked as if I was indeed in a deep conversation with the ones who'd killed our troops. The timestamp indicated it was just hours before the massacre." He went over to the couch and sat as memories of the look of horror and judgement stared back at him from his team's faces.

Brooke came and knelt in front of him, her palms on his thighs. "Look at me and tell me you didn't do it. I don't need to see video or proof. You tell me the truth, and I'll believe you."

"I would never have betrayed anyone, let alone my friends and brothers. I'm not saying I haven't killed, because I have. I've had to in order to survive, it's part of war. Never has it been an innocent, and certainly not one of my friends or brothers. Every single time I've had to...it's left a mark on my soul, but it was either them or me. The people I've come up against are the epitome of evil. In my line of work and with the SEALs, we serve a purpose and that's not just to put on an outfit for looks. It can get ugly, and sometimes lives are lost. However, I would never take a life or endanger lives for shits and giggles."

"I believe you. You're a good man, Jase. I don't know why your team didn't see that, but I do."

It felt like a ton of weight was lifted off his shoulders. Sure, he knew others believed him innocent. However, hearing the words from Brooke was like a balm to his battered soul.

"Come here," he said pulling her up off the floor and into his lap.

She came to him without hesitation, wrapping her arms around his shoulders and burying her face in his neck. "I've missed you, Jase."

He laid his cheek on hers and just held her for a moment, luxuriating in the feel of her in his arms; something he didn't think he'd ever get the chance to do again. "I've missed you, too, Brooke."

Her left hand began making patterns on his chest. "I missed the feel of you holding me. There were nights I dreamed of you, only to wake up crying and cursing you for leaving me."

His hand caught hers, bringing it up to his lips, he kissed the palm. "I can't change the past, but I can promise to make the here and now as good as possible. I wish I could promise you tomorrow, but...Brooke, I don't know what tomorrow will bring. You and Jack are the two most important people in my life, but I have a mission to complete. As much as you two mean to me, other lives are at stake if I don't do what I came here to do."

She turned to straddle him. "I understand. Although I want to be selfish and beg you to forget about your mission, I know what you're saying is true." Taking a deep breath, she looked away then back down at him. "I'll help you get into my dad's office. I don't think you'll find anything, but if I don't do it, you'll find a way inside, and then, I'll…I don't know, be left on the outside wondering. At least this way, I'll know because I'll be there."

Jase opened his mouth then closed it. The words no way in hell hovered on the end of his tongue, but the fierce determination was stamped on her features. "Brooke, I don't think that's wise."

"You can't get in without me there. My mother is like…crazy when it comes to the house. She tried to make me give back my house key when I moved out, but dad argued on my behalf. Heck, I wouldn't be shocked to find out she'd had the locks changed as a matter of fact."

Brooke tried to act as if it didn't hurt her, but he could tell her mother's callous behavior had. "If she has, we'll find another way in. What about Jack?"

"I want him with us, if you think he's safe. My friends who kept him during the funeral…they would watch him for me, but I'd feel better having him with me, especially after last night." Her breath hitched on a sob as she'd mentioned the funeral, but she'd soldiered on.

"I've got a plan, too. It's getting late. We should get some sleep," he murmured watching her lick her lips. His body was getting hard with her's pressing against his.

"Bed sounds good. Of course, so does this couch." Her head bent, and she brushed her lips over his. "Make me forget for a little while, Jase."

She wanted to forget, and he wanted to remember. Shit! He wanted to build memories and hopes and dreams that he could live the rest of his life on, with her, the one and only woman he'd ever loved. "Brooke, you don't know what you're asking for."

Brooke bit his bottom lip. "Yes I do. I'm asking you to make love to me."

He opened his mouth to respond, but her tongue slipped inside. There was no tentative young girl in the woman now. No, his Brooke decimated any and all his protests as she kissed him with passion that ignited his blood. His arms came around her, hugging her to him as he took over the kiss, thrusting his tongue into her mouth, imitating what he wanted to do with his dick inside her.

Her moan echoed his groan as she shifted on top of him, making the tight confines of the black cargo pants press against his erection. If she kept moving in the circular motion, he feared he'd have more than blood wetting his clothes. The thought had him shifting their positions until he had her beneath him on the large leather sofa. Its squeak as they moved the only other sound in the quiet of the room.

Glazed hazel eyes stared up at him as he loomed over her. "Are you sure, B?" he asked.

She smiled, her hand trailed between them until she could grasp his dick through his pants. "Most definitely, sure. I wanted you three years ago, and I want you now."

He took a deep breath. "I have a condom, but clearly that didn't work last time."

"I'm on the pill. Not because I'm sexually active, 'cause I'm not, but because it leveled out my hormones and monthly visits from aunt flo." Her cheeks turned a rosy red as she spoke.

"I'm clean, but I'll wear the condom for extra protection. Not because I don't trust you, but clearly we're potent together." He thrust his hips into her hand that still held his dick. "Woman, if you don't stop stroking me, I'm gonna make a fool of myself and come in my pants."

"Oh, I'd love to watch that. I'd video it for future spank bank times." She giggled up at him as she continued to massage him.

He narrowed his eyes. "Spank bank, huh. I'm gonna give a hard pass on that." He pulled her hand off him, settling them beside her head and covered her mouth before she could protest. He hadn't been lying when he'd told her he was close to coming. It had been a long time since he'd been with a woman and having Brooke under him was almost enough to have him blowing his load right then and there.

His lips sipped at hers, plucking at her top lip then her bottom, before moving down her jaw and then her neck. He remembered from before how much she enjoyed it when he sucked and nibbled just beneath her ear. Her body shivered at the first press of his lips on the sensitive spot he'd filed in his memory box. Scraping his teeth down, then sucking slightly, had her bucking up into him. Jase chuckled, making her shift from side to side. Oh, he was a hundred percent sure if he reached into her panties, she'd be wet.

"Oh god, yes," she whispered as he sucked her earlobe into his mouth.

Jase sat back on his knees and reached for her shirt, pulling it up and over her head with her help. The plain nude colored bra had her arms coming up to cover her from his view. "Hey, don't hide from me," he admonished. "You're bigger." He traced her hardened nipples with his pointer finger. "You said you breastfed?"

"They got a little bigger after Jack and yes for almost a year. I would've nursed longer, but when he started getting teeth, he was really bitey."

Reaching under her, he unfastened the bra and drew it away from her. "I like to be bitey, too. It must come naturally to him." He gave a wolfish grin then bent to take one tiny bud into his mouth. Looking up at her, he let her see his teeth just before he tugged on her nipple playfully.

"Son of a biscuit eater," she moaned.

With a laugh he moved to the other, giving it the same treatment. "I love your breasts. They're perfect. So responsive." He flicked his tongue over one tip then the other.

*****

"You're killing me." She ran her hand through the top of his hair.

A mischievous smile curled his lips. "You ain't seen nothing yet, sweetheart."

Brooke didn't think she'd survive, but she couldn't wait to see and feel. "Bring it on."

Jase scooted down her body, placing sucking kisses down her abdomen. He paused at one of her stretch marks. "Warrior stripes," he said then kissed each one he found.

She nearly cried as he kissed each mark left on her body from her pregnancy with Jack. The fine silver lines weren't hideous, were barely visible, but somehow, having Jase call them something so amazing had her smiling. The smile turned into a gasp as he pulled her pants down.

"Lift up," he instructed, staring up at her with such need she could do nothing other than obey.

Her pants were removed, leaving her in a tiny thong that was flesh toned. God, if she'd known someone would be seeing her in lingerie, she'd have worn something sexier.

"Son of a bitch, Brooke. You're killing me, here." He tossed her words back at her, fingering the top edge of her panties.

"They're boring," she blurted.

His gaze caught and held hers. "Babe, there is nothing boring about you. Everything about you intrigues me. From the inside out, you captivate me. I want to delve into your mind and know all there is to know, but first, I want to do this." He pulled the thong off, tossing it onto the pile and then dipped his head, fingers spreading her open for him, and then his mouth was moving on her pussy.

He urged her knees further apart with his shoulders, making more room for himself as he licked up and down again and again. God, she was so open to him, vulnerable. He brought his fingers into play, running one through her wetness. "You're fucking gorgeous, even here," he said, his voice strained.

She cried out as he pushed one digit inside her, followed by another, making her writhe beneath the pressure he applied, driving her closer to an impending orgasm. "I'm so close, Jase."

Her words seemed to spur him on as he sucked on one side of her then the other, driving her wild.

"So good, like honey on my tongue. I could eat you all night," Jase said then went back to work licking and sucking with a single-minded determination.

Struggling to catch her breath as she was swept away in a tidal wave of sensation where they were the only two people in existence. Her mind clouded, her pulse frantic as she neared an end that was surely as close to burning up in flames one could compare to. The climax, when it came, shocked her to the very core. Lost in sensation one moment, grinding against Jase's face, and the next, she was moaning while her muscles convulsed. Luckily, her body still knew she had a child in the other room, otherwise she'd have surely screamed the house down.

When she opened her eyes, her body finally coming down from one of the most glorious highs, it was to see Jase poised above her, his naked body glistening in the dim light of the room. "You ready for more?"

The fact he had to ask, of having him inside her again, filled her with need all over again. She'd longed to feel the connection like she'd had with him. The oneness of two beings becoming one while they made love. "Yes, I'm so ready for more."

"You sure?" He teased her opening with the head of his cock, not entering her just rubbing that gorgeous mushroom shaped head up and down until she thought she'd go mad with need.

Her hips bolted up off the couch of their own accord as he made another pass. "I'm not so sure. Maybe we should...check." He rubbed up and down again.

Jase was being a big tease, torturing her slowly. Two could play that game. She reached between their bodies, gripping his dick in her palm. It was so wide she couldn't quite wrap her fingers all the way around the middle. And long. Shit, she'd forgotten how big he had been. "Maybe you should put your dick where your mouth was."

He smirked. "My mouth has been all over this body."

"Jase Tyler, get in me now, or I'll have to take care of myself. My spank bank is empty save for a few memories."

His surprise at her words had her laughing and him bending to kiss her. "I can't wait to fill your spank bank, but I'd much rather fill you." He leaned back and pulled a condom out, ripped the foil packet open and slid the latex down his impressive length. When he turned back around, she didn't miss the slight wince.

"Are you okay?" Her hand reached for the wound on his side.

Jase stopped her before she could touch him, placing her hand over his heart. He moved back between her legs, got into position, and slid home. "Better than okay," he groaned.

Her body arched to meet him, hips thrusting up, and she cried out. "Oh, yes. Perfect," she whispered. The stretch and burn of having him inside her was almost too much, but then, it was like magic, like they were made for each other.

Chapter Seven

Jase knew they should take things slow, but buried balls deep in the one woman he couldn't forget, her body a perfect fit for his, slow was no longer in his vocabulary. He'd never felt the same bone deep satisfaction as he had with Brooke, like he was feeling as he powered into her again and again. In the last three years there had been no other women, and now he realized there never would be. He shifted up onto his knees, hooking his arms under the backs of her legs, forcing her to open wider for him, making her body take him deeper. God, he wanted to imprint himself on every inch of her, inside and out. Her hard little nipples beckoned as he pushed in and out, bouncing with the movement of their bodies. He leaned down, running his tongue over one then moved to the other tip and ran it through his teeth.

Brooke gasped his name, her nails raked down his back, making the option to go slow non-existent. He powered into her harder, making her breasts jiggle, fueling his desire. "I'm close," he warned. His hand slid down the center of her body, and he pressed his thumb over her swollen bundle of nerves.

"Yes, right there!" she cried.

As he pumped his hips and rubbed her at the same time, thrusting and rubbing, moving faster and faster, her walls began constricting around him, pleasure rippling along his dick until it was all blending together into one ball of sensation. He could feel her getting closer and applied more pressure, knowing he could get her there quicker.

Harder, faster, utterly swept away with the need to make Brooke come, he fucked into her like he'd never done, a primal sense of ownership overtook him. "Come for me. Let me feel you squeeze my dick like a vice, baby."

"Oh my, Jase, Jase, fuck me, Jase," she chanted over and over. Her hips lifted, writhed as she made sounds he'd forever remember as long as he lived. His Brooke was the perfect woman, complete blend of femininity and sexy badass mixed. And she was his.

He lifted her ass higher, his fingers spread over those luscious curves, his groin hitting her clit with each forceful slam forward. "I can feel you, Brooke, you're right there."

"Yes, right...there," she moaned, her body bowed, inner walls squeezing his cock, taking him with her. He let out a groan as he flooded the condom with come.

Completely and utterly spent, he collapsed onto his forearms, still conscious enough not to let all his weight fall onto her much smaller body. "Woman, you just about killed me," he said as he rested his head next to hers trying to catch his breath.

Lying under him, she ran her hands up and down his sweaty back. "I thought you were this big bad SEAL. Don't you have more stamina than that?"

Jase laughed and gathered enough strength to lift up onto his arms. "Not when you suck the life right out of me."

She looked down to where they were still joined. "I'm pretty sure that is not your life pole there."

He pulled out of her body, hating to leave the snug embrace but needing to dispose of the condom. Damn, if that small separation was a bugger, what was it going to be like when he had to leave for an assignment? He'd cross that bridge when he came to it. "Be right back." The future wasn't clear for him, not with the SEALs or the CIA.

Walking to the bathroom, he tossed the used condom into the trash after tying it off. It didn't appear to have broken. He wondered how it had happened last time as well. He hadn't double checked the condom when he'd taken it off afterwards three years ago, assuming they'd worked. Now, he'd do anything to make love to Brooke with nothing between them. "One day at a time, Jase."

When he entered the living room, Brooke was in the middle of dressing. He paused mid-step, raising a questioning eyebrow.

"What if Jack wakes up?" she asked, standing up and wiggling into her pants.

He grimaced as he realized he hadn't thought of the intricacies of having a toddler in the picture. "Does he normally wake in the middle of the night?"

Brooke paused as she clipped her bra on. "No, not usually, but this is not a...normal situation. At home, he's normally in his own bed by eight and sleeps until around seven the next day. He's potty training, but he wears Pullups for bedtime. He hasn't had an accident in a while. I just don't want him to wake up and find me naked in the living room."

Jase nodded then grinned. "So, he's never found you naked in the living room with a strange man?" he asked as her head disappeared under her shirt. When she pulled clear of the fabric, she was glaring daggers at him.

"Don't go getting a big head, mister. I just don't make it a habit of bringing home strangers to my house is all. I don't want to have a parade of uncles in and out of his life." She made air quotes around the word uncles.

He gritted his teeth thinking of other men she had been with since he'd left her. "Fair enough. What about now? Any men expecting to hear from you? Do I have to worry some guy is going to want to kick my ass for sleeping with you? What about Derek or Darron?"

"Okay, first of all, Darron was a guy I dated in high school for like a minute. Second, fuck you, Jase. How many women have you fucked since me? Is there a mercenary wench gonna pop out and want to kill me for poaching on her man?" Anger had her face turning red.

His anger faltered then evaporated. Shit! He was screwing things up and doing a damn good job of it, if the hurt stamped on her body was anything to go by, hearing another lie had been told to him by the admiral wasn't as shocking. "I'm sorry. I didn't mean any of that. You don't owe me any explanations. You've single handedly brought up our child and are doing an amazing job as far as I can see. Plus, I deserve anything that you've done with other men and then some. Although it wasn't my choice to leave, I still allowed myself to be bullied into going. You're a remarkable woman, and any man would be lucky to have you as his partner."

*****

The intensity of the moment nearly felled her, but a truth held her in place. She hadn't allowed another man into her life. Not because of Jack, or not solely because of her son, but because none had measured up to Jase. "Let's not hurl insults back and forth. I don't want to ruin what time we have together." The depth of her feelings hadn't shut off because he'd left. She didn't know how to convey that to him, nor did she want to. Not now, maybe never. Jase was here for a mission and would want to be a part of his son's life. She wasn't going to profess her undying love for the man just to make his guilt even worse.

"Let's be real clear, Brooke. I'm not giving up on us. You, me, and Jack. When this is over, we'll figure it out. I want us." He reached out a trembling hand and brushed her hair back. As soon as his skin made contact with hers, she sucked in a breath from the pleasure the simple touch elicited.

How can being brushed by his fingers send zings of pleasurable sensations throughout her? For the past three years, she'd had memories of his unique scent, the feel of his skin rasping against her as he brushed his hand along her cheek, the look of awe in his eyes when he would see her. None of those things could be replaced, yet they had her craving for more. "What am I going to do with you, Jase Tyler?"

He pulled her into his body. "Trust me again," he said. His head bent, and he covered her lips with his. He nipped her lower lip then forged inside her mouth when she gasped. "I'm gonna make you trust and believe in me, in us. Not just for Jack, but you and I."

She blinked back tears. God how she wanted what he was offering. A family with her and the two men in her life who meant more to her than anything in the world. "I want that too."

The sound of Jack crying out had her pulling away. "You better put some pants on."

Jase blinked then looked down at his dick. "Do I gotta?" he asked with a wink.

Laughing she ran her fingers along the underside of his hardness. "I'm afraid so. This is what being a parent is all about."

Jase gave her a quick kiss then released her. "I missed so many firsts."

She nodded but moved toward the back of the cabin to see to her son. "We can't go back in time Jase, ain't that what you said?" Looking over her shoulder as she reached the doorway, she saw him stepping into his pants.

"Live for today and treat it like the gift it is. You and Jack are the best fucking presents I've ever been given. I'm gonna be like a fucking dragon and hoard you like you're my gold." His eyes clashed with hers, complete truth echoed through every word.

"For some reason, that's reassuring to me." She ducked inside the room to see Jack sitting up in bed, rubbing his eyes. "Hey, little man, what's wrong?"

"Mama, I gotta go potty," Jack whined.

From past experience, her little guy probably already went in his Pullup, but she scooped him into her arms and carried him into the bathroom, glad the light had been left on with a dimmer switch, keeping it from being too harsh on their eyes. "Here we go." She placed Jack on his feet and spent the next couple minutes helping him sit on the too big potty without falling in. He woke up completely by the time they were done, proud he hadn't wet himself.

"Can I have a sandwich? My tummy says it's hungry." He pushed his belly out and rubbed circles around it with his little hands. "See, look at it mommy, it's so hungry." Jack blinked eyes so like his father's up at her.

She tapped his nose with her finger. "You're a little stinker, you know that?"

He scrunched up his nose. "I didn't go poopy, mommy. You silly."

"Your mommy really is silly. My tummy is hungry too. What do you think sounds good?" Jase asked from the doorway as he leaned against one side with his arms crossed over his chest wearing another dark T-shirt.

Jack moved closer to Brooke. "I'm Jack. Who're you?"

Jase moved into the room and got down on one knee. "My name's Jase." He held out his hand, waiting for Jack to put his into it.

Like the little soldier he was, Jack slapped his father's hand before he shook it, laughing as Jase gripped with two fingers and shook all over as if the little boy was doing it. "Wow, you're a lot stronger than you look, big guy. Let me see those muscles."

Brooke watched as Jack held up his arm and flexed and fell a little more in love with the father of her son as he measured the width of Jack's little bicep, pretending to be impressed. "Alright you two, how about a late-night snack?" Usually she would deny the request, distracting Jack with a story instead. Tonight though...tonight, father and son were meeting for the first time.

"Peanut butter and banana sandwiches coming right up. Want a piggy back ride?" Jase asked a clapping Jack. In that heartbeat in time, they both forgot about her as Jase placed Jack onto his shoulders and headed out the door. He paused and turned to look back at her. "You coming?" Jase asked, the purest delight glimmering on his face.

God, if she wasn't already head over heels in love with the man, she'd have fallen right then and there. "Oh, you bet I am."

"Mommy gonna eat one, too?" Jack asked in a gleeful tone, his fingers twisted in Jase's hair, probably so tightly he was ripping a few out by the roots.

"Does your mommy usually eat one?" Jase asked once they entered the kitchen and settled Jack on the counter.

Her son giggled, rubbing his tiny fist over his eyes. "She eats my crusts."

Jase glanced at her over his shoulder, raising his brow. "Hey, don't judge, I like the crusts. Plus, I smear lots of peanut butter over the edges. Don't I nugget?" She swooped in and kissed Jack on the neck, blowing a raspberry. He tried to squirm away, laughing like she knew he would. God, she'd missed this. Missed out on what having Jase in their lives would've been like. She had to shake herself from the thoughts of what ifs, knowing things happened for a reason.

"What can I do to help?" she asked, standing close to Jack while Jase pulled out the milk from the fridge. Jase was busy getting the fixings for their sandwiches out, but he didn't know that he couldn't leave a two year old on the counter unattended. Of course, she needn't have worried. Jase being the super SEAL he was didn't stray far from their son, his arm always within reaching distance. The instant Jack began to try to get down while she was pouring a glass of milk, Jase was the one to swoop in and catch him first.

"Easy there, little man." Jase didn't put him on his feet like expected. No, he placed Jack on his hip as if he'd done it a million times. They looked perfect together. The image brought a sting to her eyes, but she blinked several times to keep from letting the tears fall. She tried to never cry in front of her son if she could help it.

"Here, I'll cut the edges off of Jack's. Do you want me to do the same for yours?" Brooke held up a knife, waiting for Jase's answer.

He grinned at her. "You just want all the healthy nutrients from the crust. I see how you operate, ma'am. I'm gonna have to decline your polite inquiry with a negative. Ain't that right, Jack?"

Jack nodded. "Decline," her son parroted.

Jase tickled their son, loving the interaction of the simple late night snack and moved around to the small kitchen table with their sandwiches. She grabbed the glasses of milk and followed, feeling a little left out. Dang, why was she being such a...bitch. Yes, that was the word she was looking for. Jase had a right to spend some one on one time with his son, and it wasn't as if she wasn't invited.

After setting the glasses down, she scrubbed her hands over her face. The cup with the lid for Jack wobbled as her son reached for it, falling over without spilling a drop. "Wow, that's a neat trick. Maybe I should get a cup like that. Do they make them in extra-large?" Jase asked picking up his own glass and smiling behind the rim.

The look he gave her made her think of other things that were extra-large and had her blushing, if the heat in her face was any indication. "You're a naughty man, Jase Tyler."

Jack sat his cup down. "Uh oh, is he going to have to go to time out? Mommy, he's sorry. He didn't mean to. Tell mommy you're sorry. She's a good mommy. If you pinky promise to be good, she'll give you a pass."

Her heart melted at her son's words and the way he pronounced his words, his r's still had a bit of a w to them, reminding her he was still her baby. The men who'd come after her this evening wouldn't have cared that he was innocent. That she was innocent. Her gaze jerked to Jase's, and she could see he was thinking the same thing. He'd almost missed getting to know his child.

"I'll keep you both safe," he promised.

The conviction she heard in his tone had her taking a deep breath. With a nod, she sat next to where he sat holding Jack. Her son picked up one of the squares of his sandwich that she'd cut up for him and held it out for her. "Here, mommy. I share with you." Heart melting, she took the proffered sandwich with the peanut butter and bananas. Looking at her two favorite people in the world, she took a huge bite and moaned around the gooey goodness.

"Mmm, so good," she murmured.

Jase groaned, shifting Jack on his lap. "Yeah, it is."

*****

Jase watched Brooke clean their son's face and hands after they finished their late-night snack. Jack was already nodding off while she did the little routine. He couldn't believe how much he loved the pint sized little guy already. Hell, he'd love the kid even if he hadn't been his, but knowing he was, made his heart swell with pride and joy.

Standing between the bedroom and the bathroom while she lifted Jack into her arms, she turned startled eyes toward him. "Oh, I didn't know you were there."

He shrugged. "I wanted to...I don't know, say goodnight to him."

The smile she gave lit up her face. "I totally get it. Come on," she said, tilting her head to the side.

He'd never thought he'd be one to blindly follow a woman, but damned if he wasn't ready to do just that. The bathroom light switch had a dimmer, so instead of shutting the light off, he turned the dial, keeping the room softly lit. Inside the bedroom, Brooke placed Jack in the center of the bed, then laid down on one side, tapping the other. He glanced at the door to the hallway. His watch was set up to alert him if any of the perimeter alarms were tripped.

Bone tired, and weary, yet needing to be next to his family, because that's who Brooke and Jack were—his family, he sat and took off his shoes before he lay down. Grabbing the blanket from the end of the bed, he pulled it over the three of them.

When he looked over to where Brooke lay with Jack snuggled against her chest, his heart skipped a beat. They looked so damn vulnerable. "I'm sorry I wasn't there for you. Sorry I left you alone." He had to swallow past the lump in his throat. "If I'd have known...nothing would've kept me away."

"I was going to tell you," she whispered, her hand rubbing circles on Jack's back. "I didn't know I was pregnant until I was almost five months along. I know that sounds stupid, but it's true. I had my...you know, monthly up until six months, which my doctor said isn't uncommon. I lost weight instead of gaining. My dad flipped his lid of course. He said you were...well, he showed me the reports about what happened with you. The ones that were public knowledge. Even then, I said I was going to tell you after Jack was born, but you escaped from a maximum security facility. I had no way to tell you, and honestly I feared you finding out because," she trailed off.

"Because you didn't know what I'd do?" he finished for her.

She met his stare with a worried frown. "I didn't think the man I'd fallen for could do the things you'd been accused of, Jase. Not once did I believe those reports, but then you escaped. How did you get out of a federal prison?"

He lay on his back, letting out the air he'd held while she'd been talking. Shit! He owed her an explanation. He owed so many of his friends one, especially Brooke and his former teammates of his SEAL Team Phantom. "I had help, Brooke. It's a long story, and one I only want to tell once. I need to call in some men I trust. Men who can ensure you and Jack aren't going to be targets, or if you are, these men can and will be able to protect you. These men will come, but I'll need to explain to them, and probably get my ass kicked in the process." He grinned as he thought of the fight to come. Yeah, he could see Kai and Tay taking a swing or two at him. Hell, Coyle or Sully the biggest bastards would hurt the worst, but he'd take it if it meant keeping his family safe.

Chapter Eight

Kai looked at the unknown caller on his phone and raised his brows. Nobody had his private cell number. He thought of letting it go to voicemail then changed his mind. "Swift here, this better not be a telemarketer."

"Hello, Kai. Definitely not trying to sell you anything."

The sound of his former leader's and teammates voice coming from the other end of the line had him standing. He glanced across the room at his friends who'd gathered to celebrate the announcement of the impending birth of a baby to their crew, knowing they'd all be affected by the call. "What do you want, Tyler? Or what're you going by now, Traitor?" Silence descended around him as he spoke.

"You know there's always three sides to every story, Kai. Did you ever think to hear mine? Do you really think I could do the things I was accused of?" Jase's voice got louder toward the end.

He shook his head even though the other man couldn't see it. "You didn't deny it."

"The fuck if I didn't," Jase yelled.

Kai paced the room, thinking back to the day they'd been told Jase had been taken into custody. They hadn't been allowed to speak to him. Hell, he hadn't spoken directly to him other than to send him letters to the United Disciplinary Barracks, better known as USBD in Fort Leavenworth, which he'd never received one back. Only knew what he'd heard and read in reports. "I saw the videos, Jase. Everyone saw them."

A loud sigh on the other end proceeded a prolonged silence.

"Why are you calling me? For that matter, I thought you were dead. Is that another body you can add to your kills?" Kai knew he'd hit a sore spot as Jase cursed down the line. The sound of a woman's voice had him pausing.

"Excuse me, is this Kai Swift?"

"Yes, ma'am. And who may I ask is this?" Kai waved his hand to quiet down the murmurs of his team and the women who'd surrounded him.

"This is Brooke Frazee, Admiral Frazee's daughter. I'd appreciate it if you'd stop slinging insults and maybe listen to what Jase has to say. I think you, better than anyone, should know things aren't always black and white." Her words had him looking at his wife Alexa. She'd been a total surprise to him when he'd found her. Having survived so much, only to be tossed one curve ball after another. Yeah, there were about fifty thousand shades of grey, especially when it came to their world.

"Alright, I'm listening," he said with less heat.

"I'm going to give the phone back to Jase, but just so you know, if you so much as make his eye twitch again, I'm taking it away again. He's risking a lot to call you, and he's doing it for me and our son."

He stopped pacing at her words. Their son? "I'm putting this on speaker so everyone can hear. Full disclosure, the team's all here, including spouses."

"This is a dangerous situation, and I'll understand if you don't want to help," Jase paused. "I promise to tell you everything about what happened during that mission that went to shit, but what's going on right now has nothing to do with it. Or maybe it does. Hell, this is fucked up."

Kai could hear Jase moving around, the sound of his boots hitting what sounded like hard wood flooring. "Where are you right now?"

When Jase told them his location, Kai and his team all grinned. "We can be there in two hours; give or take a few minutes, we're just south of there in a place called Hot Springs. That is of course, if you're ready to explain what the fuck truly happened?"

"There are some pretty crazy switchbacks as you traverse your way up here. It's a little town called New Underwood to the East of Ellsworth Air Force Base about a half hour. Be sure and bring vehicles geared for a rough terrain. And, Kai?" Jase waited a beat. "I have a two year old son. He's my world. You fuck with him, and I'll rain Hell fire on you and anyone who thinks to harm a hair on his perfect head."

"If that's true, then congrats first of all. Second, fuck you for thinking we'd ever harm a child. See you in a few hours." Kai hung up, stunned at the turn of events.

"So, we going off on a great adventure or what?" Alexa asked.

Kai shook his head. "No, we are not," he annunciated each word before continuing. "You and Jaqui are going to sit tight while we check things out. If everything is safe, we'll..."

Jaqui snorted. "Not gonna happen. I'm going. Do you really want to leave her all alone?"

"Now, Jaq, be reasonable here. We have a little one to think about." Tay placed his palm on her stomach.

They were all on vacation and had just found out Tay and Jaqui were expecting a baby. Jaqui rolled her eyes. "I'm not the first woman to have a child, boys. Get over yourselves. Either take us along, or we'll trail behind. Imagine that scenario. Pretty sure that would make us easy targets. What do you think, Alexa?"

Kai nearly groaned as his wife nodded vigorously, making a big circle with her arms around her head. "Such a target. Oh, look at me. Come get me," Alexa said in a scared tone then snorted. "Palease, don't be a moron, Kai."

"Fuck, you women are gonna be the death of me." Kai pulled Alexa into his arms.

Alexa stood on her toes. "Remember the last time we were holed up in a cabin?"

He thought back to the time she was referring to. "Yeah. You were kidnapped out from under me, and those two," he pointed at Oz and Tay before continuing, "were almost killed."

Oz raised his hand. "Almost only counts in hand grenades and horse shoes."

They all said *shut up Oz* in unison. The big guy grinned and tossed his hands in the air. Sully, the smart one quirked his lips but stayed silent.

His wife put her lips next to his ear. "You're remembering the bad stuff. How about when we played cards? More specifically, strip poker?" She licked a slow path beneath his ear then bit his lobe, making him shiver. If she hadn't been standing in front of him, his team would've gotten an eyeful of his erection straining against the front of his jeans.

"Woman, how we gonna recreate that with a houseful of people," he muttered.

Alexa laughed. "I didn't say we were gonna be able to recreate, just trying to bring back good memories."

The little minx stepped away, but he pulled her back to him, placing her back to his front. "Alright, team. This is not just my decision. What do you say? All for one and one for all? I know Jase...well, he said he'd explain, so let's set aside the fact he was charged and convicted of the most heinous crimes that a soldier can commit. He was our brother. It sounds like he's in need of us, and we made a pact a long time ago. If any of us were ever in need, we'd always be there for one another. He made a call for help. I'm willing to stick my neck out, and I hope like hell he isn't setting us up."

Tay came back in from the living room, his computer in his hands. "I did some searching while y'all were doing your thing. Brooke is the only daughter of the late Admiral Frazee. She had an older brother Mark who committed suicide. Her father was killed in a car accident recently." Tay sat the computer on the counter and pointed at the screen. "Take a look at this."

"Holy shit, Tay. Did you hack into the Navy data base?" Kai squinted at the blinking red and black words TOP SECRET.

The big blond man lifted one shoulder. "Hack is such a strong word. I sort of slipped into a slight crack and am just looking around."

Jaqui snorted. "You're so cute when you hack, baby."

"So says a fellow hacker," Oz said, standing over her shoulder.

"I've seen him before." Coyle lifted his chin his dark gaze staring at Kai. "He was there that night when everything went to shit. The night Jase was supposedly meeting with the enemy."

"Alright, let's vote. Are we going or no?" Kai had already decided he was going, but was giving the other guys a chance to choose on their own.

Each member gave him the middle finger then walked out of the kitchen except for Alexa. "I'm taking that as a unanimous yes," Kai muttered.

His wife turned in his embrace. "Did you really think it would be any different?"

Before he could say a word, she stood on her toes and kissed his lips then moved away. "Must pack. We've got places to go, an ex-teammate to save."

Running his hand over his buzzed head, he shook his head. "You realize I'm in charge of this mission?" he called out after her.

*****

Jase hung up the phone and stared at it before he finally met Brooke's eyes. "Thank you for...your words."

Brooke took the phone out of his hands. "Don't thank me for saying the truth. But, you can't get angry at them for how they feel either."

He swung away from her. The familiar anger simmered to the surface. Back then, he couldn't believe they hadn't believed him. Believed in him. How could they think he'd done the crimes he'd been accused of? "I don't want to talk about this, Brooke." No, if he talked about it, or thought about it, he'd lose his cool. And right now, he needed to keep his head on straight. Without stopping to think, he shot a quick text to Erik, letting him know about the team coming in. His partner's response back was short and to the point, making his lips curl in a smile.

"I just gave Erik an update of the situation. He said if anything feels off, to shoot first, ask questions last." Jase shook his head and placed the phone back in his pocket. He hadn't turned the earmic on, wanting privacy between he and Brooke.

"Right. So, what do you want to talk about?" She asked, hands on her hips, glaring at him with her hazel eyes spitting fire at him.

Oh, he knew what he'd rather be doing, but the sound of a little boy waking up had them both turning toward the bedroom.

"You're going to have to talk about it sometime." Hurt echoed in her voice.

Stopping her just inside the bedroom with his hand on her arm. "I know and I will. Let's just enjoy this little bit of time with just the three of us before we're invaded by my, by Kai and the team."

Her hand covered his. "They were your team too."

That damn lump was back, but he swallowed it down and nudged her toward Jack who was fighting to get out from under the blanket.

"I gotta potty. I gotta potty," he squealed.

Brooke laughed and hurried to help their son out of the bed and into the bathroom. Their energy was infectious as he watched them move into the bathroom. While they took care of business, he made the bed out of habit, making sure the corners were tucked in properly. When Jack raced out ahead of Brooke, a grin on his face, Jase swore he'd never seen a cuter kid.

"I did it, Jase. Mommy said I'm the biggest." He pumped his fist and jumped in the air.

Jase knelt on one knee. "Good job. Give me five." He held his hand up for Jack and pretending to wince when his son smacked his little palm against his. "Wow, you sure are the biggest. So, what do you want for breakfast, and don't say a peanut butter and banana sandwich. We big guys need some variety." He lifted Jack into his arms. "How about some scrambled eggs with cheese on top and bacon? Do you like bacon, Jack?"

His son grabbed ahold of his chin and forced his gaze to meet his. "Pigs go oink oink."

A laugh escaped him at the comment. "They sure do. What do cows say?"

Jack went through all the animal sounds while he and Brooke worked together making breakfast for them. It didn't surprise him that their son was so smart. At just over two, he spoke really well, knew animal sounds, and could pick them out in books. "You've done a great job, Brooke," he said once they'd eaten and cleaned up the dishes.

She glanced down at Jack who had tired of the adults and was now on the floor playing with Lincoln logs that they'd found in a closet. "He's an easy kid to love. Not to mention teach. Seriously, he soaks up stuff like a sponge, so watch your words, or he'll repeat them."

Jase sat back and placed his hands over his stomach, the bandage over the wound had been dry when he'd checked this morning as he'd replaced it. With his feet extended in front of him, he crossed one booted foot over the other. "Now that, sounds like an interesting story. Do tell."

Color flooded her cheeks. He always loved how easily she blushed, remembering the way her body would flush during sex as well. Shit! He needed to keep his mind off of sexy time, or his son would get a whole new education.

She glanced down at the bulge in his pants then back at him. "What were we talking about?"

Jase adjusted his erection, winking as her eyes followed the action. "Ignore him."

"Easy for you to say," she snorted.

"Not so easy, actually. I mean, it's really quite...hard," he joked. Her blush got even redder. "God, I love it when you get all red like that. I can imagine how it spreads all the way down and how hot it makes you inside."

She opened her mouth then closed it. "You can't say stuff like that." She looked over at an oblivious Jack.

"Quit trying to change the subject. Come on, spill. What bad things did you teach our son?" Just saying the words our son out loud made him...happy. Hell, he hadn't planned on being a father, yet knowing he was one now was something he'd never regret or change.

"I don't cuss as a rule, or I try not to, especially in front of Jack. Well, one day I was arguing with my mother over something stupid. I thought Jack was sleeping, or I'd have watched my words more closely. After I hung up the phone, I was so angry I called her the B word. Much to my horror Jack was not only awake, but right behind me. He calls out, loudly, the B word in perfect annunciation. Lord, my heart dropped to my stomach. I couldn't very well get onto him when he was repeating my words, but I had to try to explain it was a bad word." She shook her head and smiled ruefully.

"So what did you do?" Jase sat up, placing his elbows on his knees, wondering how she handled the situation. He'd have just brushed it off and hoped for the best.

Brooke bit her lip then grinned. "I told him mommy said a bad word. That that was a bad word, and I was sorry I said it. I asked Jack how I should be punished, and he told me to go to timeout." She chuckled. "Now, being a good mommy, I went to timeout, and my sweet boy went with me. When I asked him why he was going to time-out, he said 'because he said bad word too'. He made me pinky promise not to say it again."

Jase barked out a laugh, picturing the entire thing in his head. Jack turned to peer at them from the floor and laughed. "God, he's precious."

"He really is, isn't he?" she asked with her hands folded against her chest.

Although he'd known the reasoning behind why he hadn't been a part of their lives and missed so many firsts, he still wished things had been different. Without thought, he reached for Brooke, lifting her out of the chair she was in, and sat her in his lap. "I don't want to miss one more smile, or story like that. Never again." His heart felt like it was going to burst out of his chest.

Brooke wet her lips. "Me neither. I mean, I don't want you to miss being a part of Jack's life."

He caught her chin between his fingers. "I don't just mean Jack, and you know it, Brooke. I came back here not knowing about him. I love him. God, do I love him. It's crazy, this all-consuming love for a being I just met, but it was like click, click, boom. You know?"

She nodded. "That's how I felt when I found out I was pregnant. By then, he was big enough that he was moving, only I thought it was gas or butterflies." She laughed. "I was old enough to know better, but it's the truth. When I fainted at work, they called the ambulance. From there I was taken to the ER, and the rest, they say, is history. It was like a light went on, and Jack decided to let me know he was there. My body seemed to grow overnight, which explains the stretchmarks. I didn't care if my entire stomach became one big roadmap of angry red lines as long as my baby was healthy."

Jase's body went still. "What do you mean, healthy?"

"At the hospital when I was going through all these tests and found out I was pregnant, they kept saying I might miscarry or spontaneously abort. Since I'd been having my monthly periods and hadn't gained any weight, had actually lost weight, they said it was a possibility. I placed my hands over my stomach and had a talk with our baby. I promised him or her that I would be the best mom in the world if they would just hang in there."

He put his hands over her stomach. "You did good. Better than good. I wish...I wish I'd been there." His hands flexed.

She covered his hands with one of hers, twisting so she could look him in the eyes. "Things worked out okay. Now, let's talk about something else."

Jase placed his forehead against Brooke's then felt the vibration on his wrists. "We've got company coming. Take Jack to the bedroom and don't come out unless I come get you," he said standing in one motion with her in his arms and placing Brooke on her feet.

"Is it your team?" Brooke hurried to Jack, picking him up in her arms.

He went to the computer he'd set up and looked at it before answering. "Yep. Three vehicles full of people. Looks like Kai and the boys brought their women with." He looked at the small cabin and thought of all of them crowding into the space.

"Do you still want us to go into the bedroom? I'd feel better out here with you." Jack grumbled to get back down and play.

Seeing that his son wasn't too keen on being sequestered away, he looked up at the ceiling. "What if yelling begins and fists get thrown?"

Brooke took Jack back to the toys, murmuring to him before coming back by his side. "First of all, I think you're wise enough to keep your cool in front of your son. Second, if they're not, I trust you to make sure they do. None of you are teenagers with out of control hormones. And besides, they'll see Jack and know they can't just brawl in the living room like a bunch of idiots."

Jase laughed, hoping Brooke was correct. If not, he'd do his best to teach them the error of their ways. His son and the woman he loved lives were on the line.

"Just remember, if the shit hits the fan, you grab Jack and keep him out of harm's way." Jase wrapped his arms around Brooke, giving her one last kiss before the sound of vehicles pulling up in front of the cabin could be heard.

"Trust me, nobody wants to mess with a mama bear. When it comes to Jack, I will rip the head off of anyone who tries to harm him. A mama bear in a full out frenzy would look tame compared to what I'd do if he were injured, especially if it were done because of some stupidness between men old enough to know better."

"Damn woman, that actually made me excited. Does that count as male stupidness?" Jase asked as he kissed her temple.

She slapped his chest and laughed. "Go greet your friends."

He didn't correct her assumption that they were his friends. The fact she told him to go greet them let him know she wanted him to take it outside away from their son. Smart woman. If the guys were going to say or do anything that would hurt her or Jack, he'd rather it be done outside of both their hearing. "I'll be right back. Hopefully, they'll be with me."

"Jase, they wouldn't have come all this way if they weren't your friends, and they sure as heck wouldn't have brought their wives with them if they didn't trust you not to hurt them. Remember that."

Brooke's admonishment had him pausing with his hand on the door, his gun tucked into the waistband at his back felt heavier than normal. As he opened the door, he saw Kai with the woman he recognized from before next to him. Alexa, the daughter of Russian spies looked nervous. Tay had his arm around a woman with long blonde hair. Her petite form next to the large SEAL had Jase's lips twitching as she elbowed Tay in the stomach and moved forward first.

"Hi, my name is Jaqui, and if you hurt any of my friends, I'll make sure they never find the body." She held her hand out as she walked toward him.

He shook his head and gave a wry chuckle. "I'd rather shoot myself than harm one of them," he agreed, walking to meet her halfway and taking her hand in his. She gave him a firm handshake.

"I'm with that big lug." She jerked a thumb over her shoulder at Tay who was right behind her.

"Good to see you, Tay." Jase held his hand out to Tay, waiting to see if he'd take it.

Tay looked at the hand then at Jase. "Let's hope it is," Tay agreed then shook hands.

Jase pretended it didn't hurt that Tay didn't give him the usual back slapping man hug they'd always shared. Hell, that was how they'd always greeted one another in the past. However, that was before. How his life had become so fucked up he had no clue. Always there was a divide when he thought about his time; there was the before the night and after the night.

Coyle and Oz leaned against a big jacked up truck along with Sully. As one they shoved off and came toward him. His body tensed, waiting to see what they'd do. If they came at him as one, he would be hard pressed to take the three of them on. The small gash on his side would give them an extra edge. With a couple side steps, he moved away from the slight form of Jaqui, not wanting her to get injured if punches or kicks were thrown.

"See, I told you he was a good guy."

Jase turned his head to stare in Jaqui's direction, not seeing the big fist that was thrown at him from Oz. He went down on one knee from the impact, and spat blood onto the dry dirt. Shaking his head. "We gonna do this, boys?" He looked up at Oz and Coyle as Sully stayed back shaking his head.

Oz rubbed his knuckles. "No, we ain't doing nothing. I lost the coin toss. One of us had to punch you. Now, it's done. Can we go inside?"

"Jesus, when did you decide someone needed to punch him?" Kai asked as he held his hand down to help Jase up.

Coyle shrugged his shoulders. "When we started out on this here journey. Figured it needed to be done. So now it's done."

Kai placed his hands on his hips. "What kind of logic is that? Figured it needed done, so now it's done? Why the hell didn't we discuss this as a team?"

"Cause you two had women, and we didn't. Therefore, you'd have estrogen in your rigs telling you no. We used that logic and the fact he never wrote us back. Do you know how many letters I wrote that fucker, and he never wrote me back? Not once, did you write me back. So, a split lip ain't so bad, I figure." Coyle stabbed an accusing finger at Jase.

"I never got a letter from any of you. It was like you all washed your hands of me, turning your backs like I was a pariah when I could've used a friend," he yelled back.

The sound of the door opening and shutting behind him had all their gazes focusing on the porch and on Brooke and Jack. "Hi, everyone. Jack and I heard voices, and my little man here wanted to see what was going on. He's only two but is very inquisitive. Tell everyone hi, Jack." Brooke rocked her hips back and forth.

Jase could see her daring any one of them to say a negative word. Damn, she was fierce without even trying. "I didn't get any letters," he reiterated quietly, too low for Brooke and Jack to hear, but he saw Coyle and Oz's eyes narrow while Sully tilted his head to the side. All three men would know he wasn't lying. He had no reason to at this point.

Chapter Nine

Brooke hid the fact she was shaking by holding Jack a little tighter. She'd watched as one of the men had punched Jase when his head was turned and wanted to run out the door to help him. Of course, the guy who'd done the hitting was twice as big as her and a couple inches larger than Jase.

Jack waved his right arm but ducked his head against her chest.

Jase ran his thumb over his lip and spat on the ground. She could see his split lip from the porch and hated the man who'd done the damage. "Guys, I'd like you to meet Brooke and my son Jack. We haven't told Jack I'm his father yet, and I don't want him hurt."

She watched as he walked backward toward her, keeping the people in the yard within sight.

The tall man who had gotten out of the first vehicle wrapped his arm around the woman next to him. Lord, he was handsome, reminding her of the actor the Rock. Yikes, she'd always had a thing for him even when he'd wrestled back in the day.

Jase came to stand on the top step next to her, waiting.

"Afternoon, ma'am. I'm Kai, and this is my wife Alexa," Kai said from the bottom of the stairs.

"Hi, thank you for coming." She held out her left hand while keeping her right under Jack. She noticed Jase didn't offer to take their son, figuring he wanted both arms free. God, she hated this. Hated the uncertainty.

Kai took her hand in a gentle but firm squeeze stepping aside as the others came forward. Alexa took her hand next, but instead of shaking, she placed both of her hands around Brooke's. "We're here to help you, no matter what it looked like out here."

Jaqui snorted and muttered *amen* before walking forward and up the stairs. "Ignore them, they're a bunch of assholes most of the time, but they're our assholes."

Jack's head popped up. "Mommy, she said bad word. You gotta go timeout now." He pointed his finger at Jaqui.

Brooke laughed at Jaqui as she covered her mouth with her palm, muttering she was sorry.

Tay groaned as he followed up the stairs, kissing Brooke on the cheek, which stunned her. "I'm not an asshole, just so you know."

Her son pointed his finger at Tay. "Him too, mommy. You say asshole, too." Jack's eyes widened. "Oh, no. They made me say bad word."

Jaqui put her arms around them both. "I think I love this little guy. How about we all go to timeout together?"

"Alright, no more bad words from any of you. You, little man, get one free pass." She pointed her finger at Jack. He nodded vigorously, making a zipping motion across his lips.

Sully came up, silently. He took her hand and kissed her knuckles, ruffling Jack's hair. "I'll make sure nobody else cuss's or they'll all be in timeout. By the way, I wasn't in on dumb and dumbers decision earlier." He pointed his finger over his shoulder at his teammates.

She tensed as both Oz and Coyle came forward. Without stopping to think, she handed Jack to his dad then stepped in front of the two men as they reached the stairs. "You got one free shot at him," she pointed her thumb at Jase over her shoulder. "You try it again, and I'll shoot you in the dick," she whispered so her son wouldn't overhear.

Both men covered their groins. Oz slapped Coyle on the shoulder. "I'm glad it was you who lost that coin toss," he muttered.

"Dang, your girl is scary." Kai slapped Jase on the shoulder, the hit was one of affection, not anger.

"Ma'am, I promise I won't do it again...for past transgressions. Now, I can't say it won't happen in the future. You need to understand, sometimes shit...I mean stuff happens, like that one time...what, why you all looking at me?" Coyle glared at Kai then Jase.

"Let's take this inside. I think little man here is ready for a nap." Jase ran his hand over Jack's back as their son lay his head on Jase's chest.

"He looks just like you," Tay said, staring at them both.

The proud smile that washed over Jase's lips, and lit up his features was one she'd remember for the rest of her life.

"Nah, I think he's perfect, unlike me." He kissed Jack's cheek then led the way back inside.

Jaqui stopped next to her, placing one hand on Brooke's arm. "How old is he?"

She shook her head to clear the thoughts from her mind. Jase thinking he wasn't good enough was written all over him. Looking at the tiny blonde, she struggled to remember what she'd asked. "I'm sorry, can you repeat that?"

"It's okay, I just wondered how old Jack was."

"Oh, he's two going on twenty," she laughed.

"He's the spitting image of Jase. I mean...wow. I hope my kids look just like Tay." She placed a hand on her stomach.

Brooke shut the front door after them, looking from Jaqui to Tay, then down where Jaqui's hand rested. "How far along are you?"

A smile split her lips. "We just passed twenty-two weeks."

"Do you know what you're having?" Excitement bubbled inside her at the prospect of new life and memories from her pregnancy.

Jaqui shook her head then nodded. "What I mean is we had a sonogram, but we had the sonographer put the results in an envelope and seal it. We're going to do a reveal of some kind but didn't want to know beforehand either."

"That is so cool. I would've loved to have done something like that." She'd had a sonogram at the ER, found out she was pregnant, and what she was having all in the span of hours. With her next pregnancy, she'd love to do something like Tay and Jaqui. Her thoughts skidded to a halt as she realized what she was doing. Building castles out of sand. "Silly child, don't you know sandcastles get destroyed when the tide comes in?" she muttered under her breath the words her mother had said to her more times than she liked to remember.

"What was that?" Jaqui asked, looking puzzled.

Taking a deep breath, she pasted on a smile. "Nothing. I love those reveal parties. I've watched some on YouTube. Have you seen some of them?" she steered the conversation toward different videos and laughed as Alexa pulled up a few failed ones.

While she and the two women sat in the living room, her appreciation for female friendship grew. Yes, she liked the time with Jase, but laughing with the two women and getting to know them made her feel as if things were normal. As if they weren't hiding out because someone had tried to kill her, or at the very least, break into her apartment.

"Jase is really good with Jack." Alexa's voice broke into her musings.

Her son had fallen asleep within minutes of them coming back inside, wanting his friend Jase to put him to bed. How she wanted to tell her son Jase was not just his friend...but his dad.

"I'm glad he likes Jack."

Alexa plopped down on one side of her on the couch while Jaqui sat on the other side. Both women laughed for a moment before Alexa sobered. "Honey, that man has looked in here at least a dozen times checking on you. I can guarantee you, if he thought we were being mean or threatening to you, he'd have been on our asses in a heartbeat."

Her head jerked up and looked across the room, meeting the intense gaze of Jase's. She took a deep breath and let it out. "Damn, he's sexy," she murmured as he winked and leaned forward with his arms on the back of a chair.

"Girl, they're all too sexy, but it's our crosses to bear. We're saving the world by taking them out of rotation." Jaqui held her fist out for Alexa to pound.

Caught between the two women, she sat back and chuckled. "So, you're saying it's our duty to be with them, because they're a menace to society? What with the good looks and muscles?"

Alexa nodded. "Oh yeah, the fights they'd start if they walked into a bar and all the women left their men to hang on ours would be astronomical. Luckily for all those men, we've taken them in...hand." Alexa held her hands out and made squeezing motions.

"What're you ladies talking about?" Kai asked, from the other room.

Alexa held up her hands. "I was telling Brooke I like to juggle balls."

Kai tilted his head to the side as Brooke busted out laughing while Jaqui began giggling like a loon. The big SEAL team leader pointed his finger at his wife and mouthed something Brooke didn't catch, but it had Alexa laughing and clapping.

"You are in trouble," Jaqui said.

Alexa nodded. "I know and I like it."

*****

Jase had worried about leaving Brooke alone with the other women but shouldn't have. After he'd put Jack down for a nap, he'd come back to find her in the living room chatting easily with the duo. He'd motioned for the men to come into the kitchen. Although it was an open concept space, he felt they could sit down at the table and hash things out. Kai took a seat at the head of the table, making his status clear as the leader. The move was fine with Jase. In the last three years, he'd come to grips with the fact he was no longer team leader of SEAL Team Phantom. Oz, Coyle, and Tay took the other three chairs, leaving him to stand along with Sully. Again, he was fine as that gave him a chance to gather his thoughts. These men were like brothers to him for years, worked as a team and had each other's backs during times most would never understand.

"First, I'd like to say thank you for coming," he said into the quite room. He met each man in eye. "Let me start by saying I've had mixed emotions about each and every one of you as I'm sure you've had about me. Let me finish before you ask any questions, alright?"

As they all nodded, he took a calming breath. "The night that I supposedly met with the leader of the insurgents wasn't what it looked like. I didn't meet with that man in the video. If it had been analyzed, they'd have seen it for the fake it was. Tay, you being the computer expert you are, you can surely pull that footage up and have it checked out in a matter of hours. I did however meet with someone that night. Everything about that meeting except the individual in the video was correct. What we talked about? Me asking about coordinates, how many were there, what I was taking my men into? All that was correct, because I wasn't taking my team into an ambush. Something felt off. I'd never had an admiral pull me aside and give me orders on a mission before. This was a man who'd told me not six months prior he'd ruin me if I didn't leave his daughter alone."

He saw Brooke's head raise at his words. "What do you mean?"

"Come here." He held his hand out to her.

"Your dad showed up in the middle of the desert and dropped a bomb on me. He said there was a hostage situation, a young American girl, and wanted me and my team to head out right then to an undisclosed location. He said he'd give me the rest of the intel once we were en route. After he'd threatened my life and career, I didn't trust him. I told him I needed to see the orders, that there was protocol to be followed. We fought and then he left. The next day we found out the other SEAL team had been ambushed and all fingers were pointed at me."

Brooke stood between his legs, trembling. "It can't be possible. My dad would never...he'd never kill, or rather have people killed. He loved his country, his fellow soldiers."

She tried to move away from him. "Listen to me. He put on a different face for you. I'm sure he was a great dad, but that's not who I saw that night outside your home or in the middle of the desert. The man who told me point blank my life would be over if I didn't do what he said. I left you alone, just like he'd demanded. Don't you think it's strange that around the same time you found out you were pregnant, he made his way to the desert where me and my team were?"

"He was really angry when he found out I was pregnant, but he was happy once Jack got here. My mom was awful too, until I had Jack. I don't know what I would've done without them and their support. It's just...to think he'd...oh god, I'm sorry," she cried.

Jase gave her a little shake. "Sssh, you have nothing to apologize for, honey. We can't control the actions of others. I could condemn myself for things I didn't do that night in the desert that would've prevented the death of the other team, but I can't change the past. We don't have the power to do that. Pointing fingers gets us exactly nowhere. However, there are things we can do. I don't believe your dad was working alone. That's why I said I needed into his office."

"You've got a plan," Kai said.

Jase nodded.

"I think we owe you an apology." Tay stood up from the table.

The sound of chairs scraping against the floor echoed around the room after Tay's announcement.

Jase held Brooke tighter. "No apologies needed. Water under the bridge and all that shit."

Oz shook his head. "No, we all judged you as guilty and turned our backs on you. We were your brothers, and we didn't trust in you. It's your turn. One free punch. Go ahead, hit Coyle."

"Hey, why do I get to be the one he punches?" Coyle glared from Oz to Jase.

"You punched him, he punches you. Even stevens." Oz stepped behind Kai as he spoke, flinching when Coyle jerked as if he was going to punch him.

"I admit I was angry at all of you for a long time. I even had the grim reaper tattooed on my chest as a reminder that my old life was dead." He rubbed his chest where the tattoo in question lay.

"Oh, you got a tattoo, bad boy," Alexa said bumping her hip against Brooke's as she stepped around to stand next to Kai.

Brooke glanced up at him. "You've got several tattoos you didn't have when we were together before."

He shrugged. "They all have meaning. Back to what we were talking about though, I'm not angry anymore. I think I left all the anger behind at that cabin I blew up."

Kai raised his hand. "Speaking of cabins, this one is kinda small. I made a call and happen to know of a place that is a lot more secure and big enough to hold all of us. It's a short drive from here, if you want to use it."

Jase's mind lit on where he thought Kai was talking about. "Rowan's place?"

"That'd be the one. He said it's all fixed up and ready for visitors of the friendly kind, if we wanted to use it." Kai waited.

Jase lifted Brooke's chin up with one finger. "Feel like a little road trip?"

Her lip trembled, but she nodded. "Yeah, but how is that going to get you into my dad's office?"

"Let me get you and Jack to safety. There's some things we need to do before we go busting into your old house. First and foremost, securing our son. This cabin," he looked around. "It's a good stop, but it's not what I'd deem the safest location. Rowan Shade has a home with a safe room. Do you know what that is?"

She nodded. "I've seen them in movies."

His smile came easier at her words. "Well, the ones in movies will have nothing on what our old teammate has. He takes security to a whole other level."

A round of hooyah filled the air as all five men raised their fist and yelled the SEAL battle cry.

*****

Brooke gathered up Jack's things while the guys talked in the kitchen. Fear for what was to come had her heart pounding. She thought of calling her mom to check on her, but shut the impulse down almost immediately. Goosebumps raced up and down her arms, making her shiver in the warm room.

"Need any help?" Alexa asked.

Startled, Brooke spun to face the door, reaching for the first thing she could find that looked like a weapon. The large piece of stone that served as decoration fit in the palm of her hand, ready to use. She froze as she met the unblinking eyes of the other woman. "Oh lord, I'm sorry. You scared me." Carefully, she sat the rock back down, exhaling the air from her lungs. Jesus, she was so on edge she almost bludgeoned the woman.

Alexa held her hands up. "Hey, I totally get it. After everything I've been through, trust me, I'm pretty skittish, too. I think I stopped jumping anytime there was a big boom, oh about...never. I'm still working on it, but with our guys' help, it's getting easier," she said, coming into the room and sat on the bed.

Brooke tried not to feel guilty as she looked around to make sure she hadn't forgotten anything. Of course, they didn't bring much, but what she did was important to her. Taking a deep breath, she sat down next to Alexa. "I'm not cut out for this...sort of stuff. Not that you were. It's just that—I have Jack and everything seems so much harder, you know? If it were only me, I'd be...I don't know, less—that sounds stupid. I'm sure you weren't less scared when you were kidnapped and tortured just because you didn't have a child. I'm being stupid and insensitive." She scrubbed her hands down her face. Jase had told her a little about the horrors both women had faced, and how the SEAL team had been instrumental in saving them, yet both women were true heroines in her eyes. If she'd been in either of their shoes, facing the same dangers, Brooke didn't know if she'd have been as brave.

Jaqui walked into the room without knocking, her long blonde hair pulled into a messy bun on top her head. "Are we bonding? We can't bond in a bedroom during the day without alcohol, and I hate to be the bearer of bad news, but this train is moving, ladies. Come on, up and at 'em." She clapped her hands. "Once we get to the cabin in the woods," she paused, "wait, that sounds creepy as all get out. Once we get to our next location, we'll get drunk and dish all the dirt on our guys. Except me, dang it. Well, I'll watch while you guys get hammered and remember every detail so I can have torment material."

Alexa stood and pulled Brooke up. "Ignore the crazy pregnant lady, besides, you've got a little guy who needs you to stay strong."

Looking at the two women who were both smaller in stature than her, she realized if they could survive what life had thrown at them, surely she could as well. Besides, she had Jase and a team of men and the two women surrounding her and Jack. "You're right. I just needed a little pity party for one. I'm alright."

Alexa looked at Jaqui before giving a chuckle. "That was your pity party? Remind me to not have one of my own in front of you, 'cause let me tell you, there are crocodile tears and cussing involved."

Jaqui held her hand up and the two ladies slapped their palms together. Jaqui wrapped her arm around Brooke's waist and pulled her into their little hug. "She cusses almost as bad as a sailor."

"Hey, I happen to be married to one and you are one," Alexa said then laughed as she pulled away. "Let's get going before our men come looking for us. You know how they are about timeframes. You'd think they had a clock wired into their brains," she muttered walking out of the room.

"I think it's part of the SEAL training," Jaqui mused as she followed Alexa out, looking back in. "You coming?"

Alexa carried her and Jack's bags, leaving Brooke to follow behind her new friends down the hall to where Jase and the other guys waited. Silence greeted them as they entered the kitchen area, making her feel as if they'd interrupted an argument. "What's going on?"

Jase was to her side in two long strides. "Nothing. We're discussing the game plan once we reach Rowan's place."

"Why do I feel like it's a lot more than that?" she asked but couldn't delve further as Jack came into the room in the arms of Tay, looking like they were best friends. Lord, when had her life changed so drastically.

"Look who I found?" Tay lifted Jack onto his shoulder. "Why, this big guy just about took me out, didn't you?" He tickled Jack's tummy, making him giggle.

"He didn't see me, mommy. I was right under the covers," Jack laughed, his words held a childish tone with the word right sounding more like white.

Tay sat Jack down on the floor, looking down at him with his hands on his hips. "You flipped those blankets back so fast and yelled BOO. You just about made me wet my pants, mister."

His words had Jack laughing so hard he fell on his bottom, the giggle was one Brooke loved and wanted to hear for years to come. "You little monkey." She bent and picked Jack up, inhaling his sweet child scent.

Jack's eyes went wide. "Oh no, big boys don't potty in their pants. You can bowo some of my pullups." He puffed his chest out like he was bigger.

It took all her control not to burst out laughing as Tay stood in front of them with a straight face, tapping his chin and pretended to think. "You know what, I think I've learned my lesson. I've got my eyes on you now. You won't be able to scare me again." He ruffled Jack's hair. Another shock came as her son leapt from her arms into Tay's.

"I like you," Jack announced, hugging Tay around the neck.

Brooke looked at Jase and could see the wish it was him his son was hugging and saying those words to. Tay, being the big softie he was told Jack he liked him too.

"Alright, people, let's load up and move out. Jase, you need to do anything to close this place up, or we good to file out?" Kai asked as his stare took in the room.

"We already loaded the perishables into your truck, so it's go time. Brooke and Jack are riding with me. I'm assuming you're leading, and we'll be in the middle?" Jase put his arm around Brooke, easing a little of her fear.

Although she liked all the men and women in the cabin, she didn't want to be separated from Jase, nor was she willing to part from Jack.

Once the riding and driving order was agreed upon, they filed out of the cabin. Jase made sure she and Jack were buckled in, before he made one last scan of the inside of the cabin.

"You ready for a road trip, honey?" She turned in the seat to make sure Jack was comfy. Jase's vehicle had a DVD player, and he'd already downloaded toddler friendly movies. Such a thoughtful man...no father. As her son clapped happily at the opening credits to one of his favorite cartoons, she turned back around in time to see Jase walking out of the cabin, head held high, with that predators gait she'd always found so damn sexy. "Damn, he should be outlawed," she whispered. Her words had her sitting up straight. The man was an outlaw...or was he?

Chapter Ten

Jase made sure there was no evidence left of them in the cabin, aside from finger prints, which unless he had a cleanup crew come in, he wouldn't be able to scrub away. Kai wasn't happy with the addition to the team in the form of Erik, but he trusted the other man. If it hadn't been for Erik Branson, Jase would still be in the USDB at Fort Leavenworth, a maximum security federal prison, doing time for crimes he hadn't committed. In the past two and a half years, he'd formed a friendship and bond with the other man, that was as close as his relationship with Kai and the other guys on his SEAL team had been. No, with Erik he didn't always have to be perfect. He could fuck up and tell Erik to fuck off, all while Erik was telling him to go get fucked, but they always had each other's backs. The other man had gotten him in and out of tight places, putting his own life on the line to ensure Jase got out alive. Not that Kai and the other guys wouldn't do the same, but Erik didn't do it out of a sense of duty but out of loyalty. He understood where Jase had been, where he'd fallen, and where he wanted to end up. Erik may not always be the one at the front of a mission, taking the chances like Jase, but that didn't mean he wasn't listening in and finding ways to get Jase out if things went to shit. When all else failed, Erik was the one who came. He was the grim reaper nobody wanted to meet.

"You okay?" Brooke asked when he settled into the driver's seat.

The leather steering wheel squeaked under his fingers from gripping it too hard. "Yeah, everything's fine. Buckle up. You can take a nap if you want. It's a couple hours' ride."

Hurt flashed across her beautiful face. "Don't. Don't shut me out. If you're upset or you don't want to talk about something, just say it, but don't push me away." Her dad had done that to her mom, and while Nancy Frazee didn't seem to give two shits, she was not her mother.

Jase gritted his teeth and waited until they got on the highway before he could form the right words. The last thing he wanted or needed was a hurt Brooke. Once he felt secure on the highway, he set the cruise control and kept the vehicle in line behind Kai. The device that was always on with Erik, he shut off with a push of his finger. For the moment, he wanted what went on between him and Brooke to be between just the two of them. "I suck at this. I'm gonna fuck up. I am a fuck up, Brookey, but I'm trying. I didn't want you to go to sleep so I didn't have to talk to you. My mind is trying to come up with different scenarios and plans for each one. I need plans in place in case this or that happens. It's how I work. I'm sorry if you felt like I was...no, I'm sorry for being a dick." He held his palm open in the center console. He didn't want to push her by taking her hand. As her small fingers ghosted over the center of his palm, a tingle of awareness went straight to his heart. That small acceptance from her meant more than if he'd scored with another woman. Brooke wove her fingers through his, looking tiny and delicate. Their son's was even smaller, reminding him he had so much at stake. "I'll keep you and Jack safe. No matter what, you two will be my top priority."

Her fingers clenched in his. "Your life is just as precious, Jase Tyler. Don't you forget that for one minute. That little boy back there needs his father."

He looked in the back through the rearview mirror, seeing the child who looked so much like him only filled with all the goodness of his mother. "He's got the team wrapped around his finger. Damn, he's smart. Are all kids his age like that?" He looked over his shoulder, taking in more of Jack with his own eyes instead of a mirror image.

Brooke shrugged. "I think there are some who are smarter and some maybe not on the same level yet. It depends on the child and how much time the parents spend teaching them. With Jack, I read to him all the time. He's like a little sponge, which makes it fun. Not to mention the daycare he goes to twice a week also helps."

He narrowed his eyes, not liking the idea of strangers watching his son. Just as he opened his mouth to question her, his phone buzzed. Releasing her fingers pained him. "Tyler here," he barked.

"You turned your earpiece off," Erik stated.

Jase rolled his eyes. "I was talking with Brooke. What's up?"

A put-upon sigh came through the line. "Man, you realize I was sitting here thinking you'd been hurt or captured, or that your old team had done something nefarious with your big ass."

Jase barked out a laugh. "Nefarious? Man, you been reading too many romance novels or what?"

"Hey, don't hate on my reading materials unless you try one. I bet you'd enjoy them, but that's beside the point." The sound of fingers clicking on a keyboard at rapid fire could be heard.

"I'll take your word for it. I will however state for the record that I hope you don't have a hidden collection of bodice ripper books with that long-haired dude on the cover."

"Hey, there is nothing wrong with those, although now they're more sexy man chest covers," Brooke said.

Erik groaned. "See, now your woman thinks I like romance for the covers. Tell her I like pussy. Lots of pussy."

Jase looked at Brooke and rolled his eyes. "Erik told me to tell you hi and that maybe you guys can swap books some day."

His friend used some inventive curse words then hung up on him. Jase took a moment to wipe the tears of laughter from his eyes as Brooke looked at him with a strange smile on her face. "You like him," she stated.

"Of course, he's my partner." He turned the signal on when he saw Kai's come on, following the other vehicle down the off ramp with Tay behind.

"No, you like him as in he's your friend. I saw how you were with Kai and the others. You were nice and all, but with Erik, you were...relaxed. I could see you truly enjoyed messing with him, like brothers do." Her hand rested on the console between them.

He placed his over hers, enjoying the connection. "I guess you're right. When I was part of the SEALs I had that with them, but that trust was broken on both sides. Now, there's a wall between us."

She brought their hands up to her mouth and kissed his knuckles. "It's not broken but bent. You guys just need to straighten it out. It'll take a minute or ten, but when you do, your friendship will be stronger than ever, like titanium. You know the saying tough as steel? Well, yours will be tough as titanium. You guys will be TAT. Much cooler than TAS." Another kiss was placed on his knuckles, before she brought their hands to rest on her thigh.

Her words made the hollow ache shrink at the possibility that he could get back to where he'd once been or forge a new place with Kai and the team. Yeah, he liked the idea of forging a new path, sort of like he and Brooke were doing. "You know, I think I can see a new tattoo in my future with something like that. Or maybe with a clock, an old fashion pocket watch that only you and I would know what it means. Sometimes, things take a minute or ten." The thought took hold and held.

"Where would you put it?" she asked, her eyes going from his face to his chest.

Loathe to release her hand, he brought their clasped palms to his chest right above his heart. Through the shirt, he could feel the solid thud thud against their fingers. "Right there," he said. There was a skull he would cover up, but it seemed appropriate. "I like your tattoos, too. They're delicate, like you. When this is over, I'm going to trace them with my fingers, lips, and tongue."

"Perfect." Her chin wobbled as if she was fighting tears.

*****

Brooke imagined what he'd look like once he got the new ink, praying he'd want her around after he got it. Sure, they'd made love and he'd talked about the future with Jack, but she wasn't going to create a world on fairy tales. One day at a time. If he left this time, she wouldn't fall apart again, she'd fight, unlike three years ago. Hearing him talk about her tattoos but not asking why she had the ones she did, made her wonder if he realized what they were.

"Almost there. You hungry? We can stop and grab something at a fast food place."

Jase's words had her glancing back at Jack who'd fallen asleep. He'd always been a good rider and seemed to find the motion of the vehicle relaxing enough. He slept if they drove for anything over an hour. "Can we stop by a store so I can pick up a few things for him that are his favorites. I hate uprooting him like this and would feel better if I can at least provide him with some things that are normal."

"Erik already took care of it. He sort of has a file on everyone. If you went to the store in the past year and there were things you bought multiple times, he's probably got a spreadsheet on it," Jase said casually.

She released his hand. "Okay, backup. He did what? That is a form of...stalking or something."

The big oaf raised one brow. "Sweetheart, this is a mission. Trust me, Erik didn't go digging in order to find anything nefarious."

Brooke slapped his arm. "Don't joke. It's another invasion. First the guys breaking in, and now you're telling me your friend knows when I bought tampons and condoms, or a vibrator."

Jase's warm hand lifted her chin. "Okay, I'm just gonna skip the condoms comment and jump straight to the vibrator. What did you buy?"

"Oh my god, you are such a guy," she growled. Heat lit up her face, or at least she was sure it did, from the embarrassment she felt from her outburst. "Oh my god, can he hear us now?" She pointed to his ear.

The man, who didn't realize he was closer to eunuch status had the audacity to laugh then sobered as she reached across the console and palmed him. "You should probably think really long and hard before you say something stupid, Mr. Tyler." She gave his balls a warning squeeze.

Jase shook his head, his lips twitching. "I turned it off."

With her hand still holding his balls, she checked on Jack. "You're so lucky."

The dick beneath her hand twitched, getting harder. "You are not getting hard right now," she whispered.

"Your hand is on my cock. Of course I'm getting hard," he groaned as she gave another squeeze and let go. "You've got a mean streak a mile wide, Brookey."

"Back to the original point of the conversation. Supplies and things for Jack. You think your buddy has stocked the place with stuff Jack likes? I thought this was a super secure place that nobody could get into?" she questioned.

The phone buzzed between them, making her groan. "If that's your superspy guy, tell him he better not have gone through my nightstand."

Jase covered his lips with his hand before hitting the speaker on his cell. "What's up, Branson?"

"You've got to stop silencing the damn mic, asshole. I was going to drop off some supplies, but that is a negative ghost rider. I was going to leave it for you outside the perimeters of the cabin, but that place is like on a whole other level of security. I could crack it, but I'd be weakening its defenses, and it would take me some time. Which brings me to the call. What do you want me to do with the goods?" Erik sounded irritated.

"Where are you now?" Jase asked as they drove through a small town in South Dakota.

His friend named the same town they were passing through.

"Hold tight. Call me back in five." Jase hung up without waiting for Erik to respond, his finger pressing another button on the phone.

"What's wrong?" Kai asked.

"Nothing. My partner is here with some supplies I requested. I'm going to swing in and pick them up."

"Negative," Kai barked.

Brooke watched the change morph over Jase. "Excuse me?"

Kai's sigh was loud over the speaker. "We don't know who could be watching and waiting. We'll have Oz and the guys grab and go. Tay will stay behind and make sure nobody follows them. Think, Jase. We have women and your son now."

*****

Jase took a deep breath, looking in the rearview mirror at their son, before glancing into Brooke's eyes. "Fine, I need to let him know of the change." He told Kai where Erik was and what he looked like, hoping his friend wasn't going to be too pissed, but the words of the other man had hit home. No matter how good of a friend, or how much he trusted him, Brooke and Jack were his main priority.

"If he's on the up and up, he'll understand," Kai said before he disconnected.

Brooke bit her lip. He hated that his little family was in the middle of his world. Hated that her father had put her and Jack there. He would make sure they never had to worry, like they were now, ever again. The thought had him pausing. How the hell was he going to keep them from this life unless he changed his entire world? Going back to being a SEAL was out. He'd figure it out once this last mission was complete. It was the mission that had kept him going, the one that had killed the other SEAL team and started the entire shit storm that had become his life. Once it was over, he'd figure out what to do with the rest of his life. One thing was for certain; he wanted Brooke and Jack in his life.

After he told Erik about the change in plans, the other man had snorted, but accepted without issue. "Turn the fucking ear mic on. You know you don't have to keep it on where I hear your convo, asshole," Erik said, explaining how he'd programmed the little device. Jase shook his head, following the directions. The small beep allowed him to hear Erik tapping away. Another press allowed Erik to hear him. Once he had the ear piece set where they wanted it, open for communications, but silenced unless activated, he and Brooke rode the rest of the way in silence.

The roads Kai took them on were almost hidden. If you didn't know they were there, you'd definitely miss them. The bouncing of the vehicle down the rough roads woke Jack. Brooke unbuckled and climbed into the back so she could get him a drink and keep him company. Their voices as she pointed out the window and talked about the trees, soothed him. "You guys okay back there?"

Jack gave him a thumbs up with a grin. How could the kid he'd just met take up such a large space in his heart? They took another turn before the road finally evened out. The familiar cabin came into view.

"Wow, it's stunning," Brooke said leaning between the two seats.

He almost scolded her for not being buckled but clamped his lips together. Rowan Shade was once a member of their SEAL team. Now he was happily married to a woman connected to a motorcycle club. When he'd tried to dig up information on the Iron Wolves, he hadn't been able to get anything past the fact they tricked out vehicles for the wealthy and owned a club that catered to bikers and rougher clientele. "A former SEAL owns it. He's in the security business now, but he also hasn't cut ties with his brothers."

Brooke's hand rested on his arm. "They'd welcome you back if you told them the truth."

Without agreeing, he came to a stop behind Kai's truck, waiting until the SEALs got out and checked the area. He wasn't letting his family outside his own vehicle until he was sure the area was secure. A few minutes later, Kai returned to his truck, opening the door to allow his wife out. Jase shook his head as Alexa jumped down and kissed Kai soundly before sauntering up the wide steps to the front door. "I can see who wears the pants in that relationship." He looked back at Brooke and thought he'd be in the same boat if she allowed him. The image of Brooke greeting him with unabashed joy, had him popping the door open before he could do something stupid like drag her back in the front seat and kiss her senseless. Or hell, maybe he'd be the one senseless.

Opening her door, he leaned in. "I'll grab yours and Jack's stuff. You need help with the big guy there?"

Jack was squirming. "I gotta potty, mommy. Gotta potty, now."

"Nope but we better hurry." She worked to get Jack out of his car seat.

Jase held the door open for her and Jack, waiting for them to get out, then moved out of the way while they rushed up the steps to the cabin.

"When we have a boy, I'm gonna teach him to go pee outside. Just drop his pants and go." Tay shook his head as he stared after Brooke and Jack.

Jaqui snorted. "Oh sure, I bet that'll go over really well. I can hear the phone calls now. *Excuse me, ma'am, but your son is urinating on my favorite fig tree. Or, 'Ma'am, your boy pissed all over my rose bush and flashed his peepee in front of the children,'* she snorted.

Tay shrugged. "Hey, boys will be boys."

He clapped Tay on the shoulder. "I'm gonna let you dig yourself outta that hole."

Oz snorted. "I agree. If the lord didn't want us being able to pull it out and take a leak anywhere, he wouldn't have made it so darn easy."

Not willing to get into the right or wrong arguments of boys peeing outside, he carried the bags inside the large cabin, whistling as he walked inside. "Damn, Rowan sure has done good."

"He's got a great security set up as well," Kai mentioned, tilting his head toward the hallway. "Drop the bags in one of the bedrooms and follow me. I'll show you."

"Which do you want?" he asked Kai.

There were two bedrooms on the top level and two on the bottom. He thought of taking their bags upstairs, but decided he'd rather them be on the ground floor. The large room he choose had its own bathroom with a tub and shower like the other. He assumed the two upstairs were similarly outfitted.

"Oh, there you are. Jack wants to know if we can go outside and explore?" Brooke and Jack stood outside what must be the hall bathroom. His son had his chin on his chest, looking sad.

Jase squatted down, lifting the little boy's face up until he looked him in the eye. "What's wrong, big guy?"

Jack's lower lip wobbled, tears pooled in his dark brown eyes. "I didn't make it to the potty in time."

He looked at Brooke and saw she held a plastic bag in her hand.

"Hey, it's okay. You did real good, buddy." When Jack shook his head, Jase pulled him into his arms, settling him on his left thigh. "Yes, you did. You rode all the way in the car without incident, and you never once complained. Heck, see that big guy over there," he pointed at Coyle, lowering his voice. "He used to whine all the time when he was stuck in a convoy for over two hours without being able to stop. We used to joke we were gonna have to put big people diapers on him. Can you imagine what he'd look like wearing those?"

Jack looked over at Coyle and shook his head. "We wouldn't laugh at him, though."

His son's compassion had him hugging him tighter. "That's right, 'cause sometimes accidents happen. Now, if you go ask that big guy if he'll go outside with you and your mom, maybe he'll show you some cool stuff."

Coyle winked at them, showing he'd heard their conversation. "Maybe we'll see a bear," Coyle stated.

His son clapped and pulled away. Jase stood back up, holding out his hand. "Want me to take care of that?"

Brooke looked at the bag and then him. "Thank you. They need to be washed, luckily I keep a spare in my purse."

"I'll take care of it after I check things over with Kai." He eyed the backpack style purse she carried.

The smile that she gave him made him realize he'd do absolutely anything to see her happy and content. After she handed him the bag with Jack's soiled clothing, she kissed his cheek then followed Jack and Coyle out the door.

"You gonna stand there and stare at the door forever?" Kai asked from behind him.

Jase lifted his finger but turned around and followed his former teammate into the room he went into. "Dayum, Rowan Shade. I need to talk with him."

Kai snorted. "Don't pretend you didn't know what he had here. Of course, he's made some modifications since the last time you were in the area."

He ignored Kai's reference and sat down in the other rolling chair. From one monitor, he saw the front of the cabin from several different angles. Kai pointed out which monitor did what then stood. "There's two safe rooms as well. One on the top floor and one down here, along with a weapons room. Come on, I'll show you, and then we'll come back and get you logged into the system so you have access."

The sight of Brooke and Jack running across one of the monitors had him pausing as he got up. "Is there audio feed as well?"

"Yeah, but it's limited at best. They have to be near one of the cameras in order for us to pick up what they're saying. I think. Shit, you never know what Rowan has done to the technology since last time." Kai lifted one shoulder, waving toward the door with his hand. "We can give him a call after the tour."

Watching as Brooke covered Jack's hair with a handful of leaves, then run away as Jack picked up some to do the same, made him wish he was outside with them. He vowed they'd have years to do just that and more.

He and Kai went through the first safe room, seeing it had a small cot and a few amenities. The second one upstairs was almost identical. As they went back down, they met Oz who had a frown on his face. "Rowan's been ringing on the secure line in the weapons room."

Kai and Jase both checked their phones but hadn't missed a call. Jase didn't expect to have gotten a call, but was shocked that Rowan hadn't reached out to Kai through his cell. "This can't be good," he muttered as they hurried to the weapons room.

As the team leader, Kai took a seat near the landline, it's red color one that showed Rowan had a sense of humor. Immediately their call was picked up. "Shade, what's going on? By the way, you're on speaker with Jase, Oz, Sully, and me."

Jase knew he was warning the other man instead of just a friendly heads up. He hadn't earned their trust back, but he didn't give a shit. Folding his arms across his chest, he checked the monitors for a glimpse of his little family. Coyle stood near a tree while Brooke and Jack sat on the porch. He narrowed his eyes as he tried to see what they were holding. Walnuts. They'd gathered walnuts in their adventure. Shaking his head, he glanced back at Kai, listening with half an ear as Rowan asked about their trip. "Why the hell did you summon us on this damn red phone?"

"Hello to you to, Jackhole," Rowan said with a growl.

Jase lifted his middle finger toward the phone but stayed silent.

"It's not nice to flip your host off."

He looked around the room, searching for cameras. "You a Peeping Tom now or what?"

Rowan's deep chuckle came through the line. "Nah, I know you, brother."

"Whatever. So, what's up?" These men didn't know shit, or they'd have believed in him. He slammed the door on the past, focusing on the present.

"There's been chatter on some lines that shouldn't have chatter. Admiral Frazee had some enemies. I hear you might have a stake in his family." Rowan's words dropped into the room like an anvil.

"Who else has this info?" Jase gripped the back of the empty chair, staring at Jack's innocent profile.

"Seems some thought it mighty suspicious that you were dating the lovely Brooke Frazee, then you left. Fast forward nine months and there's a dark-haired boy with dark brown eyes. Now, some say he's the spitting image of her deceased brother, but others say if you put a picture of Jase Tyler next to Jack Frazee, the resemblance is uncanny. Plus, she named you as the father on his birth certificate."

Jase felt like he'd been kicked in the stomach, only it was a good kick. How one would classify that as a good one, he wasn't sure, but fuck...he'd thought for sure Brooke wouldn't have listed him on Jack's records. Knowing he had a legal right, that she cared enough, even when she hated him, nearly knocked the wind out of him.

"You need to sit down, man?" Kai asked standing.

He shook his head. "Damn. She's so damn brave. I mean...how many women would've done that, knowing she could've cut me out and moved on with her life, found a new man to pick up the pieces, without me being any wiser. That would've been the easy way. The smart way. Hell, I guarantee her father wasn't happy with her decision."

"Clearly, you're aware that you're a daddy. Congrats, man. It's the best feeling in the world," Rowan said with a sigh.

"Whoa, when did you become a dad?" Kai asked settling back in his chair.

"Oh, yeah. Lyric and I had a little girl. Her name's Harlow."

Jase could hear the hesitancy in the other man's voice, figuring he was worried about sharing too much information. "About Brooke. Was there anything else?"

Rowan cleared his throat. "Frazee's best friend and fellow admiral has been taking over his duties. Looks like he's been helping Mrs. Frazee as well. They went through the ranks together from what I found, moved apart as their posts took them in separate directions, until about three or four years ago."

"I've never met him. What's his name?" Jase's eyes went back to the porch, searching for Jack and Brooke.

"I'll send over the file I have on him. He had a wife and daughter, but they were killed in a boating accident. Alright, I gotta go, my girls are calling me." Rowan made a clicking sound with his teeth that had Jase frowning.

"Got it. If you get anymore chatter, you gonna call on the big red phone?" Kai asked.

"For your info, asshole, your cells aren't secured the way this line is. The chatter I was talking about...was heard through a cell phone." Rowan hung up, leaving them in stunned silence.

"Well shit, that's scary," Oz stated with a frown as he looked at his smartphone.

"Let's get you into the system so you have access to the different systems." Kai began punching in keys.

"You trust me enough to do that?" Jase sat down.

Oz snorted. "You wouldn't be here if we didn't, dick." The big guy walked out glaring at his phone followed by Sully.

"He's gonna be stressing out over the fact someone might hear him talking on the phone now." Kai sighed. "Somedays, it's like wrangling a herd of cats."

Chapter Eleven

Jase raised a brow but didn't tell Kai he knew exactly what he meant. At one time Jase was in Kai's shoes, being the team leader and herding all their asses.

"Do you miss it?" Kai's question startled him.

"What? Being part of the team?" Jase blew out a breath. "At first, when I was arrested, I was sure I'd be freed and all would be set to rights. I kept waiting for you guys to show up and show me you supported me. Then, as the months went by after I landed in Fort Leavenworth, I was too busy staying alive to worry about anything except...well, staying alive. Being known as a traitor and getting an entire team killed didn't garner me any friends, except ones I sure as shit didn't want. I spent my days and nights working out and planning my next step. I read when I was allowed to, worked out every other minute of the day. Rinse and repeat." He lifted his shirt. "This came on day one hundred and two. It was the first time I killed a man behind bars." Jase covered the scar with his shirt once again.

"I'm not gonna apologize. It would seem hollow, and you don't want to hear that. We were shown the same evidence that they delivered to the jury. Why didn't you deny the charges?" Kai turned the chair to face him.

Jase put his elbows on the table in front of him. "I did. I swore up and down I didn't do it. Then, I received a video of you guys. My team sitting in the barracks. The video changed to the barracks being blown up and bodies that resembled you and the others being identified. Your names scrolling across the bottom. The message was clear. I take the fall or you all died. This wasn't some small-time thing. Whoever killed one team was willing to kill another, and they had access to the prison I was sitting in, waiting for trial. Do you understand what that meant?" He met Kai's dark gaze.

"This was an inside job?" Kai said, anger flashing over his face.

He nodded. "For six months, I fought to stay alive, knowing I was going to live the rest of my life as the fall guy, and that was okay as long as you guys lived. Then one day, I had a visitor. He asked if I wanted to blow this place but not actually blow it. I shook my head and thought this dude was crazy. He asked again and told me to think real hard. If I said yes, he'd have me out of there that night. I'd just gotten out of the hole for killing my sixth man. All in self-defense but that doesn't matter. I killed six men, Kai. I was done. I wasn't sure if I even wanted to continue living. So I nodded, and told this stranger, yeah, I wanted out. I figured even if I died trying, at least the agony of the daily shit I had to do would be over." He exhaled and looked over at his ex-teammate to gauge his response to what he'd said.

"Go on," Kai said without inflection.

"After dinner, my favorite time of the night. Not. I was heading back to my cell when one of the guards pulled me to the side. Immediately, my body went on the defense. I hadn't killed one of the workers there, but hell, there was a first time for everything. He held his hands up and nodded his head toward the side door. There, behind the glass was the stranger. I had nothing in my cell I wanted to grab, so I thought fuck it. I opened the door and followed that man. Erik made good on his promise as he led me out of USDB. Don't ask me how, but I literally walked out and didn't look back. From there, we've been tracking the real traitor."

"And covering our asses on occasion," Kai stated.

Jase shrugged.

"I've figured it out. All the times we thought you were killing or the one we were searching for, you were one step ahead of us, taking out a target, right?"

Again, he shrugged. He wasn't admitting any crimes. "I just happened to be in a few of the same countries as you. I might have fallen on a few guys who might have had weapons aimed at some guys I knew."

A sob from the door had him jerking his head toward the entrance. Brooke stood next to Coyle, with Oz off to the side. Sully stood back with his arms crossed, silently gauging everyone.

"You...you almost...you could've been killed and I'd have...we'd never have known. Don't," Brooke backed away.

Jase stood up. "Brooke, listen to me."

Coyle put his hand on Jase's chest as he got to the door. "I heard you. I don't know what to say, except thank you. You made a decision that cost you. Life has taught me many things, but what I just learned is brothers of the heart shouldn't be cut out without a good ass kicking. Had we come and talked to you, I guarantee there's no way you could've lied to our faces. We fucked up and allowed you to go through this shit alone. We should've stuck by you. We're a team and as such should've stuck together. We're tough bastards as one, but as a unit, we're unstoppable."

"Hooyah," Oz said.

The men he'd considered his friends, his brothers, all yelled the same sentiment. One by one, they moved forward and hugged him. The heartfelt apology lifted another weight off his chest. He'd thought they'd always think he'd been guilty, even if he claimed not to be.

"Just so you know, we ain't gonna like, make out and shit," Oz joked.

Kai shoved the big man in the chest then laughed. "Shut the fuck up, dickhead. So, what's your plan?"

Seeing his team turn to him like old times—as if he were the one in charge, had Jase taking a deep breath then letting it out. "I need to talk to Brooke first. I'll be back."

Tay moved aside, clearly knowing nothing would get done until all was right with his woman. He knew the evidence stacked against him was a lot, and his friends were men of honor. It would've been hard for them not to have believed what was staring them in the face. With one last look at their faces, he headed toward the back deck, instincts telling him that was where Brooke went. Of course, it didn't hurt having Alexa standing near the patio door with Jack in her arms, a worried frown creasing her brow.

"Jack and I are going to go build us a compound, and then I'm going to show him how Godzilla destroys it." Alexa tickled his son's stomach, making him giggle.

"Alexa said that Godzilla might be a girl." His son laughed so hard his little body bent over backward almost falling out of the other woman's arms.

Jase leaped forward, fearing his son would fall onto the hardwood floors. However, Alexa had complete control, scooping Jack back up and nuzzling her nose into his neck, blowing a loud raspberry. "Hey, you doubting my theory, bugger boo?"

As he passed them, Jase couldn't stop the urge to kiss Jack on the forehead, any more than he could contain the swell of love when he listened to his two year old tell Alexa he wasn't a bugger boo. God, he loved that little boy more than anything, save the boy's mother.

Outside, the air was cool with the promise of rain. He found Brooke sitting with her legs curled up to her chest on a lounger, looking like she'd lost her best friend. Jase hated to see the pain and anguish, caused by him on her too young features. She was almost ten years younger than him, but in her soul, she'd always seemed older, more mature. Maybe he'd seen what he'd wanted, but he'd be damned if he could let her go. He'd tried three years ago. The loss of her ate at him every hour of every day that he wasn't consumed by a mission. Yes, he continued to live; he had to as a SEAL. Nobody could accuse him of not doing his job and doing it well those six months after he'd left her on her back patio, but if he'd not been fucked up in the head, maybe, just maybe, he'd have recognized the signs of a set up.

Jase shook his head, knowing there was no sense in playing the 'what if' game. You couldn't change the past or predict the future. Sighing loudly, he strode to where she sat. "You look cold," he said, eyeing the way she ran her arms up and down her arms.

Brooke looked up at him. "Just thinking. It's nice out here." She turned her head back toward the forest.

If he'd been a gentleman, he'd have left her alone, given her space. For three years, she'd had that, or at least, she'd had space from him. Jase was done having a divide between them. Lifting his leg, he gave her a gentle nudge, moving her forward so that he could shift behind her on the lounge. Once he was settled, he pulled until she was reclining against him. Her back to his front. His arms wrapped around her middle. She sat stiffly for all of ten seconds, then he felt the moment she let herself accept his comfort.

"I'm scared," she whispered almost too low for him to hear.

Rubbing his cheek against the side of her head, he breathed in her floral shampoo. "I know you are, and that's good. If you weren't I'd be worried. This isn't an everyday thing a woman like you should have to experience. Hell, this isn't something most people deal with. The sad thing is, in our world today, it's becoming more common. With all the terrorists getting bolder and people from our own country getting greedy or just plain stupid or wanting to join a cause they think or have been brainwashed into believing is right, we have more than just a handful to worry about."

Brooke shifted so her head lay on his shoulder; her eyes met his. "You think my dad was one of those?"

Jase didn't want to lie to her. Instead he let her see the truth in his expression. Again, all the evidence pointed straight back to the admiral.

"I can't wrap my head around that, Jase. He always took his hat off when we walked in a building. Always stood for the National Anthem. I mean, if you were to ask me who was the most patriotic person I knew,

I'd have said my father. When a flag was at half mast, he'd bow his head and say a prayer as if he could feel the loss of whoever had...lost their life. He..." she stopped on a sob. "My dad may have manipulated our relationship. No, he screwed you, me, and Jack out of the first two years of our son's life together, and that was wrong. But, and this is huge, I can't believe he would intentionally kill or have people killed."

He brushed away the tears that flowed from her eyes. His words wouldn't change how she felt. They both knew the evidence and where it pointed. Jase had a deep seated hate for the man, yet he also had, at one time, a deep respect.

*****

Brooke turned back to face the towering trees, knowing nothing Jase or she said would change the mounting facts. Her father had sent Jase away. Even after he'd known she was pregnant with Jack, he didn't tell her anything about what was going on. A steely resolve settled in her heart. She'd take Jase back to her family home and help him go through her father's office. Many times, she'd used his computer and had access, even to his desk since the admiral had never thought she'd be a threat to National Security. "When do we head back?" she asked after a few minutes.

Jase's arms tightened. "First thing in the morning. We'll get a good night's rest then head out. I'd like to leave Jack here with the team. Before you object, think about it. He's in a home with not one, but two safe rooms surrounded by an elite Navy SEAL group, trained for this. I trust them with our son's life, Brooke. It's why I called them."

She bit her lip, hating the thought of being so far away from her baby for even a moment, let alone an entire day. However, the image of him going on the trip with them, of what kind of danger he could be in had her nodding. "You're right. I hate it, but I agree."

"He'll be safe and probably be spoiled rotten by the time we come back. Heck, he'll learn all kinds of things within hours that most kids three times his age do," Jase soothed.

A laugh bubbled out of her. "Oh yeah, like what?"

Her son was smart as a whip and caught onto things quickly, but he wasn't some super child or anything like that. Many children his age could read, which she wasn't pushing Jack to do. If he learned as they read, she'd be happy. She went back to Jase's comment. "What do you think those crazy SEAL friends of yours will teach him?"

"Well, lets see," he paused. "Alexa is telling him that Godzilla is probably female. Which is totally not true. Everybody knows that big bastard is a dude." He grunted as Brooke's elbow nudged his stomach then continued. "Tay will probably teach him how to play a video game, only it'll be a war game. Kai, oh, he's the one to watch. I imagine he'll have Jack out in the woods in camo learning how to walk all silent like."

She smiled, opening her mouth to ask about the rest of the team, but her stomach decided to rumble.

"Come on, I think it's time I feed you. I bet Jack's hungry too."

Jase kissed her on the cheek, meeting her eyes. "Brooke, above all else, know I'd never allow anyone or anything to hurt you or our son. I've done a lot of questionable things in my quest to find the traitor amongst us. All that would be child's play, if one of you were threatened. I wasn't team leader for nothing. I wasn't chosen as the scapegoat for nothing. Whoever was or is the traitor, because I believe your father wasn't working alone, knew if I was blamed, the government would stop looking." He stood with her in his arms, letting her slide down his body before he continued. "Their ploy worked. For three years, I've been hunted, only I turned the tables and became the hunter as well thanks to a little help. Now, let's put a pin in all this for the next couple hours."

Brooke could see Jase wanted to ease her worries. His true need to make her feel safe and happy had always been one of the things that had turned her on. "You're sexy when you get all alphaish on me."

He stared down at her. A promise written in his eyes. "I'll show you just how alpha I will be."

The slide of a door opening behind them had Jase tensing.

"Hey you two, dinner is ready. Unless you are gonna stay out here and do that moony eyed thing all night, I suggest you get in here asap," Coyle barked.

"I'm gonna beat the shit out of him." Jase rested his forehead on hers.

She rubbed her head back and forth on him, the action soothing the slight ache forming behind her temples. "No you won't."

Jase grunted, which she somehow found endearing. "Let's go eat and find Jack."

The name of her son, flowing out of Jase's mouth with such possession, made her heart melt. God, this man had the power to hurt her and Jack more than anyone else in the entire world.

She froze at the thought of what it would cost her if she lost him again. What it would do to her and their son. "Lead the way." She tried to take a step back, but his arms contracted.

His jaw tightened. "In life, we live, love, lose, miss, hurt, trust, and also make mistakes. I've done all that, but most of all, I've learned from all of those things. I won't ever do anything that will cost me you and Jack. If you believe nothing else, believe that."

Brooke saw the conviction and total honesty written on his face. If Jase had any say in the matter, she had no doubt he'd have been there for Jack and her. "I trust in you. You, Jase."

Air whooshed out of his lungs. "That's the best damn thing I've ever heard. Come on, or I'll be damned if I don't take you back to that lounge and claim you body and soul. Damn, woman. I...you don't know it, but right there, with those words." He took a deep inhale before continuing. "My entire life I've lived and breathed. I existed but didn't feel truly alive until I saw that little boy. Now you've just given me even more, something that's been missing I didn't even realize. True love. I've cared about women, don't get me wrong, but they didn't have a place in my heart. I thought I would never have that elusive thing written about in books and shit. In all honesty, I thought it was a myth. You're my very own fantasy come to life."

She smiled. "So, what you're saying is I'm your unicorn?"

Jase pulled her flush to his body. "I think I'm the one with something horny on his body."

"Whoa, did I come at a bad time?" Jaqui asked from the doorway, Jack perched on her hip. "This little guy wanted to see his mommy. We'll just wait for you inside. Want to go play with the building log things?" Jaqui asked Jack, her voice fading as they walked back inside.

Moving away from Jase took effort, especially with his strong arms and harder body so close to hers. "We're coming."

"No we're not. At least not yet," Jase muttered with a smile.

She buried her face against his chest. "You are so bad." A small inhale had her filling her lungs with his scent. In all the years they'd been separated, she'd never forgotten how he'd smelled. Clean, masculine, and a hint of citrus.

His fingers laced with hers, keeping their connection as they entered the cabin, the tangy aroma of something spicy filling the air. "Wow, something smells wonderful."

"Oz has probably whipped up something delicious."

As they entered she saw the big red haired giant of a man wearing an apron with a ball cap turned around backward. He should've looked silly, but none of these men could be described as anything but masculine. And handsome. Lord have mercy they were most definitely that and so much more. She wondered how they blended into the different places when they were on missions.

Alexa winked at her from her spot at the table, a knowing smirk on her face. "Can I do anything?"

Jase gave her shoulder a squeeze, passing her by to pick up Jack from the floor. Watching the two of them play together, father and son as if they'd done the same thing dozens of times, had her missing things they'd never get back.

"We got this under control. It's routine for us. Have a seat," Coyle said, putting plates out on the counter. His incredible green eyes showed evidence of his mixed heritage in his dark complexion. Both he and Sully had the most amazing eyes. Combined with their African American heritage, their dark good looks, and towering heights, they were gorgeous men. Yeah, blending wouldn't be easy for any of them.

"They're all dreamy, right?" Jaqui asked from her seat at the table, her chin resting on one palm.

The sound of silverware dropping had Brooke looking toward the sink to see Tay bending down to pick up something from the floor. He stood, pointing a fork at Jaqui, a frown on his face. "No, they are not dreamy. I'm dreamy," he stated stabbing the tines of the utensil toward his chest.

"Yes, dear," Jaqui agreed batting her lashes at him.

Tay was across the room, lifting Jaqui into his arms, and settling back into the chair with her in his lap.

"Jesus, can't you two not be doing that in front of children?" Kai asked, his eyes going over everyone in the room. Brooke had a feeling he didn't miss a thing.

"Hey, we're just making sure there's room for everyone." Tay didn't look the slightest bit sorry.

Kai rolled his eyes but bent and kissed his Alexa on the forehead. "If that chair breaks under your ass, you better make sure Jaqui doesn't get hurt."

"Hey, you saying something about our weight?" Jaqui glared at Kai.

"Not yours, no. That one," Kai pointed a finger at Tay, then dodged the balled up napkin the other man lobbed at him before continuing with a grin. "Hey, where's the respect?"

"Alright, everyone gather round, supper is ready. I ain't your mama so come and get it," Oz broke in with his booming voice.

Brooke looked to Jase for protocol. She wasn't sure if there was a pecking order or if it was a first come first serve. She shouldn't have worried as Oz pointed his spatula at her. "Does little man like chicken fettucine alfredo?" he asked.

Nodding, she watched Jase walk their son over and smiled when Jack slurped up a pasta noodle loudly, making both men laugh.

"Now that's the way to eat," Oz said placing a small helping onto a plate for Jack.

"Yummy," Jack announced.

Heart full of love and joy for these men, who were taking such great care to make sure Jack was welcomed and happy, she lined up behind Sully.

"Ladies first." Sully's tone suggested he wouldn't take no for an answer.

Her stomach growled loudly, putting a smile on Oz's face. "This smells and looks delicious. Thank you, Oz."

Oz tipped his head in acknowledgment. Brooke took her plate, which he'd overfilled, to the table, sitting next to Jack. "Go ahead and get yourself a plate, Jase." He had to be as hungry as her, although his stomach wasn't rumbling loudly like her own.

Jase kissed Jack's head, ruffling his hair as he whispered in his ear. "Eat it all, kiddo, then we'll play a game afterward."

Brooke knew he had other things he needed to do. Things that were pressing, but he seemed to want to spend as much time with Jack as he did her. Lord, let them have time. Time to do more than have a few stolen hours or days, she prayed.

Chapter Twelve

Jase helped clean up after they finished eating the delicious dinner Oz cooked. His little family and his old team gelled. That was a word he hadn't expected to use when it came to him and life. If he was honest, he thought he'd be the last bachelor among them, watching as they all got married and had kids. That was until three years ago. After that fateful night when his life became one shitshow after another, he was convinced he'd never have a chance at a normal life, let alone one with a woman who looked at him the way Brooke did. Now, he had a chance for more with a woman who loved him, and a son he couldn't wait to teach how to do all the things a dad taught him. If there wasn't a huge cloud over them, namely a traitor who was still working inside their government, possibly at this very moment plotting his and his family's death, life would be close to perfect.

"We'll finish up in here. Why don't you go spend a little time with your boy, then come to the weapons room so you can tell us your plan." Kai took the dishcloth from him.

"Thanks." He dried his hands on a paper towel then tracked Brooke and Jack by the sound of giggles, finding the three women on the floor around the coffee table while Jack stood on the coffee table. He leaned on the wall watching as Jack clearly was acting as if he were some sort of monster.

"I know, you're a barbie doll," Jaqui guessed.

Jack shook his head, growling and stomping his little feet. "I'm big. Huge and green." He made more growling noise.

Alexa raised her hand. "A flower?"

His son giggled. "Flowers don't growl, silly."

"How do you know? Have you heard of Horton Hears a Who?"

Jaqui put her head on her upraised knees, snorting. "You need to get out more."

"I know, you're The Incredible Hulk." Brooke clapped like she had the answer.

Jack looked up and saw Jase. "Jase, do you know?" He repeated the stomping and growling. "I'm big and green, and I stomp on things."

Jase moved away from the wall, pretending to think. "Hmm, let me see. Big and green and growls. Does he also shoot fire out of his mouth?"

His son jumped up and down. "Yes."

"Godzilla," Jase answered.

Three feminine groans filled the room as Jase swooped in and lifted Jack into his arms. "Godzilla, who is most definitely a dude. Right?" He held his hand up for Jack to slap, acting like it hurt a little, which had Jack beaming proudly. God, he loved his kid.

"Want to go outside and explore? Maybe we can find some deer tracks." He held his hand out to Brooke, wanting her to go with them.

"Oh, let me get my shoes on," she said shyly.

"Jack and I'll wait for you on the porch," he told her, watching as she hurried back toward their room.

They spent the next hour traipsing through the woods around the cabin. Jack picked up sticks and stones, sure he'd found Godzilla tracks. Now, leading the way back toward the porch, he stopped Brooke with a hand on her arm. Jack had fallen asleep a few minutes ago in his arms, something he wouldn't normally feel comfortable with on a mission; outside and exposed with his arms not free, but with Kai and the guys surrounding them, he knew they were safe. Oh, he was aware that Oz and Sully were shadowing them, making sure they had cover in case shit hit the fan. That's what they did as a team. A buzz in his ear had him re-membering Erik, his partner for the last several years, the one man who hadn't thought him a traitor.

"Hang on. My partner's trying to get in touch." He pointed at his ear. With a touch of his finger to the small device, he turned it on. "What's up, Erik?"

"And a good evening to you, too. I'm well, thank you for asking." Erik's snarky tone was grating in his ear.

"Sorry, man. I'm glad to hear you're good. Did you do anything fun?" Jase smiled over at Brooke. She grinned back at him. The little exchange felt intimate until Erik grunted.

"Oh for fucking crying out loud, man. There's some new intel. Where should I send it?"

Jase narrowed his eyes, staring at the cabin with the lights blazing inside. Darkness was closing in, which was why they'd decided to head back. He wasn't sure why, but he didn't want to have any information coming into the place where his son would be staying. "Email it to me. When I get service tomorrow, I'll look at it. Until then, give me the run down." He started walking as he spoke, feeling the need for Kai and the others to be in on the conversation.

"Tyler, no matter how secure I think this connection is, there could still be people with skills like me. I'll send you the files. They're encrypted and won't be easily hacked." The last word was their code that was exactly what was happening. He picked up the pace, hurrying toward the door.

"I think you need to get laid, maybe get out of your lair more." Holding his finger to his mouth, he motioned to the door for Brooke. She took his cue and went inside ahead of him, holding her arms out for the sleeping Jack. Jase shook his head, moving into the house and going straight for the bedroom. He laid their son in the middle of the bed, staring down at his perfect little face. They should've probably brought him in earlier and given him a bath, but he'd been having too much fun. With one last look, he let the back of his fingers run down one soft downy cheek.

Brooke stood next to the bed, fright in her gorgeous eyes. He bent and kissed her cheek. "I'm gonna go check on things in the other room. All is well, I promise." It wasn't a lie. Whoever was tagging into Erik's conversations were clearly professional but not on their level. However, they had to take extreme care in case they could hear Jase.

He shut the door then walked to the weapons room, meeting Kai's dark eyes across the room. Oz, Coyle, Sully, and Tay were gathered, their arms crossed as they waited for him to enter. He looked behind him, expecting the women to follow their men. The quiet snick of the door echoed in the room.

Kai pressed a button, making the earpiece buzz a sharp sound. "What the fuck?" Jase lifted his hand to his ear.

"That'll take care of any interference on this end. Who you talking to?" Kai's glare was cold.

Jase leaned back against the door. "His name is Erik. He's been my partner for the past three years. He's the one who got me out of Leavenworth. None of that has anything to do with the information he just gave me. He said there's new intel, but he's got a tag. That means whoever this is, is good. Or rather really bad." He paced away from the door. The weapons room was a good size, but having six large men in it, made it cramped.

"Erik can get into any system without anyone being the wiser. It was how we knew what missions were going where. I knew whoever set me up had an agenda. He's worked really hard to kill you guys, mission after mission. However, I don't think it's personal because of where you were sent. If he succeeded, it would've been a national incident. Possible war between nations. We intercepted more than just your missions. I mean, not that I don't love you guys and all, but there's more. A few well-placed shots here and there, and those missions went off without a hitch. The reason you fucktards were such a pain was because you knew how I worked. You boys had a hard on for me." He pointed his finger at Kai. "That first mission in Mexico was the beginning; this one will be the last. My family has to come first. I can't keep risking my life anymore. Before...before I found out I had a son and a chance with Brooke, I'd have continued, but after this, I'm out. You guys want to continue, it's up to you."

"Where did he say he was sending the information?" Tay broke into the quiet room.

Jase looked over at the computer expert of the team. "He said he'd email it to me, but I don't want to open any communication where my son is." In that, he would hold strong.

Tay sat back in one of the computer chairs, folding his arms across his chest. "What, do you think I'm that big of a loser I don't know how to make sure it isn't hacked?" he asked, putting air quotes around the word hacked.

He opened his mouth to tell Tay that Erik was an expert, but shut it. Tay was an expert as well, and they were sitting in a room that was equipped with enough computers that would make NASA look at them twice. Hell, he'd even noticed Kai had been using facial recognition software when they'd walked in but hadn't asked why. Now, he felt the need to know everything. "Full disclosure, guys. Erik works for one of the alphabet agencies. Which is a mystery that I gave zero fucks for. I didn't push for answers, and he didn't offer them. Now, what the hell were you doing when I walked in?"

Kai moved to the side, showing him the screen. "We were running images of everyone who passed the cameras around Brooke's building the day after you took her and Jack, seeing if anyone popped into the database for terrorist or sent off an alert."

Knowing it was best to allow others to give you answers than to ask, he waited.

"Her mother came by and a few men who we couldn't get a read on. They seemed to know where not to look. Now, what's your plan, and don't piss me off by this silent shit. We're a team," Kai growled.

Jase grabbed the back of his neck and sighed. "Tomorrow, I'd like to take Brooke back and see if we can't get into her father's home office. As for Jack," he paused, meeting each man in the eye. "It would mean the world to me if you would keep watch over him. If I didn't have to take Brooke with me to get access to the house, I'd leave her here too. Who am I kidding? I'd leave her if she'd allow it."

Tay and Kai both let out a dry chuckle, which Jase was coming to know meant the women were truly the boss.

"Your son couldn't be safer, unless you were here with him, that I can assure you," Kai stated.

The other men nodded, telling him they would protect Jack with their lives.

"We'll leave after breakfast and be back by bedtime, if all goes well." His gut clenched at the thought of it taking longer. Brooke hadn't said if she had ever spent a night away from Jack or not, but he'd just found them.

"Tell us exactly what the plan is and what plan b and c is, 'cause we all know you got them." Coyle rubbed his hands together. "Also, what else do you know about Erik, let Tay do some digging and see if he can verify his credentials."

Tay held his hands over the keyboard, his fingers dancing in the air. "Give me his name, and I'll get my bot on it."

For a moment, he felt as if he was stabbing his friend in the back, but thoughts of Brooke and Jack had him giving the other man what intel he had on Erik, down to his age and physical details.

"Alright, while my bot goes to work, let's check out this email, and before you get your panties in a twist, this server is more secure than the one at the White House." Tay sat tall in the chair, his all American good looks and southern drawl fooled many into thinking he was a hillbilly without schooling, yet he was one of the smartest and technologically savvy men the Navy had.

Once Tay had the email, Jase sat back with a loud exhale. "This shit is gonna make my hair turn grey," he remarked, running his hand over his head.

Kai kicked his feet out in front of him, resting his hands on his stomach. "Saw you acquired some ink during your time away from the SEALs."

Jase rubbed his hand over his chest. "A little," he agreed.

Tay's fingers tapped away then stopped. "Well, what do we have here? Looks like there's been someone looking for us."

Jase and Kai both moved closer, reading the words on the screen. Grainy footage of the night Jase had been set up became clearer. An email with the admiral's name on the top came next. The words 'TARGET ACQUIRED' in bold letters made ice settle in Jase's veins. "That fucker set me up." He thought of his contact, the one who'd sent him to watch over Brooke, the shadow figure with the computer voice. "Tay, if I gave you my cell could you trace a call?"

"It's possible, but highly unlikely unless I had a trace on it at the time of the call, and even then, if the person was using a scrambler..." Tay trailed off.

Jase pointed at the screen. "What about that?"

Kai shook his head. "This was to the admiral, not from. We don't know who sent it to him or if he responded. Right now, we don't have anything except that he was sent a video and this letter. The man is dead, but whoever was on the other end isn't."

He sat with his elbows on his knees, his hands dangling down toward the floor in a room filled with men he'd hated for the past three years. A feeling of betrayal washed all over him again as he thought of Brooke's dad. The admiral had been more than just a dad and soldier. He was the one Jase wanted to be like, the reason he was a SEAL. Even more, Mark had been his son's grandfather and the father of the woman he loved and hoped to marry someday. "How do I break this to Brooke?" He didn't look up as he voiced his concern.

Sully slapped him on the shoulder, squeezing the tense muscle there. "You just do and when it's all over, you pick up the shattered pieces of her heart and put it back together again with your love. I saw you two with your kid. Love like that don't just come by every day. You'll weather this storm together, coming out the victors on the other side. Maybe a little rougher from the journey, but nothing worth having comes easy."

Jase looked at the one member of their team who was the quietest and smiled. "When you decide to talk, you sure don't mince words."

With a shrug, Sully went to the door, glancing over at Jase. "My mama didn't raise no fool. She told me if you ain't got nothing good to say, don't say it. Most times, y'all are jawing away." He motioned to the room then walked out.

Oz laughed, then sobered. "He's right. We're a right chatty bunch. Like, almost like...a bunch of chicks," he gasped.

Jaqui stood by the entrance, glaring at him. "Oh please, you've always been more girlie than me."

Jase stood up, knowing they could go for hours back and forth like teenagers. He met Kai's gaze and knew without words his old friend had his back. Kai stood and held his hand out. When Jase took the outstretched hand, Kai pulled him into a hug, the other man's arm circled his head, bringing their heads to rest on each other's shoulders. "You take Brooke and get the evidence you need. If you don't get it, you get the hell out, and we'll get it as a team. You're not alone anymore," Kai said, his tone implacable.

"That's the plan," Jase agreed. "You keep Jack safe and happy 'til we get back."

Another squeeze of his neck, which Jase mimicked on Kai, and they stepped back.

"Damn, I was hoping you guys were gonna kiss," Alexa joked sauntering into the room.

Kai groaned, pulling Alexa into his arms. He walked out as she made a high-pitched noise, going in search of Brooke. If she was already asleep, he'd crawl into bed with her and Jack after a quick shower.

*****

Brooke bit the pad of her thumb and looked at the clock for the hundredth time. "What's taking so long?" she asked quietly, not wanting to wake Jack. He'd woken a little bit ago, gone to the bathroom, and let her change him into pajamas and fell right back to sleep. That seemed like ages now.

She spun at the sound of the door opening to find Jase entering. He looked tired, yet more handsome than any man had the right to. Lifting her thumb toward the bathroom, she made her way into the small room. Jase followed, a crease furrowed his brow.

"What's wrong?" he asked once the door was closed.

"What's wrong? Are you serious?" She looked up at his face and thought of smacking him upside the head.

He placed his hands on his hips. "You're cute when you're all fired up. Now, before you hit me, can I take a quick shower?"

Those lines of worry and exhaustion were stark in the bright bathroom. "Fine, but you can talk while you're showering. Two birds with one stone," she said.

He lifted her face with one bent finger. "I'll tell you everything. You know, you could always take a shower with me. Two birds with one stone." He grinned down at her as he tossed her words back at her.

She looked at her body and the little smudges of dirt from their foray outside earlier. Taking a step back, she pulled the shirt over her head. No sexy strip tease, just an efficient removal of her clothing, one article at a time, not once meeting his eyes until she stood naked before him.

"Fuck, you're beautiful." His hand brushed her hair off her face, the pads of his fingers traced down her collarbone to one hardened nipple.

"I'm not, but I like that you think so." She shivered in the cool of the room.

He leaned back, turning the shower on with one hand. "To me, you're the most gorgeous woman on the planet, and I'm the luckiest bastard alive 'cause you're standing in front of me, letting me touch you, see you like this. It's enough to make a man like me feel like he's almost worthy."

Brooke grabbed his hand and laid it over her chest where her heart was beating like mad. "You are more than worthy, Jase Tyler. You're an amazing father to a son you didn't even know about until a couple days ago. You accepted him and love him without question. I loved you three years ago for the man you were, and I love you now for the man you've become. But do you want to know what's crazy?" She didn't wait for him to respond before continuing. "I'm going to love you even more tomorrow than today and every day after more than that. My love for you and Jack will know no bounds."

Jase lifted her up, covering her mouth with his. There was no gentle brush of lips. This was a hard, almost desperate clash of lips, teeth, and tongue. Finally, he pulled back, his breathing choppy. "God, I've hoped...prayed you cared about me, that I hadn't killed any chance at you and me." A tremor shook his big frame.

She clasped her hands on each side of his face. With her own face so close to his from him holding her, she stared into his eyes. "Never, Jase. You're it for me. I kept saying to myself, 'tomorrow I will move on'. I prayed for you and hoped you were happy. Only the next day came and I didn't move on. I couldn't because you still had my heart."

He sat her back on the tile floor. His eyes held hers while he undressed, each article of clothing joined the pile she'd made. Steam filled the room by the time he was naked. He pulled the door to the shower open and led her inside. "I'll spend the rest of my life showing you how much I love you, too," Jase promised, shutting the door as he whispered those words, but she heard them through the sound of the running water.

Ever the gentleman, Jase allowed her under the running water first. She was conscious of him filling his hands with shampoo. Maybe she should have been slightly embarrassed. However, that wasn't even close to what she was feeling as he told her to switch places with him. Only instead of him concentrating on himself, he worked the shampoo into her hair, paying close attention to her every sigh, it seemed as his fingers massaged her scalp. "You could make a fortune at my salon," she moaned. Heck, women would line up around the block if he were the one to do all the wash and rinse jobs.

Jase grunted. "No thank you. I think the only hair I'd like my hands buried in is yours. Switch," he commanded."

Brooke moved under the water, closing her eyes while the suds were rinsed away. When she opened them, she found Jase's eyes staring at her chest. "I can't believe you're here with me." One finger ran over her puckered nipple, wiping away a drop of shampoo. Jase grabbed the conditioner off the shelf, poured some in his palm then motioned for her to change spots with him.

"Ya know, I can do this myself." Brooke offered but turned around. Having Jase's hands on her, even when he was doing something simple like washing her hair, was exciting her to the point she was sure it would take only a few flicks of his nimble fingers down south, and she'd come.

Once Jase worked the conditioner through her hair, she was prepared for him to move them around again. Her heart pounded in anticipation. Two strong arms came around her, pulling her back to his front, letting her feel the hardness between his legs. Oh, she knew he was affected by her nakedness. It had been impossible to miss seeing his erection when he'd stripped before ushering her into the shower. Yet, he'd always had supreme control when they'd been together.

"I'm aware you can wash your own hair. I find I like doing it. In fact, I like it a lot." His palms smoothed over her stomach then down her thighs. "Tilt your head back and close your eyes," Jase said as he brought his hands back up her body, creating tingles everywhere he touched. "Tell me about your tattoos."

The water ran down over their heads while Jase rinsed her hair. The scent of raspberry filled the room, making her open her eyes to see him squirting body wash into his palm. Still, with her back to him, he continued his delicious treatment, washing every inch he could reach until she was sure she'd go mad with need. His words had her breath catching.

"The phoenix represents me and what I felt like after I had Jack. I don't know how to explain it, but it was like I had a new purpose...a new life. Like the mythological phoenix that recycles its own life when it perceives its impending death, igniting itself on fire only to reemerge from the ashes stronger, that was how I felt after...well, after you left and I had Jack." She took a deep breath. "The semi-colon is for my brother, but I put my own stamp on it. Instead of the standard dot on top, I have a heart and the bottom swirl is also made up of a heart with a swirl." Brooke wiped away a tear.

Jace traced his finger up the side of her ribs. "They're gorgeous, like you."

"My turn." She moved out of his arms, taking the fragrant soap and filling her own palms. Jase raised one brow but allowed her to run her soapy hands over his shoulders and down his pecs. Under his tattoos she could feel scars and paused at the feel at what was clearly a puckered wound. "Is this a bullet hole?"

Jase's jaw flexed before he nodded. "War is ugly, Brookey."

To take the look of anguish off his face, she allowed her hands to smooth down his flat abdomen, skimming over the healing wound on his side. She looked up as she traced the muscles downward until she reached the fine line of hair. "You know why they call this a happy trail?" She grinned up at him while teasing him with her almost strokes toward his flexing cock. She could feel him, hard and thick, pulsing against their lower half.

"Because it'll make me really happy if you get to the end of it?" His gruff words made her smile, but she didn't look up, keeping her concentration on teasing him.

Sliding her fingers down, she scraped her nails along his thighs and stepped back to give herself room. She looked up to see if she had Jase's attention, the heated look in his dark gaze was exactly what she wanted. He widened his stance, making room for her as she went to her knees, clearly knowing exactly what she planned.

Jase reached down, circled the base of his cock and stroked himself in a slow glide. She couldn't take her eyes off his hand as he continued the sexy act again, making her heart pound.

Unable to contain herself, she leaned forward and took the flared head into her mouth. Using his legs for support, she licked and sucked, angled her head to the side and stared up at him.

Their eyes met as a shudder went through him. She took as much of him into her mouth as she could. Feeling the tip of his dick hit the back of her throat she gagged and had to pull back. Over and over she moved on him, loving the way he moaned.

The hand in the back of her hair tightened, pulling her off and up until she was standing before him, and then he had her against the wall, his lips covering hers with a fierceness that she knew she would crave for all time.

"Wrap your legs around my waist." He ordered even as he helped her, both hands going under her ass while he pressed himself deep inside her. "God, yes, you feel so good. Hot, warm, and willing woman. My woman." He pumped his hips with each word.

She looked down and saw the way her breasts looked smooshed against his slightly hair roughened chest with the sexy tattoos, the water from the shower background noise, the cool air hitting her overheated skin. All the while, Jase continued to move inside her, faster and harder, and then he bent, taking one of her breasts into his mouth, biting down hard enough it stung. The small bite had liquid fire shooting straight to her clit, making her cry out on his next inward thrust. "So close," she gasped.

He released the tormented nipple with a slow lick, moving to the other and giving it the same treatment. Her breathing was coming in ragged pants. With every move he made, she shifted, trying to get him to hit that bundle of nerves down below. He cupped her chin with one hand with exquisite care, his thumb brushing back and forth over her lip. "Tell me what you need. What you want."

Every nerve in her body felt exposed as he continued to rub his chest on hers, his cock moving in and out. Yet, she needed more. "Touch my clit. Please."

Jase's smile was bright before his head dipped to her neck. "Your wish is my command." Nipping and sucking, he left a trail of kisses down her neck until he captured her nipple in his mouth again. At the same time, his fingers reached between them and flicked over her mound, finding the bundle of nerves. He tugged with his teeth on her nipple and gripped her clit between two fingers, sending her over the edge.

The combination took her breath away. Complete and pure pleasure, so erotic and sinful she couldn't think as her body milked his. "Jase, right there. Yes, yes, oh fuck, don't stop."

Her arms cradled his head as he pumped his cock in and out at an amazing speed. His body jerked, a full body shudder as his cock spasmed inside her.

She closed her eyes, savoring the feel of the two of them connected.

"You have a really dirty mouth when you're coming." Jase's words were said with a hint of satisfaction.

A shiver shook her even with his warm body still pinning her to the tile wall. "I guess you bring out the bad girl in me. Um, are we running out of hot water?"

Jase helped her stand while he pulled the lever farther to the hot side, blissful warmth flowed back out of the water spout. "Why don't you hurry and clean back up. I'm used to a wash and go in any condition. Besides, the view is great."

Brooke made quick work of washing and rinsing, all under the heated perusal of Jase. God, she loved the way he seemed to be mesmerized by her. Oh, she was aware of every flaw her body had but embraced each and every mark made from carrying Jack. Yes, they were an honor to have.

When she moved to switch spots, Jase caught her face between his palms, kissing her in a completely different way than the frenzied kisses from earlier. Soft brushes of his lips back and forth over hers, followed by a lick of his tongue, he pulled back with a groan. "You better get out of here, or we'll be frozen and wrinkled by the time I'm through with you."

A peek down between his legs showed he was already hard again. "Wow, someone has been eating their Wheaties. Or is that for something else?" She winked and got out before he could swat her on the ass as he reached for her. They hadn't used a condom this time, but she did a quick mental calculation and hoped the contraceptive pill worked. Although she loved Jack with all her being, she and Jase needed time to make their relationship stronger for the three of them, not add another baby into the mix. However, if they did end up with another she knew they'd love him or her as much as Jack.

Chapter Thirteen

By the time Jase got out of the shower, Brooke was already dried off and dressed in a pair of shorts and shirt. He wrapped the towel around his waist and walked over to where she stood by the mirror brushing her hair. "Tomorrow, you and I are going to head back to your parents' home. How do you truly feel about leaving Jack here with the SEAL team?"

The brush paused in her hair, her eyes meeting his through the mirror. "You trust them with him? With our son?"

He watched the tension in her body while she waited for him to answer. Without a second thought, he nodded. "Absolutely. I wouldn't have mentioned it if I didn't. They were the first I thought about when I realized I needed backup. When it comes to the safety of you and Jack, if it's not me, they would be my backup plan." The truth hit him square in the chest. Yes, he'd been more than a little pissed at his team for not believing in him, but he still trusted them with the lives of those who meant the most to him.

"Then, that's good enough for me. I wish he could go with us." She swallowed, taking a deep breath. "I know that sounds stupid, but having him with me, where I'm the one keeping him safe, makes me feel...in control. Does that make sense?" Brooke sat the brush on the counter, her voice wobbled slightly only to have firmed at the end. So damn tough his woman.

He caged her in with his body behind her, his hands going around her slim waist, rocking them side-to-side. "If you didn't have that instinct, it would probably be abnormal. You're a mama bear wanting to protect her cub. In this instance, you're protecting him best by letting five big SEALs and two women, who I'm pretty sure are just as fierce as those men, take care of the most precious thing to you. You, Brooke

Frazee, are the most amazing woman I've ever met, let alone been lucky enough to call mine. After this is over, you, me, and Jack are going to have a big discussion."

"You know, that sounds pretty ominous, but I'm not scared of you or your talk." She picked the brush back up.

Jase took her hand in his and kissed her knuckles. "I'm going to get dressed and check in with Kai. I'll be back in a little bit. Don't wait up though. Tomorrow's gonna be a long day." He kissed the side of her head before stepping away. If he didn't leave then, he didn't think he'd be able to anytime soon.

Back in the bedroom, Jack slept on, peacefully, knowing his mother was near. Jase made a silent promise to his son, and himself that one day in the very near future there would be no secrets between them. Jack would know he was his father and hopefully call him dad. He'd make sure Jack went to bed every night secure in the knowledge both his parents loved him and would protect him, always.

Quietly, like he'd done hundreds of times, Jase pulled on pants and a shirt followed by socks and shoes. It was a habit to dress completely when leaving his bedroom, just in case the need to flee arose. He ran his hand over his face, the slight stubble reminded him he hadn't shaved after the amazing bout of shower sex with Brooke. One day, he wouldn't always be looking over his shoulder, having to always be on guard. He shut the door behind him without making a sound and came to a stop. The sight of Oz standing across from his room with his legs crossed over one another, casually leaning against the wall like he had been there for a while, made him raise his brows in question.

Oz lifted one shoulder. "Before you go into the weapons room I wanted to ask you or Brooke what some of the little guys favorite foods were. You know, for tomorrow. He's a cute kid and seemed to like all of us well enough, but sometimes, comfort food is needed."

To say he was stunned would've been an understatement. Jase gave a nod, unsure if he spoke if the words wouldn't come out a bit raspy.

Oz's simple action reminded him what he'd been missing for the last three years. Brothers. Men who had his back and those of his family. If something had happened to him before he'd found out about Jack, Brooke would never have had these men stepping in to help her if she needed it. Now, she not only had him, but the five men he'd once been closer to than his own family. "He likes peanut butter and banana sandwiches."

"Ah, shit. What is that...like in your damn DNA that you passed off to him?" Oz shook his head but smiled, his dark red hair glowing in the hallway light.

Jase punched him in the arm. "I told you to try it. You're too big a pussy though, so don't judge asshole. My kid has great taste."

Oz punched him back but didn't say a word until they walked into the weapons room where the rest of the team, minus Tay and Alexa, were holed up. He relaxed when he saw that Kai wasn't sitting with a tension filled stance. He'd always known when something wasn't right by how the big man sat or stood. Now, he was leaned back with a satisfied smirk on his face. Clearly, he wasn't the only one who'd been doing some extracurricular activities in the shower. Clapping his hands together twice, just 'cause he knows how that always annoyed the shit out of Coyle, he looked around the room before he sat down. "Alright boys, here's the game plan. Tomorrow, I'm taking Brooke with me to try to get into her father's home office. I appreciate you taking care of Jack while we go there and back. Thanks to Oz here, he already knows what my little guy's favorite snack is. Oh, and he loves to share the most amazing treat with his friends so don't hurt his feelings."

Kai lifted his right hand, middle finger extended. "Fuck and no, would be my answer. I'll just tell him I'm on a diet or something."

Jase shook his head. "You'll hurt his feelings."

"Ah come on. Peanut butter and bananas? How the hell did he? Never mind. It's a genetic flaw or some shit. Fine, we can deal with it for a day." Kai glared at Jase.

Coyle rubbed his stomach. "I don't know what you all are bitching about. None of you tried it, but I did." He looked at Jase. "After you went away, I had a hankering for it. I think it was like pregnancy sympathy shit, only you weren't pregnant. Anyway, I got up at like four in the morning and made myself a plain ole PB sandwich. Just as I was getting ready to take a big ol' bite, my eyes fell to a bundle of bananas. And BAM, I've been hooked ever since. I thought of going to counseling or BA, you know, Bananas Anonymous but then thought, nah, better not."

He looked at Sully, who had started laughing about the time Coyle had mentioned pregnancy, then to Kai, who was rubbing his hand over his mouth, knowing his friend was trying to keep from smiling. "I love you man," Jase said to Coyle.

His friends all stood at once, yelling 'Group hug' in unison. Jase felt like he finally came back to where he belonged, almost. They stayed locked in a five-man hug, laughing and swaying back and forth, until the sound of Tay whistling brought their head up. "Whoa, did I miss the kumbaya and shit?"

"Get your ugly ass over here, Tay. Jase's kid likes PB&B. And now, Coyle has admitted to the weirdness, too." Sully dodged Coyle's hand as it shot through their circle.

Tay nodded as they made room for him. "I like it, too. It's some good eating. I say we have it for breakfast."

Jase laughed at the sound of several male groans. "Alright, you knuckleheads, I need to get to bed. I want to head out fairly early, so we can get back quicker. Jack's an early riser too, but with our schedules, that won't be an issue."

When they all pulled away, he could see the emotion he felt written on each man's face. After a few more minutes of talking, he left the room and walked back down the hallway to where Brooke and Jack slept. Tomorrow, they'd hopefully piece the last of the puzzle together, putting an end to the nightmare that had been his life for the last three years. What the fallout to it would be, he had no clue, but he'd be damned if he allowed it to cloud Jack's or Brooke's life the way it had his.

*****

Brooke cracked one eye open when Jase eased out of the bed. That slight movement had her waking up, knowing today they were heading back to her family home and possibly upending her world.

"I'm sorry, I didn't mean to wake you," Jase whispered, looking over his shoulder.

She sat up, rubbed her eyes and looked at her watch. "It's the ass-crack of dawn. What time are we leaving?"

His lips tilted up in a grin. "Not yet. I was going to shower and check in with Erik and the team. You can sleep for a little longer if you want." He stretched his arm across the short distance, brushing his fingers through her hair. "Damn, you're beautiful in the morning even when you're grumpy."

Her cheek nuzzled into his warm palm. "I need coffee before I can do human," she mumbled.

With his thumb he traced her jaw, then took his hand away. "I'll see what I can do for you. Can't have my girl not humaning." He got up without causing the bed to jar Jack, amused at her incoherent speaking.

She sifted her fingers through their son's hair, smiling at the fact they'd all three slept in the same bed all night. Poor Jase. He'd probably never thought he'd be hanging onto the edge of a mattress because a two year old liked to sleep sideways. "I'm not that bad. Well, I am sorta growly, but at least I'm not biting your head off. Before Jack was born, I could barely function. I've trained myself to be better. Thank you for last night." Their son had woken up just hours after Jase had come in, and had asked if Jase would tell him a story. Instead of going over to the other bed after Jack had fallen back to sleep, Jase had stayed next to

Jack. Never had she thought in a million years would Jase not only be in their son's life but hers as well.

Jase paused in the process of buttoning his pants. He'd slept in a pair of boxer briefs, something she'd wondered if he did normally. "You don't have to thank me for anything, especially not when it comes to Jack. I've missed out on so much." He closed his eyes. When he opened them, they shone brightly. "If I can help it, I'll never miss another milestone in his life," he said, the words a promise.

The lump in her throat was hard to swallow, but she nodded, knowing nothing she could say would turn back time or ease the hurt from time lost. They could only move forward and concentrate on the here and now. Without disturbing Jack too much, she too got out of bed. "I'm just going to use the bathroom."

As she went to walk past him, Jase caught her arm. "Don't feel bad. Not for me or what's done." He kissed her forehead, pulling her into his arms. The gentle swaying back and forth was something Jase did all the time. She often wondered if it was a memory from when he was younger.

Wrapping her arms around his back, she breathed in his scent, hugging him to her. "I love how you hug. It's one of the things I missed most."

"There was so much I missed about you." His voice rasped quietly.

Knowing they had a big day ahead of them, she took a step back. "I'll just be a moment. Jack'll be fine out here by himself, if you want to go do whatever you were gonna do."

The sound of Jase's beard scratching against his palm was the only sound in the room for long seconds. "Do you want me to bring you back a coffee?"

An image of him carrying a cup of the warm brew was almost enough to make her say yes, but it would only delay them. "No, I'll go get me some. You go do what you gotta do. Go on, I'm fine." She stood on her tiptoes and kissed his cheek above the stubble.

"I need to shave. I'll do that before tonight." His words sent a thrill through her.

Before she could make a fool of herself, she walked into the bathroom, closing the door behind her. As she leaned her back against the hard wood, she reflected on how different her world was compared to a week ago. "If only my father were still alive, life would be almost perfect." Shoving away from the door, she turned the light switch higher so it wasn't quite so dark. Once she used the facilities, she washed her hands and face, then went back out to the bedroom. Jack slept on, blissfully unaware his world had changed so much. "I love you, Bugger Boo," she whispered to him like she did every time.

The rest of the morning flew by while they got ready to leave. Jack woke up happy as always, ready to eat and play. Her worry about leaving him was quickly allayed as Oz and Tay, along with Jaqui and Alexa, played a game of 'Catch the boy' around the living area, much to Jack's delight.

"Go on, this ain't our first rodeo with a kid," Kai assured her.

His words and Jack's happy face allowed her to climb into Oz's large truck. "Why aren't we taking the SUV we came in?" she questioned after buckling up.

Jase waggled his brows at her then gunned the engine. The sound of gravel flew up as he drove around the cabin, bumping through the yard like he was enjoying the fact he was off-roading on his friend's property. "Cause Oz's truck is made for climbing and pushing through shit. Plus, nobody can see through the tint on these windows. Not to mention, ain't nobody looking for us in something like this."

She gripped the o-shit handle as he fishtailed it down the drive, the clang of rocks hitting the bed of the truck making her wince. Yeah, her mother wouldn't be looking for such a truck. The big black thing looked like it belonged on one of those Monster Truck shows where it ran over other vehicles. "How big are these tires, anyhow?"

"I'd say they're somewhere between thirty-six and thirty-eight inches, but I'm no expert." He stopped talking as they reached the turnoff to the main road.

"You realize, he's probably going to kick your ass for messing up his vehicle." The sound of rocks pinging off the shiny black of the truck's exterior had her wincing.

"Nah, that's what this truck is made for. He's had it specially coated and shit, so it's tough all around. If I know Oz, he's even got the underbelly of this beast done with a special armor. Trust me, he takes his rigs seriously." Jase reached over, taking her hand in his. "Relax, we have a long drive ahead of us."

Instinctively, she looked around for her cell phone, but they'd had her leave it at the cabin in the weapons room. Their worry it could be traced or bugged bothered her, but she was trusting them with Jack, so trusting them with her cell was a small thing. "They'll call if Jack needs us right?"

He brought her fingers to his mouth and kissed them, taking his eyes off the road for a moment, giving her a reassuring smile. "Yes, mama bear."

The teasing tone eased her worry, some. For the rest of the trip, she and Jase talked about anything and everything. By the time they passed the sign that told them they were entering Rapid City, her nerves were on edge.

"Want me to stop and get a latte for you?" Jase pointed at the big green sign with the mermaid logo of the famous coffee shop.

She almost said no, but the scent from the brewing goodness wafted through the window Jase had open. "I'd love one. There's a drive-thru, but I'm not sure if this thing will make the clearance." Luckily for them, there wasn't a restriction, and he was able to pull up and order their drinks without issue.

At the window, the teenager took a second look as they pulled up to the window. Jase, ever the gentleman, handed her cash and told her to keep the change. Brooke took a sip of the hot drink, sighing in pleasure from the delicious taste. "Seriously, if they could just hook me up with a home delivery daily, I'd be in heaven."

Jase's eyes were watching her lips when she looked over the rim of her cup. "I love that sound," he murmured. "I can't wait 'til this is over, and I can hear it when you're naked."

Her next drink was too large, making her cough. "Lord, Jase Tyler, you need to come with a warning label."

He sat his cup in the holder then winked at her. "You should, too."

They lapsed into silence while Jase drove them just outside of the city limits to her family home. The closer they got, the tighter the ball in her stomach was. The clock on the dash told her it was almost half past ten in the morning. If her memory was correct and her mother was back to her regular routine, Nancy Frazee wouldn't be home. Being an active member of the Country Club, her mother went to the club to meet with other society wives for brunch every day like clockwork. However, since her dad...Brooke couldn't think about why her mother would no longer be going. No, she hoped life was back to its regular programming in at least that small way.

"Try to relax. Remember, this was your home, too. Surely, your mother wouldn't find it odd for you to drop in for a visit?" Jase's voice broke into her thoughts, his deep timber reverberated through the quiet cab of the truck.

Brooke thought of her mother and how she'd changed since Mark, her older brother, had committed suicide. God, she hated all the terrible memories flooding her. Leaving home had been a no-brainer at the time. Nancy Frazee had been a wonderful mom to her and Mark Jr. She could still remember the laughter and picnics they'd go on during the summer. However, once they'd discovered Mark had killed himself, their world had stopped. At eleven, she was old enough to know what was going on. She'd loved her big brother. He was her best friend and confidant. But her mother took it the hardest. She became cold and distant. Nothing Brooke did was ever right or good. If it hadn't been for her father, Brooke was sure she'd have been sent off to a boarding school. As it was, she'd been left alone except when her dad was home. Even then, he was busy a lot with work or soothing Nancy. It wasn't until she'd had Jack that Nancy had warmed to her, or rather Jack. "I'm pathetic," she muttered.

Jase glanced her way before turning down the road that would lead to her parents' house. "Why do you say that?"

She shrugged. "My mother hates me. Like, she literally has zero tolerance for anything I say or do. The only time she ever calls is to ask me for something, which is usually if she can see Jack or borrow him to show off at one of her social things. I think, if I'm truly honest with myself, she only tolerated me before Mark died. He was her pride and joy. Makes me wonder how she'd have treated Jack if he'd been a girl. I think she hates me because she sees me as competition or something. I don't know. It's silly."

Chapter Fourteen

Jase pulled to the side of the road about a mile before the Frazee's home. Brooke had her head turned to where she was looking out the window, her elbow on the window sill, while she bit on one of her fingernails. He listened to her words and wanted to tell her she was wrong. Wanted to tell her Nancy Frazee loved her. Heck, who wouldn't love her? But the words stuck in his throat. He didn't know the dynamics of their family. He only knew that he'd make for damn sure she never questioned how much he cared for her and Jack, and god willing, any other children they were blessed with. "Brooke, I don't know anything about your mother. The few times I was around her, she always seemed like an...ice queen to me. I thought she just thought I wasn't good enough for her daughter. Maybe she does have issues with you because some women don't get that maternal gene that comes so easily to others. That's her loss. You've become so much more than she'll ever be, if that's the case." He waited until she turned to look at him. "You're not only a sweet and compassionate woman but you're a terrific mother. I'm proud to know Jack had you to raise him. When this is all over, you, me, and Jack, we're going to go on a family vacation."

Her hand went up to her cheek, brushing away a stray tear. "Thank you. Now, let's go do this and get the hell out of here."

He put the truck back in gear and continued on toward their destination. The long driveway brought back his last memory of being there. His grip on the steering wheel make a squeak from him squeezing it too hard. One finger at a time, he eased the hold he had on the leather. "Everything looks the same as it did three years ago," he remarked.

She nodded. "My mother has a landscaping service who takes care of the yard. She doesn't like change. Or I should say didn't, but that was before. I barely recognized my parents' house the last time I was here.

The only thing she hadn't touched was my dad's office, which I'm hoping that works in our favor when it comes to today."

They didn't say another word, while he drove around to the side of the house where the garages were located. The privacy fence to the backyard was locked, but Brooke hopped out of the truck as soon as he shut it off. He cursed that she hadn't allowed him to make sure all was safe. Touching his ear, he turned the device on. "Erik, how's things looking on your end?"

"*All's good here in the Boondocks. Mama Frazee is lunching with the old biddies at the club.*" Erik's tone was nonchalant, but an undercurrent of anger was there.

"Alright, what's wrong?" he asked as he followed Brooke to the back patio. She looked over her shoulder when she heard him talking. He pointed to his ear, to which she nodded but didn't say a word.

A loud sigh came through the ear piece. "*I don't know. I have this strange feeling you don't trust me. What's going on?*"

"Nah, it's not you or me. The other guys...they don't know you and weren't willing to trust their lives, or that of their wives for that matter, to someone they didn't know. Since I was asking them for a favor, I had to respect their wishes. Erik, I trust you." The man had gotten him out of a federal prison. He'd been instrumental in keeping Jase working on a team, of sorts, for the government, kept him from being killed on more than one occasion. Erik was a loyal friend. He just wasn't one of the team members from before; therefore, they didn't trust him like Jase did.

"*Good to hear. Now that we got the girlie shit out of the way. If my timetable is correct, you and your little lady have approximately an hour and seventeen minutes before her mother returns. At that point, you'll need to be prepared with a cover story, just in case.*" Tapping could be heard, making Jase think of Tay and his hacking abilities.

"How do you know all this?" He followed Brooke as she entered the house, watching her push a code into the security system. The breath he held eased out as the flashing red turned green. "Should you reset it in case she monitors it while she's away?" he asked Brooke.

Brooke shook her head. "She won't, or at least, she never has before. I don't think she's become paranoid in the last couple weeks either. Come on, let's get this over with. Do you have any idea about what you're looking for?"

Following closely behind her, he kept his senses open, looking around for anything that might seem out of place. His inner alarm was going off. Something wasn't right. "Erik, did Mrs. Frazee leave here alone today?"

"I don't know. I've only been monitoring the movement of her vehicle. Want me to look into the security footage at the country club, see if I can find her?" Erik asked.

"Yes, and while you're at it, see if you can't watch her progress backwards. I want to know who she arrived with and who she talks to." The admiral had smoked a cigar on occasion, but Jase didn't think the man had regularly smoked in the house, nor did he think Nancy Frazee was a smoker. Yet, the faint scent of menthol lingered in the air. The memory just out of reach of who he knew smoked a similar smelling brand.

"What's wrong?" Brooke glanced back at him, worry in her tone.

He searched the rooms as they passed, heading toward the back of the house where the admiral's office was. "Does anything look out of place to you?"

Brooke shook her head. "No, mother always kept everything tidy." Outside the entrance to her dad's office, she stopped and put her hand on the heavy oak door, her deep intake of breath proceeded her leaning her forehead on one of the panels that made up the custom-made door.

He wanted to take her into his arms and tell her she didn't need to go in with him. That he'd take it from there but knew she'd balk at his words. His Brooke was a fighter. "Erik said we have a little over an hour before your mother returns," he said instead.

"Let's do this." She turned the knob. Clear surprise showed on her lovely face when the door didn't open. "Well, it looks like someone has locked it. I gots keys, though." She held up a set with a smirk.

Good god he loved this woman. "Damn, you're sexy when you're sassy and speak all cute like that. I'd love to *gots* you," he mimicked her words.

"Why thank you, kind sir." Her key fit into the lock, opening the door with a quiet snick.

Inside, he could smell the menthol a little heavier. "Do you smell that?" he asked, not telling her what he meant, wanting her to acknowledge the scent on her own.

Her nose wrinkled. "It reeks of mint and nicotine. My dad smoked cigars on occasion, but he always made sure the window was open. Usually, he'd go outside on the patio if he had one, and they never had that nasty smell." She waved her hand back and forth in front of her nose. "He used to say, and I quote 'That's god damn offensive to my nose', and then he'd wink." Her voice had gone deep when she'd imitated her dad, followed by sadness.

Jase wished he could say her dad was a good man, but from all the evidence, the admiral was a traitor. The man had sent Jase to prison on false charges and tried to have him killed on more than one occasion. He couldn't find any remorse for the loss of the man other than the ache it caused Brooke and Jack. Standing near the door, he took a few seconds to scan the interior, getting a feel for the place. With a roll of his shoulders, he shrugged the pack off his back, unzipped it, and pulled the things he'd need out onto the floor. First order of business would be to make sure there were no listening devices installed. If his suspicions were correct, the admiral wasn't working alone. As Brooke turned to ask him another question, he placed his finger over his lips, shaking his head. Her eyes were troubled, but she nodded.

The tiny box lit up as he walked around the perimeter of the room until he reached the bookcases behind the desk. There, right behind where the admiral would sit and do his talking, or presumably work, Jase found, not one but two high-tech recording devices, cleverly hidden among the books and awards. Once he identified them all, he pulled out another handy electronic. This one, Erik liked to call the scrambler. Whatever it was truly called, Jase had no clue and didn't care. He only knew it blocked any recording device, even video. "We're clear to speak freely. Can you open the drawers on his desk and this cabinet?" Jase tugged on the top drawer of one of the built-in drawers.

Her fingers fumbled the keys as she attempted to open the desk first. "I can't believe there were bugs in here. Who would do that?"

Jase abandoned his task to comfort Brooke. He'd forgotten she wasn't accustomed to the life he'd been leading for the past several years. "Who knows, love. Let's just get this done and get out of here. If you want, you can unlock these for me and wait out in the living room." It would be easier on the both of them, especially if he found incriminating evidence.

She gave him a tight hug then pulled away. "No way. I want to see whatever it is you think you're going to find firsthand. I need to...see it to believe it." Resolve was set in every line of her slim figure.

His finger went under her chin, tilting her face up to his. "No matter what we find, or don't find, remember I love you. This," he looked around the room. "It means nothing. Changes nothing between you, me, and Jack."

Brooke closed the small gap between their mouths, giving him a sweet kiss. "I know, but thank you for saying that."

This woman had no clue, but he'd give her the moon, if he had the ability. "Let's get this done, so we can get back to our son."

"I like the sound of that." Brooke's hands still had a tremor in them, but she made quick work of unlocking the drawers.

Jase went through each one, finding nothing that was of interest. He booted up the man's computer, finding it password locked. "Shit!"

"Here," Brooke said, moving the mouse over the box and entering a series of letters and words. "My dad was cautious, but I knew all his passwords. He just didn't know it."

He shook his head. The fact a civilian could open up an admiral's computer that could very well have sensitive material on it was mind boggling, even if the person in question was their daughter. Jase didn't stop to look a gift horse in the mouth, though. He went to the history file, searching to see what Admiral Frazee had been doing, or looking at, before his death. His finger froze when the timestamps were for earlier that day and on days prior when the man in question was deceased. He copied the links and opened a browser, pasting them into it. When he saw what the first link led to, he froze, shocked to the core.

"What is that?" Brooke asked from over his shoulder.

How did you explain to the woman you loved that she was looking at coordinates to military locations in the Middle East? Locations that were top secret. The next one floored him even more as it was the blue print to Brooke's building. Inserting the thumb drive into the computer, he typed in the keys that would copy everything. Erik and the team, or rather Tay could scour the entire thing in a matter of hours, where it would take him days to search through the damn thing. What was clear to him? Someone who'd been on the computer in the last few days had been passing information on. Information that would be endangering US soldiers, along with details of Brooke's home and business layout. The only reason he could come up with for both wasn't good.

"Erik, I've got a shitton of info that needs to get in the right hands. Right now though, we need someone to get word to troops in the Middle East. Their locations are compromised." He gave the coordinates that he'd seen.

"*Are you fucking kidding me*?" Erik snarled, the sound of things dropping then keys tapping filled his ear.

"Wouldn't joke about this. I'm going to check the rest of the room, but there were a couple bugs. Want me to take them? Maybe you can see where they came from?" His fingers flew across the screen, searching through a few folders.

Erik let out a puff of air. "*I'd kill to get my hands on one of them, but if you take it, they'll know someone is onto them. No, it's too risky.*"

"I'm going to go through a few more things, then we need to get out of here." Jase could see his conversation had upset Brooke, but they were running out of time. He gave her what he hoped she took as the sorry he felt. She nodded, sitting down in one of the leather wingback chairs heavily.

"*Be careful. Contact me as soon as your safe.*"

He logged off the computer once the thumb drive indicated it was done downloading. The speed amazed him. Damn fine technology when it was working on your side.

Rifling through the drawers behind him, he didn't find anything that stood out, until he came to a video camera. The cleverly hidden device looked like an old book, but what had made Jase pull it out was the fact it looked too new, especially as it sat next to the older ones. He looked at his watch, grimacing. They were pushing their luck, but he wanted to see what, if anything was on there.

The small digital device came on when he pushed play. He arrowed back to the beginning, narrowing his eyes at the date. The day the admiral had died is the first day recorded.

*****

Brooke got up when Jase pulled down what appeared to be an old collector's book of her father's. "What's that?"

Jase shook his head, opening the book and pulling out a small black device.

She sucked in a breath as she realized what he held. Someone had been recording what went on in her dad's office. "Who put that there?"

"I don't know. Let's take a look." Jase held it out from his body, hoping like hell he wasn't making a mistake.

Her hand flew to her mouth, stifling the cry. On the screen, she noticed, not for the first time, that Mark Frazee Sr. was a handsome man, especially when he was dressed in his Navy uniform. He walked with the same sort of lithe grace she noticed Jase and his friends did. Like they'd been trained, or maybe it came naturally. Whatever it was, she hadn't noticed her father's walk until seeing it on the camera.

A gasp escaped through her covered mouth when the door flew open. She'd never seen her mother raise her voice, let alone screaming like a mad woman. Her hair was mussed, and her clothing looked as if she'd just thrown them on. A look of hurt and another emotion flashed over her father's face before he turned to face his wife.

His words low, clear, and final. 'I want you out of my house within twenty-four hours. I've put up with your coldness, your lack of respect, all without so much as a negative word. Even your...don't touch me attitude for the past fifteen years. I would've put up with it for the rest of my life, or yours, because god help me, you were my wife. I took those vows to heart. Today, I learned you weren't a cold fish. No, I learned the hard way exactly what you are, and that's a whore who sleeps around with a man I considered my friend.' He raised his hand when Nancy made a move toward him, backing away from her. 'Don't. Don't ever touch me again. I can't stomach the thought of looking at you, let alone having your hands on me. Look at you,' his head moved up and down her half-dressed form. 'Get out of my sight. I'll be gone in ten minutes, but when I return tomorrow, you best have what you'll need for an extended vacation. Whatever else you need from this house, you can contact my lawyer.'

Brooke listened as her mother pleaded while her dad gathered up his laptop and a few things from his desk. He glanced around the room, made sure his desk was locked, and walked out of his office, pausing outside in the hall. His mouth moved, but she couldn't hear what he said. The next thing she saw was her mother, head hung down, walking out of the room and shut the door.

"Oh my god, my mother was sleeping with someone my dad considered a friend." Her heart ached for the pain her dad must've felt. Although she hadn't thought her parents had a loving relationship. Not like the ones you'd see on television, but they'd seemed happy. Content. God, she hated that word. She would never settle for what they'd had. It was going to be all or nothing for her.

Jase's eyes were still glued to the small screen on the video. His patience much better than hers. She paced around the room, biting her thumb nail while she thought of who could've been the man her mother slept with. Mark Frazee had lots of friends. He was a likable man, but having a man that he would feel gutted by was the million-dollar question. "Jase, do you think he was so upset after his discovery that he wrecked his car?" She couldn't continue her question. The memory of her brother Mark taking his life was like a knife waiting to slice open a scarred over wound. Every wound heals, just like she knew the heartache of losing her dad would, just as the loss of her older brother wasn't the same gut wrenching pain as it was when she was eleven, but those scars on her soul would always be there.

"No, honey, I don't. Your dad was many things, but suicidal wasn't one of them. If I knew your father, he was probably thinking of ways to kill the bastard. Maybe not in real life, but in his head, he'd probably already offed him." Jase, looked back to the camera, then sucked in a breath.

She hurried to his side. "What?"

"Watch." He rewound and then hit play. The door to her dad's office opened, allowing her mom to enter with a man Brooke knew. He too was an admiral for the Navy. He was a man she'd known all her life.

Brooke shook her head when he strolled to her dad's desk, holding out his hand toward her mother. "What is she doing?"

"Looks like your mom has a key to this desk as well." Jase didn't look at her as he spoke.

She told him how close Admiral Davis and her mother had seemed at the wake after her dad's funeral. Now, watching the video, it was clear who her father had caught in bed with his wife. "I think I'm going to be sick." Brooke covered her mouth with her hand, her stomach rolling.

Jase pushed pause. "You don't need to see anymore. I know his name, thanks to you. I'll relay it to Erik and Tay and get them started on searching through the databases for any link to our missions. Why don't you go get a glass of water? By the time you get back, I should be done here."

Taking a deep breath, she tried to swallow the lump in her throat. The churning in her gut wasn't settling. In one day, she found out her father's heart had been broken, and that her mother was a lying cheating whore. "Do you want one too?" she asked, glad her voice didn't come out a croak.

"No, thank you."

Without another word, she let herself out of the office which had once been her dad's sanctuary. Now, it would forever be tainted by the memory she'd witnessed on the video. She made her way into the kitchen, noticing the slight changes that had been made. "I wonder if these are thanks to the new maid or my mother?" It took her three tries before she found where the drinking glasses had been moved to. After she filled the glass with water from the fridge, she went to the dining room and looked out at the back patio through the french doors. The treehouse where she and Mark had laughed and played beckoned her. She had thought that one day Jack would get to play there like they'd done. Now, Brooke didn't think she'd ever come back to the house where so much betrayal happened.

"Hello, Brooke. What brings you out here?"

The deep voice behind her stunned Brooke, making her spill what little was left in her cup all over the floor as she spun to face Admiral Davis. "Oh my word, Admiral. You scared the crap out of me. What are you doing here? Is my mother with you?" She looked behind him, searching for her mom.

Admiral Davis looked around the kitchen, his eyes seeming to miss nothing. "No, I believe she's at the Country Club with her lady friends. Whose truck is that out there?"

She noticed he hadn't answered her question about why he was there but didn't ask again. Goosebumps were racing over her flesh. "That big jacked up thing? It's a friend's. My car wasn't acting right, so he offered to let me drive his spare. I had no clue it was a monster truck when I accepted his offer." She tried to sound flippant but was sure she missed the mark.

Moving away from the patio doors, she headed back into the kitchen, rinsing out her glass before putting it into the dishwasher. The admiral watched each thing she did. His shoulders seemed to relax when he saw only the one glass inside. "You here alone? Where's Jack?"

"He's with my friends. I just came to check on my mom. I forgot she went to the Country Club, well, not forgot, but thought maybe," she trailed off, sadness filling her for why her mother would've missed her daily brunch with the ladies.

The admiral sighed. "Yes, well your mother is a strong woman and understands she can't mope for the rest of her life, and you shouldn't expect her to," he chastised.

Her hands bunched into fists as she thought of punching the man in the face. "I'm well aware of that, Sir." A thought struck her. "Since you knew my mother wasn't here, why are you here, and how did you get in?"

A second ticked by then another. Brooke began to think he wasn't going to answer, but he shocked her even more as he lunged over the granite counter top, tackling her to the ground. The attack had come out of nowhere and knocked the air from her lungs, keeping her from being able to scream for help.

"You always were a nosy little brat. Why do you think I needed to get rid of you and that little brat of yours," he gritted out, grabbing her hands in one of his. The other he gripped her throat. "Who knew you were coming here?"

She tried to think. Tried to buck him off of her, but he had a good eighty pounds on her, most of it not muscle, but she couldn't unseat him. "Get off me. Get off me, you fucker," she yelled as her jarring back and forth got his hand around her throat to ease.

Admiral Davis laughed, the sound one of a man who knew he had the upper hand. He pulled his arm back, fist doubled. Brooke struggled under him, her head moving back and forth to keep from making it easy for him to hit her in the face. Time slowed as his arm came toward her, his knuckles aimed, heading for any part of her that he could. She closed her eyes and froze, waiting for the blow.

All of a sudden, his weight was gone. Looking up, she saw Jase toss the other man back over the island. The sound of glass shattering echoed around the once pristine kitchen. She scrambled to her feet. Jase and the admiral were evenly matched in height, but her man was so much more. His fists lashed out, hitting the other man several times in the face. She heard him yell something about hitting women, making her smile for a moment.

The admiral fell to the floor, blood seeping from his nose and split lip. "Do you know who I am?"

"Yeah, you're the motherfucker who set me up. You're the mole who had an entire team killed and probably a lot more good men and women, too," Jase growled.

His words didn't make sense at first, when they penetrated her fogged brain, a gasp left her. "It was him? Not my dad?"

Jase turned his head to look at her. "No, baby, not your dad. He was setting your dad up to take the fall."

"It's too bad you won't live long enough to tell anyone," the admiral said.

They both turned to see the other man moving to a standing position, a gun with a silencer on the end pointed at Brooke.

"What are you going to do? Kill us both?" Brooke asked him.

Chapter Fifteen

Jase counted to ten in his head trying to calm his first instinct to lunge at the admiral holding a gun aimed at Brooke. He could see the resolve to kill her in the other man's face. "Listen, you don't have to do this, man. I'll let you walk out of here right now, but if you pull that trigger, you're a dead man," he warned Jase.

The admiral's lips tilted up in a grin. "You think I don't have a back-up plan. Where's little Jack, Brookey?"

Brooke's eyes widened, fear like a living breathing thing wafting off of her. He wanted to go to her and hold her, reassure her his team wouldn't allow anything to happen to their son.

"He's somewhere you'll never find him."

With a snort, Admiral Davis shook his head. "You know, your mother loved our son Mark. I didn't understand why. I mean, sure I admired how good he was at sports, figured he got those genes from me. But when he came out as gay, I was done. I'm glad nobody knew he was my kid. Now, she feels your son can replace the one she lost. I told her I was fine with it. Hell, she's a little crazy, but I've loved that woman since we were kids, long before she met your dad. She and I, we should've gotten married, but I messed up. It didn't take Nancy long to realize her mistake. If she wouldn't have gotten pregnant with you while I was overseas, she'd have left your dad. That stupid fucker was all about his vows, though," he spat.

As the other man was talking, Jase could see each word was like a dagger to Brooke. Not only had her mother had an affair, but it had gone on since the beginning and her beloved brother was this man's son. His mind caught onto the mention of their son. "What does any of that have to do with Jack?"

"Why, she's going to raise him as her own. We're going to be a family. What with everyone else gone, she'll become his mother, and I'll be his dad." The admiral said it in a casual tone, like he was talking about the weather.

"Does she know you tried to have the both of us killed?" Brooke asked.

Admiral Davis waved the gun back and forth. "No, and now she'll never know. Little Jack will be brought up right and be the son I never got to raise."

"Over my dead body." Brooke had moved farther away as the other man spoke, getting closer to the large island in the kitchen.

Nodding he waved the gun up and down. "That's exactly the end game."

Jase saw the other man's eyes, knew he was going to fire. He didn't know how good a shot the admiral was, or wasn't, only knew there was no way he could reach him in time to stop it. In a blink of an eye, his world flashed before his face. He threw his body to the right, praying he could block the shot with his own flesh, yelling for Brooke to run in case he did get hit. He pulled his gun from the back of his pants; in a move he'd done hundreds of times, he swung his arm, firing off two shots. The admiral's eyes widened and two wounds appeared on him. Two on the chest directly above where his heart was located. They were kill shots.

He rolled, coming up onto his feet in a crouch. His body didn't exhibit any signs of being shot, which had him running toward where he'd seen Brooke. "Brooke," he yelled, skidding around the tile floor. Never on a mission had he ever lost control, but now, he found himself shaking as he rounded the counter, praying she was okay.

Brooke rolled over, wincing as she pushed herself up onto her hands and knees. "Are you hurt?" she asked, hurrying toward him. Her hands went up and down his torso, checking him for injury.

"No, dammit, Brooke, stop that. Are you hit? Let me see?" Jase pulled her hands off his body while he looked her over. There was some blood on the side of her shirt. He lifted it but found only a small cut. "What happened?"

She pointed to the broken piece of pottery. "I must've fallen on that when I jumped. Is he?" she sucked her bottom lip into her mouth.

Jase pulled her against his chest and nodded. "Yeah, I need to contact Erik. Fuck, a goddamn admiral from Washington. I'm so sorry, baby."

"Do you think he had anything to do with my dad's accident?" her voice wobbled. "Oh god, my mother. What do you think he meant about taking Jack as her own?" She tried to get up, knocking her head into his chin.

"Ow, settle down. He's with Kai and the team."

Brooke shook her head. "She's his grandma. He loves her, and she looks so sweet and innocent." Her words tumbled out of her mouth.

Jase tucked the gun back into his pants, thinking about what she said. "There's no way she'd know how to find him. Sweetheart, Jack is safe."

"Are you sure?" Hope and love stared back at him from her hazel eyes.

He tucked a lock of hair behind her ear. "Positive. Why don't you go out on the patio while I contact Erik so we can get a cleanup crew here? I'll need to find out how to proceed since officially I'm deceased."

Her arms went around him, hugging him tightly. "Thank you for saving my life."

He laid his head on top of hers. She had no clue he could do nothing else. Sure, he had Jack now, but without her, he would only be half a man. "You're my life, Brooke. Without you, I'd be half a man."

A tear dropped from one eye, but she wiped it away. "I wish my dad was here. I wish he could see what a good man and father you are. But, wishes and rainbows aren't something you get every day. I wished for you to come back and I got you, so I guess I shouldn't push my luck. Can I call Kai, or one of the others, to check on Jack? I have this overwhelming need to hear his voice."

"If you go out to the truck, turn it on and hit the button that has the phone symbol. All you gotta do is say 'call Kai', it'll connect him for you." Jase walked her toward the patio doors, keeping his body between Brooke and the dead man on the floor.

A small kiss on the lips, and she was heading toward their borrowed truck. She didn't know it, but he had an inkling everything wasn't as it seemed. "Did you hear all that, Erik?"

"Loud and clear, my friend. I'm on my way there now. I should be arriving in five, give or take a minute. Fuck, that is one fucked up mama. Not your woman but her mama." The sound of gears shifting sounded through their connection.

"You got a cleanup crew coming in, or is the alphabet crew handling this?" He pulled what looked like an older sheet out of the hall closet. The dark blue color would be better than nothing.

The door to the patio flung open with a crash. "Jase, my mother came and took Jack. Kai said she showed up, and they assumed we knew. That we must've told her where he was; otherwise, how would she know? She has my baby," she sobbed.

"Fuck," Erik snarled. *"Hold on, I'm almost there. I can pull up the tracker on her car. Did Kai say what she was driving?"*

Jase pulled his cell out, dialing Kai before Erik had finished speaking. The other man answered on the first ring. "What kind of vehicle was she driving?" he asked without a hello.

"Shit! I'm sorry man. She was driving a silver Lexus four door." Kai didn't make any excuses.

Jase relayed the info to Erik. The sound of a throaty engine floated through the open doors. "Erik is here," he told Brooke, pulling her behind him. Still, his hand went to the gun at his back.

Minutes later his partner walked in, his head going left and right taking in the scene.

"Easy, no need to shoot," Erik said. He ambled over, setting a bag on the counter, pulling out a computer. Within minutes he had a program up and running. "Alright, I got her. Oh, looks like mama is coming home."

Jase and Brooke looked at the body lying on the floor. "We need to hide the vehicles. If she sees ours, she's liable to keep going." Jase looked at Erik, gauging his thoughts.

"I agree. They live out here without another house on either side, it'll be hard to stash and get back here before she arrives." He didn't look up from the screen as he spoke.

"Let's put them in the garage. She never parks in it," Brooke said.

"That was the old Nancy. What if she does now?" Jase had to state the obvious. Her mother wasn't the woman Brooke thought she was.

Erik lifted his hand. "She's gotta drive around to the backside here to access the garage, right? At their nod, he continued. "Well, if she starts to leave, I'll shoot out her tires. Done."

The decisive way Erik handled things was one of the reasons he was an effective operative. He didn't overthink things; he did them and did them well, the first time. If a roadblock appeared, his mind went to the best way to get through them, over them, or around them. To him, nothing wasn't doable. "Alright, give me your keys, Erik. I'll move your car in after I get the truck in."

"No can do, Jase."

Erik's negative answer had Jase dropping his hand. "What?"

The other man shook his head, typed in a few more things then shut his laptop. "I'll drive my precious into the garage. Nobody drives my precious but me."

At Erik's words, Jase laughed. "You realize that's crazy don't you? I mean, I've driven cars that are worth hundreds of thousands of dollars." Jase walked out with Erik.

*****

Brooke listened to Jase and Erik arguing, but her fear and worry for Jack had her wringing her hands. She wanted to call her mother and demand answers. Looking down at her shirt, she grimaced at the blood stain. "I can't let Jack see me like this."

She'd left clothes at her parent's house but wasn't sure if her mother had moved them or not. Heck, she wasn't sure about anything anymore. Going back down the hall, she tried to erase the image of the dead body in the other room from her mind. She opened Mark's bedroom door on impulse. Her mother had kept it exactly how it had been before he'd died. Standing in the open doorway, she wondered if her dad suspected that Mark wasn't his biological son. Not once in all her eleven years had she suspected. Of course, she'd been young, too young to have picked up on anything unless it was said outright. But, she could remember how proud her dad had been when Mark had made varsity. Their dad always went to games, even when their mother wouldn't. No, if he knew, he didn't care one way or the other. She shut the door and moved to her old bedroom. Unlike Mark's, her room had been renovated. No longer was it the somewhat girlie room she'd had. Being a tomboy, she didn't want the pink bedroom, instead she wanted a pale blue, like the sky. Her bed had been a full size, with a patchwork quilt made from different pieces of fabric from rock bands she'd liked. One of the ladies at church had sewn it for her, and she'd loved it. Her mother hated it, but because her dad had proclaimed it perfect, she was able to keep it.

Now, looking into the room that was once hers, she couldn't believe the difference. Thomas the Train was painted on one wall, with the theme continued throughout the room. At the time, she'd thought it was great the way her mother had embraced Jack. However, now it took on a whole new meaning. Walking around the room, she ignored all the toys and went to the closet, amazed at the clothes for little boys inside.

"Fucking seriously?" In a box at the back labeled Brooke, she found some of her clothes. Quickly, she pulled out a top and slid it on.

"Jase," she called as she walked out of the room, stopping in her tracks as she came face-to-face with her father.

"Hi, Brooke."

She froze, clutching the stained shirt in her hand. "Dad?"

He nodded. "It's okay. I'm not here to hurt you or Jase. I had no clue he was alive. I…I've been working to find out the same thing as him. Come on, I think it's best I explain this once to both of you. You have my word, Brookey. I'm not a bad guy, no matter what's going through your mind."

He had no clue what was going through her mind. She wanted to throw her arms around him, feel if he was real. She wanted to demand answers. Wanted to know why he'd let her think he was dead. "You…you let me think you were dead. Do you know what that did to me?" she hated the way her voice broke, but dammit, he's her dad, and she'd thought she'd lost him.

Mark Frazee reached for her, but she jumped back. "No, don't. I'm not…I don't know what's going on, but your wife has my son. Her lover," she swallowed. "Admiral Davis tried to kill me and told me some awful things. Now you show up, and I don't know what to believe."

The feel of Jase moving in behind her gave her the strength she needed to stand there and confront her dad. "Tell me what's going on, dad."

From the beginning, her dad explained how missions were being compromised. Missions he'd been somewhat a part of. When he'd been implicated, they'd taken measures to find the source. It was then Jase had shown up.

"So you thought I was a spy? That was why you didn't want me with your daughter?" Jase asked.

Admiral Frazee nodded. "Then you were caught on tape and the rest…you know. Only now it's clear who orchestrated it all."

He looked down the hall toward where the body was. "So you didn't know about his and mom's affair?"

Her dad shook his head. "Not until the day we faked my death. Yes, it was planned. We found out where the trail inside had led, and it went all the way to Washington. The only thing we didn't know was how it went from here to there. He made the mistake of moving another couple pieces around since my death. I've been holed up with security twenty-four-seven. They had no other recourse but realize it wasn't me. The higher ups also knew I didn't have the access to DC the way he did. I just don't understand why he hated me so much. I've known him for over thirty years."

"People, it's show time. Crazy granny is pulling in," Erik called from the other room.

Brooke bit her lip, wondering if she should tell her dad what they'd learned. Time ran out as the sound of a door shutting had them all moving.

"I need you to promise to stay calm until Jack is away from her. We don't know how she'll react, when she finds out her lover is dead." Jase pulled her face toward him.

Brooke took a calming breath. "I'll try."

Jase nodded once then pecked her on the lips. "That's my girl."

The sound of her mother talking to Jack set her teeth on edge. She hated the hoity-toity way she spoke to him, as if he were an adult instead of a two year old child. Jack's sweet, childish voice brought a smile to her as he asked if he could have a snack. Her son was always hungry.

"Jacky, you'll get fat if you continue to eat like a horse. Those idiots who had you said you just ate. Now, why don't you go into your room and play while I make a phone call?"

"Yes, grandma," Jack said in a subdued tone.

"What did I tell you to call me on the way here?"

"But you not my mommy," Jack cried.

Brooke slapped her hand across her mouth, keeping the cry of outrage from spilling out.

The sound of her mother's heels clacking across the tile proceeded her next words. "Jack, your mother left with that man. You know, the one you told me about. She told me to come get you and that I was to raise you as my own. That makes me your mother. Now, do as I told you, or I'll have to punish you."

Her mother had never sounded the way she did, in that moment, in all the years Brooke had known her. Snobby, bitchy, and conceited were things Brooke would associate with Nancy Frazee, but this crazy woman, speaking to her son, was not her mother. She shook her head at Jase when he raised a brow. She watched from the safety of the hall closet as Jack trotted past, a stuffed toy in his tiny hand.

"Children. I'll bring this one up right with the help of a good man," Nancy muttered.

Brooke eased out of the room, making her way down to where her son had gone. She'd leave her mother to Jase and her dad. Right now, she wanted to hold her baby and let him know she didn't leave him. That she would never leave him. Her heart ached at the dejected look on his face as he'd walked past.

*****

Jase tilted his head toward the kitchen. They could hear Nancy mumbling to herself. He made a swirling motion with one finger near his temple, wondering if the woman was certifiable or not. Admiral Frazee shook his head then shrugged his shoulders. Jase wondered where Erik and the body had gone. If they had still been in the room, Nancy would've been freaking out by then.

"Davis, where are you. I've called you over ten times. I'm getting worried. Have you taken care of our pest problem? Remember, she's my child, so try to make it look good, and if you can make it painless, that would be great, but if not," she stopped talking. Jase could picture her lifting a shoulder.

Brooke's dad appeared shocked at the words coming from his wife's mouth.

Admiral Frazee stepped out of the room, his shoulders back like he owned the world, not just the house, His footsteps loud as he walked into the kitchen. "Hello, Nancy, you're looking rather unwell. Did you see a ghost or something?"

Jase wanted to applaud the man as he looked behind him and all around before facing his wife.

"You. You're dead." Nancy pointed her finger at Mark.

"Clearly, not. I'd ask you if you wanted to touch me to prove how wrong you are, but I think we both know how much you abhor that thought. Not to mention, I find it truly distasteful myself these days."

Nancy backed away as Jase rounded the corner. He saw Erik enter from the other room, and more men were out in the back. "Mrs. Frazee, I need you to stay calm."

Her face angled toward him. "You. What are you doing here? Where's my baby?" She took a step, stopping as her husband put his arm out. "Don't touch me, you fiend."

Admiral Frazee laughed. "Believe me, I don't want used goods."

"I'll have you know, Davis is twice the man as you. You all thought you were so smart, trying to hide from us. Jack always takes his stuffed bear with him. I always know where he's at. Brooke was never trustworthy enough to keep him. I had to make sure I knew where he was at all times. Davis made sure I had everything I needed, even access to Jack. He was my first and only love. If you would've only been a better father to Mark, he wouldn't have turned out the way he did. Davis would've loved him. If it wasn't for Brooke, I wouldn't have stayed with you and your damn morals. Well, guess what, Mr. Morality, I've been sleeping with Davis since long before you and all the time we've been together."

"Nancy, do you really think I care? I loved Mark just the way he was. Every day I wake up and wish he were here so I could tell him how much he meant to me. As for Brooke, well she's the light of my life that I'm glad we created together. Sticks and stones, baby."

Nancy gave a bitter laugh. "Mark wasn't your son. He was Davis's. If I could've made it so, Brooke would've been his as well. The only reason she wasn't was because he was overseas when she was conceived."

Jase could see the pain lash across the admiral's face at her words. She was talking in circles. Mark would never have been good enough in her eyes, not as a father. It wasn't his fault Mark Jr. was gay, but the woman wasn't prepared to listen.

"Be that as it may, I still love them both." The admiral waved his hand, acting as if her words hadn't hit their target.

He watched Nancy as she kept backing up until she hit the cabinet behind her. In a blur, she pulled open a drawer and came out with a gun, a small caliber one that would do some damage if she knew how to shoot and had good aim. "Mrs. Frazee, put the gun down. Right now," he ordered. "You don't have any major offenses against you." He didn't mention they were working on it, or the fact she'd kidnapped his son, had probably aided in the murder of US soldiers by giving information to the man she professed to love. All that would be up to the government.

Brooke's mother laughed, the sound maniacal. "Oh, you all think I'm stupid. I'm walking out of here, and you're going to let me. Davis is a very powerful man. He can and will bury both of you."

"I'm sorry, ma'am, but Admiral Davis won't be assisting anyone," Erik spoke from the other room, his deep baritone voice ominous.

Nancy's head whipped to the side, the gun jerking toward the sound. Chaos erupted as a single shot rang out, followed by several more. Jase dove for cover, his weapon out. Nancy ran toward the darkness, stopping with a gasp. Eyes wild, she pinned him with a hate filled glare then turned the gun toward her head.

"No," he roared as she pulled the trigger. He looked toward the room she'd stumbled toward and could see what she'd found. The body of her lover.

Where was Erik? Jase looked around. "Status?"

"She shot me, man." Erik leaned against the wall, holding his side.

Jase squatted down, moving Erik's hand off the red stain. "Oh, shut up, pussy, it's only a graze."

Erik used the wall to get up, cursing the entire time. "Mothereffer, that shit hurts. I don't get shot when I'm just chillin'. I mean, have you ever?"

He raised his hand up. "Shut up. I can't even believe we're having this conversation. Just chillin'. You were in a room with a dead body for crying out loud."

The other man nodded. "And? We weren't in some godforsaken country getting shot at by a bunch of enemies, sweating our nuts off. Hence, chillin'. Come on, why you walking away?"

"I need to check on my son, and you need your head examined," Jase called over his shoulder.

"You try getting shot when the adrenalin isn't pumping. It hurts twice as bad," Erik called to his back.

"Why is this guy whining like a little bitch?"

Jase stopped at the entrance to the hallway at the sound of Oz's voice. "What the hell you doing here?"

Oz shrugged. "Something seemed off with that one. I thought I'd follow and make sure the little guy was alright and shit."

Jase's chin hit his chest, emotion swelled inside him. "I fucking love you, too, man."

"Hey, I followed the kid, not you." Oz raised his arms.

"Same diff." Jase walked over, pulling Oz into his arms. "Thank you for coming to protect my son."

The big red haired man's eyes searched around the room. "Yeah, well it looks like I missed out on all the fun."

Jase nodded. "It was definitely a fuckshow."

He and Oz walked side by side down the hall. "So, that's clearly a lot worse than a shitshow, huh?" Oz asked outside the closed door.

"You've no clue man. At least Jack is still too young and innocent to know what went down. Let's go say hi, shall we. How do I look?" Jase waved his hand at himself.

Oz looked him up and down. "Well, you ain't got no blood and guts on you, and I don't see no bullet holes. I call that a damn fine day."

The other man's words made Jase laugh as it was a familiar saying they'd say after a mission. "Hooyah," he said.

"Oh, I forgot to ask if my truck was okay?"

Jase winced, pretending he had bad news. When Oz took a step back Jase clapped him on the shoulder. "I'm just fucking with you. Your rig is just fine."

"You're still a dick," Oz mumbled.

"Love you, too."

Chapter Sixteen

They walked into a room filled with trains, but Jase found the two people who meant more to him than anything in the world. "Hey you two. Whatcha doin?"

"Jase, Oz, look what mommy did," Jack yelled.

On the table that had an elaborate train setup, Brooke had clearly derailed her train. "Wow, buddy, remind me not to let your mom drive my rig."

Jack giggled, adding a lightness to the room. He wasn't sure how to break it to her about her mother. "Hey, Oz, you wanna keep Jack company for a second. I need to speak to Brooke for a moment."

He helped Brooke to her feet, walking out into the hall with her tiny hand in his. He could feel her trembling. They both stared down the hall then at each other. "We heard gun shots. Jack asked if someone was making popcorn."

Hating the thought of what he had to tell her, Jase buried his nose in her hair, inhaling the sweet scent. "I wish it was just that. Your mom...she didn't take it well, the loss of Admiral Davis broke something in her. She took a wild shot, and...I'm sorry, Brooke, she killed herself."

Brooke pulled away, tears flowing from her eyes. "She...she's dead. That can't be. She wouldn't...I mean, she said it was a coward's way out. I heard her crying, talking to Mark like he was here, telling him how selfish he was for leaving her here without him," she sobbed, burying her face against him. "Oh god, she loved him so much. Why didn't she love me half as much?"

He had no words, no answers other than her mother was the selfish one. Not for taking her own life, but for not loving her daughter the way she deserved. He looked down the hall and met the dark gaze of Brooke's dad. With their eyes locked, he hugged Brooke tighter. "I swear to all, I'll love you and all our children with every fiber of my being. If anyone tries to harm one hair on any of your heads, I'll hunt them to the ends of the earth and beyond. They'll wish they were never born, by the time I get through with them." Not once did he take his eyes off of Admiral Frazee. The other man needed to understand and accept the fact he was here, and he was staying.

"You're a good man, Jase. I'm glad my daughter and grandson, your son, have you. You'll always be welcome as I hope I'll always be welcome in your home. Nancy...I loved her, and thought she'd loved me at one time. Sometimes, love on one side isn't enough." He ran a hand down his face, a tremble shook his frame before he continued. "Maybe we should've divorced a long time ago when I knew she wasn't happy, but I was too stubborn. She said my morals kept me here, and she was right to an extent. Now, it's too late to change the past, but I want you to know I never, not once regret you or Mark. No matter if what she said was true and Mark wasn't mine by blood, he was still my son." He pinned Jase with a hard stare. "I didn't go to you in that desert to get you killed. I was trying to figure out who was the mole and...I let my prejudice cloud my judgement and you got blamed for something you didn't do."

Brooke moved away, or tried, but Jase pulled her next to him. Nodding at her dad, he took a deep breath. For the last three years, he'd lived with the need for vengeance at his core. Now, all the people who'd set him up were dead, and he felt all the weight lifted off his shoulders. "At any moment, we all have a choice, Admiral. That decision will either lead us closer to where we need to be or further away. You see, it all comes down to us in the end and the choices we make. I plan to choose wisely, how about you?"

Admiral Frazee moved closer, his arms loose at his sides, stopping a foot from them. "I choose my family's happiness. Brooke, Jack, and you, Jase. In the coming days, I'm going to have to face a firestorm from the fallout of everything that happened in there, but knowing I have my family, I can, and will, get through it."

"I love you, dad. When I thought you...and now mom," she swallowed. "I can't lose anybody else. I need you guys to get along."

Her dad tucked a lock of hair behind her ear. "Little girl, you'll never lose me. Even when I had to fake my death, I was aware of where you were and who you were with. Don't give me that look, Tyler. You think I'd let my little girl down. Those men trying to get into her apartment were the only surprise we weren't expecting. Who do you think told you to secure her? After that, we had eyes on you until you headed into some damn mountains. By then, I knew she was in good hands. When I recognized you as the man she was with I only felt relief, knowing you'd do everything to keep my...our family safe."

"Well, hell." Jase wasn't sure what to think as he remembered the call the night outside of Brooke's apartment. No matter what else happened, they were together now, he, Brooke and Jack. "I'm sorry about your wife and about what she said about Mark Jr." Jase held Brooke a little closer.

Admiral Frazee gave a sad smile. "You don't have to touch something to love it or be part of its creation. Look at Jack. Tell me you don't love him," he nodded at the closed door. "Before Mark was ever born, I loved him more than anything in the world, only matched when Brookey came along. Whether he was my flesh and blood, or not, changes nothing with how I feel in here." He tapped his chest.

Jase nodded. "I know what you mean. When I see Jack smile, it's like the world lights up. If anything were to happen to him..." He stopped and cleared his throat. "Yeah, I would lose my shit."

Brooke's arms contracted. "Nothing would be worth living for, if I lost him," she said.

Jase and the admiral both nodded. Maybe that was the straw that broke Nancy. They'd never know for sure, but one thing he did know, was from this day forward, he and his little family of three now had a fourth member, if Brooke's dad wanted to be a part. He held his hand out to Mark Frazee. Her dad looked at his outstretched arm then at him. With a shake of his head, Admiral Frazee closed the small gap between them and wrapped them both up in a hug. "We're family now and this family hugs," the admiral announced.

Brooke laughed. "I always did love your hugs, dad."

The door behind them opened. An excited squeal from Jack was followed by their little man yelling papa over and over.

"You came back. I knew you'd come back, papa." Jack latched onto his grandpa's legs.

Jase watched as Brooke's dad picked his grandson up and tossed him in the air as if there weren't two dead bodies in the other room. "Of course, I came back. I wanted to be here when your daddy finally came home."

He and Brooke both froze, neither had discussed when they'd tell Jack the truth.

Mark turned with Jack in his arms. "You see that man right there?" He pointed at Jase. "He's your daddy and one of the bravest men in the whole world."

"Even braver than you?" Jack asked.

"Yep. Even braver than me."

"How bout braver than batman?"

The old man pretended to think. "Yep, I'd say braver than even him."

Jack whooped, then launched his upper body toward Jase. Luckily, both the admiral and Jase had fast reflexes and were able to keep Jack from falling onto the floor. Jack's dark eyes lit with happiness. "Can I call you daddy?"

Unable to say a word with the lump in his throat, Jase nodded.

Jack placed both his hands on either side of his face, making sure Jase couldn't look away. His son had no clue there was no way Jase could ever look away from him in that moment. "I'm glad you're my daddy. Can Ozzy be my unka?"

Brooke burst out laughing at the request, but Jase nodded. "Absolutely. Yo, Unka Ozzy, my son has adopted you," he yelled down the hall.

Oz's red head appeared. "Um, is Ozzy what I'm being called?"

Jack clapped. "Unka Ozzy, you my best friend."

"Hey, I thought I was your best friend?" Jase tickled his son, making him giggle.

His son squirmed in his arms, laughing. "No silly, you're my daddy."

If someone would have told him his heart would melt over three simple words, he'd have called them a liar. Now, with Jack in his arms and Brooke next to him, he finally understood what it was to be redeemed after years of feeling like nobody gave a damn about him. Life can throw you a lot of curves, but he'd be damned if he didn't learn to swerve with them and come out the victor as long as he had his family and friends with him.

"You have a really bright smile on your face right now," Brooke said, sliding her arm around him.

He kissed her cheek then Jack's. "That's because I'm happy."

Oz groaned. "Ew, get a room. Come on, buddy. Let's get the heck outta here. I think someone said the cleaners were coming." His head jerked toward the kitchen.

Admiral Frazee sighed. "Why don't you take Jase and Jack out through the doors in the master bedroom, the view is nice that way."

In other words, that way they wouldn't have to see the death and destruction in the kitchen.

"Are you going to be okay, dad?" Brooke asked, her hand rested on his upper arm.

Admiral Frazee took a deep breath. "Yeah, I will."

As Jase walked out of Brooke's family home, he was counting his blessings for all he had. One day in the very near future, he planned to make an honest woman out of Brooke and give both her and Jack his last name. Until then, they were going to take a much needed vacation.

"You can drive my truck back to the cabin, but I'm following you. I took the liberty of getting the little guy's car seat out of that silver car over there." Oz's words reminded him they still had friends.

"You're such a giver, Oz," Jase joked.

Oz nodded. "I know." He took Jack and expertly buckled him into the car seat in the back of his truck.

One thing was for sure. Life with his old team definitely wasn't boring. "When I get you alone, I am so going to..." Jase was stopped by Brooke's hand over his mouth.

"Don't even say it. I'm already on edge. If you even mention," she looked in the back at Jack, where Oz had strapped him in, happily watching a movie. "Tonight, after we put him down, it's you and me time."

"Damn, I love you," Jase swore.

She leaned over the center and kissed him quickly. "I love you, too. Now, let's go. I need to get away from here for a little while."

Jase understood her need for distance and did as she asked. He wasn't sure what their future was going to bring, but it would be together.

Two months later...

Brooke looked around the house she and Jase bought near her dad's. She was still having trouble believing it was real, having the man she loved, the father of her child, in their life.

"What's that sigh for?" Jase asked slipping his arms around her waist from behind.

She leaned into him, looking over her shoulder to meet his dark gaze. "Is this real?" She waved her arm in front of her.

The living and dining room were large, with hardwood flooring, opening up to a kitchen that would make a chef happy.

Jase kissed her cheek, hugging her tighter. "If it's not, I don't want to wake up."

Turning in his arms, she locked her arms around his neck. "You feel pretty real to me."

His finger dug into her hips a moment, then he lifted her up until they were at eye level. "How about if we just make for sure."

Her legs wrapped around his waist, locking around his back as his lips covered hers. Instantly, their tongues dueled, stroking against one another while he began walking toward the master bedroom. The older ranch style home had been completely renovated with dark wood floors that didn't make any sound as Jase carried her almost past Jack's bedroom, but he stopped outside the door with the little plaque that had their son's name written on it. "Let's make sure he's sleeping," Jase murmured.

Love swelled in her chest even more. Her first priority had always been Jack. Now, knowing she had a partner who loved him just as much made her realize how much she'd missed Jase all this time. The fact Jack was Jase's biological child was the icing on the cake, for she knew if he hadn't been, Jase would've loved her son anyway.

With one arm under her ass, he eased the door open. The nightlight let them see a sleeping Jack snuggled under the blankets, with a teddy bear hugged tightly to his chest. Jase quietly closed the door before continuing to their bedroom.

"I love you." The words came out a raspy exclamation. God, this man was the epitome of what a father and lover should be. One day, she hoped they would become more, but she wasn't going to push him.

The bedroom was lit with candles, surprising her from her thoughts.

"I love you, Brooke. I love our son, but I came back for you. Thank you for forgiving me and giving me another chance." Jase released his hold on her, allowing her to slide down his body.

She shook her head, covering his mouth with her hand. "There is no need to thank me or for apologies anymore. We're so far past all that now. Besides, I believe we need to christen that bed." She looked around Jase at the gorgeous bed they'd bought together. The black leather head and footboard, with the four posters on each end, was truly decadent. With the white and turquoise bedding and the light grey walls, the room was a perfect mix of masculine and feminine.

"Woman, I love the way you think."

Brooke squealed when Jase lifted her off her feet and strode to the bed. In one, not so smooth move, he pulled the gorgeous comforter back, throwing it and the mound of decorative pillows onto the floor. "I'll pick those up later," he assured her, tossing her onto the bed.

She bounced once then was covered by Jase climbing on top of her. "You did all this for me?"

Lying sideways on the bed, she tried to take in the flowers on each end table she'd only barely seen and the myriad of candles lit around the room.

Braced on his elbows next to her head, he traced her eyebrows with his thumbs. "I wanted our first night in the bedroom where we begin the rest of our lives together to be memorable."

The soothing motion of his fingers on her brows had her smiling. He knew just how to touch her, and where, but that wasn't where she wanted his talented fingers. "I think you are the most romantic man in the world. But, I do have one complaint." She bit her lip, waiting for him to ask.

His body froze above hers. "What? Anything you want or need, if I can do it or get it, it's yours."

She smiled, wiggling beneath him. They'd both showered after the long day of putting the finishing touches on the house, each putting on clothes again. "We're wearing too many clothes. I want to feel your skin on mine with nothing between us."

Heat flared in his dark gaze as he inhaled deeply. "Woman, that is a wish I can totally rectify." Jase reared back, lifting his arms behind his head, whipping off the shirt he wore.

Brooke began pulling her own T-shirt off, flinging it toward the foot of the bed, hoping it landed where she could find it easily. Thoughts of her shirt fled when Jase's hands cupped her breasts. His fingers deftly unsnapped her bra, pulling the edges apart. Her nipples puckered in the cool air.

"I love these. They're like ripe little berries, begging for my lips." Jase bent his head, spreading kisses along her collarbone, and down the swell of her breasts, not quite touching where she really wanted him.

"Jase, please." Her fingers sifted through his hair that had grown longer in the time since her father's fake funeral.

The diabolical man maneuvered them so she was lying with her head near the headboard, moving so he was now between her thighs, his dark hair and eyes gleaming in the candlelight. "I always aim to please you, B."

She opened her mouth to tell him how to please her but then, his tongue came out and licked over one nipple then the other, silencing her. They'd made love several times since he'd returned to her life, each time always better than the last. The rest of their clothes were removed without finesse, both their hands joining in, making her laugh and him groan when he couldn't get out of his cargo shorts without getting off the bed. "Don't you move," he ordered.

Brooke found herself grinning at his highhandedness, and figured she'd tease him a little. Lifting her legs up, she pushed them open allowing him to see her hands ghost down between her thighs. Jase growled, climbing back onto the bed, his fingers trailing up her legs. She hadn't realized the backs of her knees were sensitive until he lifted her right leg up and placed a kiss there.

Her thighs shook and her toes curled at the feel of his lips brushing up her inner thigh then down the other. "You're trying to kill me."

"No, I'm loving you slowly." No sooner had the words left his lips than he was lying between her spread thighs, holding her open with one hand while his lips and tongue ate at her.

She fisted her hands in the sheet, gasping each time he swiped across her clit. "Oh god, Jase, I'm so close. So damn close."

He looked up. "You said a bad word. Want me to put you in time out?"

Looking down at his face, her juices coating his lips and chin, she reached down with one hand, running her hand through his hair. "I'll take my punishment another way."

Jase's look turned positively wicked as he kept his gaze locked with hers and pushed two fingers inside her pussy, making her arch up into him. In moments, her arousal went from almost there, to over the top. She gasped out his name, careful not to yell, worried she'd wake Jack. "More, I want more, Jase."

Her demand earned her a nod, and then he was licking his lips, moving up her body. Jase shoved into her. There was no allowing her to get accustomed to his size, the slight stretch from his entrance another pleasure that ratcheted up her own excitement. "I'll give you more. All of me," he promised.

In seconds, he was buried to the hilt, so deep Brooke didn't know where he began and she ended, only that they were together. He set a fast pace, taking her with him. Meeting him stroke for stroke, their bodies strained together as they reached for the ultimate prize.

"I'm close, Brooke." His arms flexed with each movement, sweat glistening on him.

She lifted her legs higher, opening herself wider for each hard penetration. "Me too," she moaned. "Yes, right there. Faster. Oh...fuck me. Yes," she gasped, eyes going wide. Her body constricted around his, pulse after pulse.

*****

Jase slammed into Brooke at the feel of her pussy squeezing his dick, the tight constricting muscles pulled his own orgasm out of him. "I love you. God damn, I love you, Brooke," he roared, forgetting his son was sleeping down the hall.

His thrusts slowed, wanting to prologue their pleasure, feeling her body's little tremors still squeezing him moments after she'd come.

"It keeps getting better." Brooke ran her hands up and down his back.

He rolled to the side, his semi-hard cock slipping out of her, but he kept his arms locked around her, taking her with him so she lay on his chest. They hadn't used a condom, a conscious decision they'd both made over a month ago. She was still on the pill, the low dose. If they were blessed with another child, he would be over the moon happy. However, he wanted to do it right, starting now.

"You know you and Jack are my world," he said, letting his arm roam up and down her back.

She stiffened above him. "Yes," she said hesitantly.

He wrapped both arms around her when he felt her try to pull away. "I love you both more than anything. I want to be a part of your lives for the rest of mine, but there's something missing." He gave her a hug, rolled so she was lying on her back, staring up at him with a frown. He traced her brows with his finger.

"Okay. You've lost me, Jase."

With a slight shift, he pulled the drawer open on the nightstand grabbing the little box he'd placed there earlier out. "I'd planned to get down on one knee and do this the right way, but damn it all, you're too sexy and I couldn't wait to christen the bed, like you suggested."

Brooke looked at the box in his hand then at him. "What do you mean?"

Jase pulled her into a sitting position, shoved up and knelt in front of her on their king sized bed. "Brooke Frazee, I love you more than life. You've given me a reason to come back into the world as the man I was before…well, before my world went dark. I'll never be good enough for you and Jack, but if you give me a chance, I'll do my best to be the best husband and dad to our children." He opened the box in his palm, waiting for her to speak.

A tear fell from one eye then the other. Brooke struggled to her knees, placing her palms on his chest. "You are so much better than good enough for us, Jase. You're the man I've loved and wanted to marry since I first laid eyes on you. Of course I'll marry you." She held her left hand out, waiting for him to place the ring on her finger.

The moment would be one he would remember for all time. No, there wasn't some moonlit beach setting or fancy restaurant proposal. Hell, he nearly laughed as he slipped the white gold band with the diamond solitaire onto her ring finger, imagining the conversation as they retold the story of when they got engaged. "You realize when we tell people about our proposal—we might have to edit it, right?" Jase asked Brooke while she stared at her ring.

Brooke looked down at her naked body then at his. "I don't know; I think we have the best story in history. I mean, who else can say they were asked to marry the man of their dreams, in a roomful of roses lit by candlelight, all while said man ravished you?"

Jase pulled her into his arms. "Ravished you, huh?"

She smiled against his chest, placing a kiss over where his heart beat frantically. "Most definitely, ravished. It's in all the best books."

Hours later, Jase woke to the sound of laughter. His son and soon to be wife were trying to sneak up on him, but little Jack wasn't the best at the quiet game. He lay with his arm over his eyes, pretending to sleep, waiting until he knew Jack was close to the bed. As soon as they were within arm's reach, he sat up and pulled the startled boy into his arms. "Gotcha," Jase growled.

"Daddy," Jack giggled.

That one word melted Jase's heart every time he heard it come out of Jack's mouth. "What are you two up to so early?"

He looked over the side of the bed, making eye contact with Brooke who stood wearing a pair of leggings and a tank top. "Well, this little guy said it was time to wake you up so you two could do something special."

Jase, holding onto his son, swung out of the bed. Now that they were living together and had a small child, he'd began sleeping in a pair of boxer shorts. Didn't help the usual morning wood, but luckily, it had gone down once he'd realized Jack was stalking him. God, he loved his family. "Yes, we are, and no, you can't come. This is a guy's only thing. Right, little man?"

Jack nodded vigorously from his perch on his hip.

Brooke folded her arms over her chest and glared at them. "Fine," she said then turned to leave.

"Wait, can mommy come too?" Jack asked.

Jase sighed. "Oh, but it's a surprise for mommy, so she'll get to see it when we're done. Now let me get dressed. Brooke, you aren't allowed outside until we holler for you."

Since he'd been officially cleared from all his charges and honorably discharged, Jase had thought long and hard about what he was going to do for the next fifty years, give or take a few. Of course, Rowan had offered to let him become part of his security company, but Jase was used to being in control. No matter how much he liked the other man, he didn't think two alpha personalities like theirs would mesh on a day-to-day basis. Like before, Erik had come in with an offer he thought was too good to be true. Even after three years, he was still learning things about his partner. Their new private security business was going to partner with Rowan Shades, a perfect compromise and one that already had a great foundation. "If I don't end up beating the shit out Erik first," he mused out loud as he looked at his cell phone. Seeing a text from Erik with an image of him sitting on a beach drinking a margarita with what he thought their business should be called written not only on the cup, but his shirt, and spelled out in the sand in front of him, Jase sent back an image of his middle finger. Short but sweet, that was how he had to deal with Erik.

The ding on his phone had him groaning. Instead of looking to see what smartass response the other man sent back, he tucked the little device into his pocket and headed in search for his family.

He and Jack went outside after he got a pair of shorts and shirt on, pulling the weeping mulberry tree and the things they'd need out of the garage. His son wore a matching outfit to his with a pair of gloves and had his own little shovel for digging. "Alright, let's get to digging." They found the perfect spot in the front yard, knowing the tree would get bigger. Brooke had always loved the trees shaped like an umbrella, she'd told him. Now, they'd have one in their front yard and be able to watch it grow like their family, god willing.

"You wanna go get your mama?" He stood with the shovel facing the ground admiring their handy work.

Jack jumped up and down. "Yes," he whooped.

A couple minutes passed, Jase thinking Jack got lost turned to go in search for them, stopping as the two he referred to as his life walked out. Mother and son, hand-in-hand. Brooke looked at him then the tree. Her free hand covered her mouth. She picked up Jack, and raced to Jase. "It's perfect." She kissed Jase, an open-mouthed kiss, until Jack put his hand between them.

"Mommy, don't. Look at the tree we planted."

Jase wrapped his arms around both Jack and Brooke. "This is only the beginning of our lives. As we watch it grow, so will my love for you both. Thank you for redeeming me. For giving me the chance to be a better man, Brooke."

"You were always a great man, Jase. Now, you're ours. Forever!

The End

DARK EMBRACE

THE DARK LEGACY SERIES
BOOK 1, Coming 2017

Jenna rolled to the side, the taste of copper filling her mouth making it hard to swallow. She squinted, trying to figure out where she was without making too much noise. The room was huge. Like something out of a fairytale. The thought had the breath freezing in her throat. Her hand went to her cheek, feeling for the cut that had burned like acid soaking straight to her bones. When her fingers felt nothing other than smooth skin, she exhaled, thinking it had only been a nightmare. "Then where the fuckity fuck am I?" she whispered into the quiet of the room.

Shoving the blanket off her legs, Jenna scooted to the edge, her main thought was to blink her way back to her realm now that her mind was clearing. With every inhale of breath, she knew her guys were near, but she couldn't get a clear read on where exactly. Damien and Lucas Cordell, the princes...of, well, she wasn't sure exactly what as their father was the Vampire King who was mated to a shifter. Being the eldest of their children and twins, she guessed they were next in line to take over if he should ever step down. The last time she'd seen the powerful man, he was no sooner to releasing his title than she was.

As her feet touched the ground, her legs wobbled then gave out. The feel of the cold tile slapping against her palms had her crying out even as her knees slammed into the unforgiving surface. "Shit," she moaned.

Why nobody had come at her cry was a little alarming, but it gave her a moment to get her bearings and stand up, or attempt to stand. Hell, she'd take leaning on the bed while standing on her two feet at the moment as a step in the right direction. "You can do this, Jennaveve," she cheered herself on but in all reality, it took more effort than she'd thought. "What the hell happened to me?" A fine sheen of sweat covered every inch of her body like she'd been working out for hours.

She remembered allowing herself to be kidnapped by a scumsucking vampire freak who'd mated with a panther shifter. The jackhole had tried to kill his wife, but had planned to make his daughter watch. In his mind, which she still wanted to gag when she thought about the things she'd seen, the bastard wanted to teach his daughter a lesson or something. She rubbed at her temples as she thought back to the night in question.

Yes, she'd only been in his clutches for a couple hours. Her Iron Wolves were coming, she remembered sensing them, along with Damien and Lucas. Everything was going according to plan, until a stranger came out of the darkness.

Fear had her looking around the quiet room, opening her senses in search of the being who'd come out of nowhere that night. His essence had reminded her of the Cordell's only darker. Sinister. Goddess, she'd never felt such a being before and didn't want to ever again. A shiver stole up her spine. "Please tell me I'm not his prisoner?"

No, she couldn't allow herself to think that way or she'd lose whatever sanity she had left. She needed to get to the Fey Realm and recharge. Once she was back to herself, she'd return and speak, or mate, whatever the wolpires did. Jenna nodded, then opened her heart reaching for her home. When nothing happened and she was still leaning against the large four-poster bed, real anxiety nearly felled her. "I'm just overly tired. Lula can come and help a girl out." Like before, she reached out for her friend, only a vast emptiness met her quest.

When she reached for the familiar link with her friend Kellen Styles, the invisible bond she'd created and could reach in her sleep, the same thing happened. Never in all her thousands of years had she not been able to communicate with whom she wanted, when she wanted. Never, had she been unable to move between realms. Until now.

The door opened to the right, it's slight creak like a shotgun in the quiet room. Jenna raised her right hand, preparing to defend herself. With what, she had no clue as she could barely stand on her own two feet, but she'd be damned if she'd go down without a fight. Of course, she'd probably go down in a stiff wind, but the young female who entered paused, her startled gaze appeared friendly.

"Good afternoon, miss. I came to check on you. We weren't sure you'd be awake just yet. Let me go get..."

"Who are you and where am I?" Jenna demanded hiding the tremble that shook her by forcing rigidity into her body.

Eyes as wide as a baby doe, the girl kept one hand on the door. "My name is Beth. I'll just go let the others know you're awake. Is there anything I can bring for you?"

Jenna wanted to run across the room and make the girl stay, but her body was shaking from standing already. "Please, tell me where I am."

"You're in the guest wing, of course. I'll just go tell them you're awake." Beth began walking out the door.

"Wait. Who are you going to tell?"

"The Cordell twins of course." Beth bowed and backed out as if she thought Jenna was a crazy person.

Hearing the name Cordell had her relaxing. If she was in their home then she was safe. They'd help her figure out why she couldn't access her realm, or reach out to anyone. The way she was feeling, it was as if she was...human.

The air stirred near the large fireplace. What made her look she wasn't sure, only knew something seemed familiar. She expected to see Damien or Lucas, heck her heart actually sped up at the thought of seeing them. However, her body froze as the man from the darkness appeared. "What are you doing here?"

She whipped her head toward the door the young girl had gone out. Although Jenna's senses weren't on track, she was sure she'd been a human, especially since it was daylight. The being in front of her came out of the shadows, allowing her to get her first real glimpse of him without the cover of night or a trick of his keeping his identity hidden. Oh, he was gorgeous, there was no doubt of that. But, what was most startling was his resemblance to Damien and Lucas.

"Hello again, Fey. You are looking slightly ill. Are my...family not treating you well?" His eyes flashed from obsidian to red. Where her men had gorgeous eyes, she wanted to get lost in, this man's were cold and lifeless.

His words finally registered. "Your family?"

He raked his claws together, making them clack in a way Jenna was sure he did to scare his victims. Newsflash asshole, I've faced bigger, badder, uglier, and hopefully deadlier foes, she thought.

"I'd love for us to stay here and chat, but I fear the big guy is waking, and well, I'm not in the mood for a reunion just yet. By the way. Sorry, my pet. I don't usually put females as pawns, but in this instance, it's a must." He flew across the room, eliminating the space separating them.

Jenna fell back against the bed, nearly falling on her ass. His quick reflexes kept her upright. "What the hell are you talking about?" She pressed her hand to his chest, trying to put space between them.

He shook his head. "You'll find out in due time, my pet. Now, we must go before father-what-a-waste, awakes."

She knew the telltale signs of magic and could feel it as the man in front of her began to manipulate the fabrics of time and space. "Who are you?"

He flashed her a smile, white teeth with two canines much longer than the others prevalent. "My name is Khan, son of Zahidda. Bastard son of Damikan at your service."

The door flew open, giving her hope she'd be saved. The sight of Damien and Lucas had her shoving harder against the rock-hard chest. "Let me go, asshole. I'm not your pawn." It was like trying to move a mountain if you were a mere human. Goddess, she hated being so weak.

"Jenna, flash away," Damien growled.

"Ah, but your female can't. It seems I'm her cure, little brothers," Khan taunted.

Lucas stepped forward. "Who are you and what do you want?"

Khan tilted his head to the side. "You have nothing I want. Tell your *father* I'll be in touch. Oh, here," he tossed a necklace onto the bed. "He'll know who I am with that. If not, then you're little plaything will become mine...until I tire of her."

Blackness swirled around Jenna as she heard both Lucas and Damien roar her name. A sick feeling hit her square in the gut, one she knew all too well. Khan was playing a game with the Cordell's. One only he knew the rules to, and he had zero compassion for anyone getting in his way. Jenna just happened to have gotten in his way, or more aptly, given him something to use. Shit, she so could use her Fey powers, or her bestie Kellen right about now. Or even better, if she'd not have been so stubborn and mated with Lucas and Damien, instead of waiting, then none of this would have happened. "Well, what if's do nothing but make big girls cry over spilled milk," she muttered to herself.

"What?" Khan asked as he opened the portal allowing light to filter in.

She blinked a few times. "Huh?"

"You mumbled something about girls crying and spilled milk." He carried her over to a couch and set her down. His gentle touch and actions at war with his words to Damien and Lucas.

The light airy room reminded Jenna of a lake cabin, one that families would go to on vacation. "Oh, um, nothing. I talk to myself sometimes."

Khan shrugged his shoulders. "Make yourself comfy, you'll be here for a spell or two." He winked.

A growl rumbled in her throat. "Hahaha, very funny."

He was next to her in a blink. "No, I'm not funny at all. What I am is deadly. You will do best to remember that." He raised his nails, the longer lengths looking ominous now, reminding her of the night he'd cut her cheek.

"You did something to me when you sliced my cheek open." If he was going to kill her, she'd at least know the hows and whys.

"I didn't realize I'd poison you the same as those ghouls. I spelled these." He clacked his nails together before continuing, "to kill with maximum efficiency. I thought I'd scented something different on you and was just going to take a taste. When I smelled my...the Cordell's blood in you, I realized my chance to finally exact justice on their father was now."

Her world righted itself as she realized why he looked and smelled like her men. "You're their brother?"

"Ding ding ding. Give the girl a prize." Khan walked away, his stride not quite as smooth.

"But...how? I mean, are you?" She was at a loss for words. She'd met both the elder Cordell's, Damikan and Luna and couldn't imagine either of them giving up one of their beloved children.

Khan turned around, his eyes glowing red. "Damikan seduced my mother, then left her for his queen, the shifter bitch. My mother was ruined in the eyes of her clan, tossed out like trash since the Vampire King wouldn't acknowledge her or her child. We had to fend for ourselves, fight for everything we could get, including the ability to sleep without fear we'd be staked at sunrise. All the while, his greatness lived in his grand home with his Hearts Love and created a new family, while me, his eldest son was a beggar in the streets. The things my mother had to do in order to keep us safe would turn your hair grey, until I was old enough to help. Would you like me to tell you some of them, Fey?"

Jenna swallowed, knowing what he was implying. The thought of anyone, man, woman, or child being forced to do anything made her want to rip the nuts off of the ones who did the making. "No, I don't need the details. However, I don't believe for a second that Damikan knew. He's an honorable man."

No sooner had the words left her mouth, before she found herself against the stone floor, an angry Khan looming above her. "You don't know anything. What have you ever had to suffer?"

She wanted to reach out with her powers and soothe his pain away, but had nothing except her arms, yet she didn't want to touch him. "I'm sorry, Khan."

He flashed across the room. "They will come for you, and when they do, I'll kill them and then Damikan will know what suffering is."

Jenna gasped, a spark of her powers flared to life at the thought of Damien and Lucas being hurt. "Over my dead body."

Khan raked his gaze over her prone form. "That can be arranged as well."

In a blink he was gone, leaving her on the cold floor with nothing but a small bit of her former powers. "Goddess, wherever you are, help me please." The last thing she wanted was for her guys to try to save her, only to be hurt or worse, killed in the process. Khan had powers that rivaled that of Damikan, only darker. No, she'd find her Fey spark, and save herself, then figure out what the fuckity fuck happened all those years ago. How the heck could Damikan have fathered a child, a son, and left him with his mother without giving them his protection? By her calculations, he was...thousands of years old at the least since Damien and Lucas were over three millennia. Luna was going to rip his dick off. Jenna smiled in spite of her situation. It was either that or curl up in a ball and cry. It had been thousands of years since she'd indulged in a pity party for one and didn't think this situation merited one, yet.

*****

Damien looked at the empty space where Jennaveve had been only moments before, then at the shocked face of his brother, knowing his own reflected the same. "That couldn't be who it appeared to be." He paced away, his wolf scratched beneath the surface of his skin.

The bedroom looked as if a F10 tornado had been through it in the short amount of time since they'd entered and watched the bastard disappear with their woman. He knelt next to the bed, scenting Jenna's blood. A small smear of her precious life force coated the tile flooring. He ran his finger over the red stain, bringing it to his nose, inhaling, focusing on what had caused the injury. Instant jarring took him into the exact moment their Hearts Love had fallen onto her knees, her cry of pain was like a blade slicing through his own chest. "Why did one of us not stay with her?" Anguish and regret filled him.

Lucas's roar had the windows rattling, his wolf every bit as angry as Damien's. "I don't understand this, but we were both only away from her short periods of time. Whoever...that being was, he knew when to strike. It was as if he had a connection to her."

Distaste soared through Damien. He glared at Lucas, wanting him to take the words back. Their Jennaveve didn't belong to anyone but them. "We must summon father. This happened in his household. Surely he has a way to track whoever came and went."

His brother's eyes flashed blue. "Whoever he was, he's a dead man."

Damien nodded. "In that, we agree."

The door flung open, wind pushing him and Lucas backward as Damikan entered, their mother Luna rushing behind their father. "What the hell is going on? First, I feel a breach in my wards, then I'm summoned," he paused, pointing at his chest. "Me, summoned to a guest suite as if I'm not the King. You have thirty seconds to explain before I teach you and your brother why I am the ruler." The air crackled with power.

It took all his control not to cower in the face of his father's fury as the King of Vampires blasted his dominance at them the very air became heavy, threatening to push him to his knees. He and Lucas both stayed on their feet, fighting the power, holding their bodies straight by sheer will. Blood seeped from his nose, but he wasn't willing to show any weakness, not now, not when Jenna's life was on the line.

"Enough," Luna yelled, stepping between them, holding her arms out. Their mother's head whipped back and forth, tears falling down her cheeks, blood ran from her nose as well.

"Someone took our Jennaveve from your home. He was right here, looking just like you." Lucas stabbed an accusing finger toward Damikan.

Damikan's deep rumble made Lucas's from earlier seem tame as he took a step forward. "What are you saying?"

Damien glanced between his mother and father. No matter how pissed he was, the thought of hurting his mom was something he didn't want to do, but Jenna's life was on the line. "Look into my memories," he said instead of speaking out loud.

"Oh no you don't," Luna spat, blood on her face from where Damikan's dominance had pulsed through the room.

Their father broke his gaze from them, sucking in a breath. "Luna, what...come here." His gentle tone at odds with the anger still simmering in the air.

Luna shook her head. "I want to know what is going on and I won't be brushed aside. Speak, Damien."

With a nod, Damikan wrapped his arms around their mother. "Whatever you have to say, you can say in front of your mother. We have no secrets." As he spoke, his right hand went up and down her body, cleaning the evidence of blood from her.

Luna relaxed into his embrace, the strain melting away.

Lucas came to stand next to him, folding his arms across his chest. "This is the most fucked up thing we've ever encountered and let me tell you, between the two of us, we've seen and done a lot. I know you're both older than dirt, but you've been together since you were both basically kids. In our world, it's unheard of for two to find their Hearts Love so young the way you did, father."

Damikan nodded, his chin resting next to their mother's ear. Damien wondered how they were going to react to the next words that came out of Lucas's mouth. He looked over at his brother, waiting for him to finish.

Lucas shrugged. "I started, you get to finish, old chap."

"Fuck," he swore.

"Damien, really, was that necessary?" Luna asked.

Damikan growled.

Every moment they stood there and put the conversation off, the longer Jenna was in the other man's hands. "Use your senses, dad, tell me, us, what do you smell. Who do you sense when you enter? You felt the breach to your wards, track the intruder and tell us who it was, or who you think it was. Then I'll tell you who was here."

"Enough of these riddles, Damien. Your Hearts Love has been taken and you want to play games? If it were my Luna, I'd rip the very fabric of this world apart to reach her." His father's eyes flashed to obsidian.

Damian nodded. "It seems there was a woman before our mother who you must've felt something for since you gave her a son."

His words fell like stones dropping down the side of a mountain. Again, the pressure built in the room. His mother's gasp and shocked disbelief was clear on her beautiful olive complexion.

"What the hell are you talking about? I have no other sons." Damikan turned Luna to face him.

"He is not mother's child, but yours. Look into my memories. Both of you." Damien wasn't willing to force himself into his parent's mind, but he opened his memories for them, allowing them to see and hear what the stranger had looked like and said.

"How?" Luna asked, her hand cover her mouth, the other over her heart.

Damikan released her, moving around the room in a slow methodical way. His head tilting this way and that. When he reached the far corner near the fireplace, he stopped, inhaled deeply then disappeared.

"Shit, where did he go?" Damien tried to trace and follow, calling out for his father's elite soldiers as he did, only to come up against a solid shield, keeping him locked inside the castle. "No," he roared.

Lucas reappeared next to him, his fist bloody. "I tried to break out through the back gates, but he has us warded in. Why would he do that?"

Pain and betrayal slashed at Damien, echoing through the twin bond he shared with Lucas. Looking over to where their mother stood, she seemed smaller, more fragile than ever before. He took a step toward her. "Mother...I," he stopped.

Luna held her head up. "Do not apologize for something you have no control over. We will get Jennaveve back, and I will handle your father." Her eyes flashed blue, fur rippled over her and then their human mother was replaced by that of her wolf. Anytime she needed time or space, she'd always told them she needed her fur. Now, was clearly one of those times.

"Fuuuck," Damien roared, his wolf and vampire being battled within him. He wanted to shift to his wolven form and rip through the walls of the castle until he found Jenna, but knew she was not anywhere near. The link that bound them was tenuous at best, and it seemed to be fading.

"What about the Iron Wolf? They have a...special connection," Lucas spat.

Walking over to the shredded bedding he picked up what was left of the pillow case, pulling it to his nose. "I think I just threw up in my mouth when you said that, but it has merit. Can you link with the asshole?"

*****

Lucas opened his mind and concentrated on Jenna's best friend Kellen Styles of the Iron Wolves. He knew the shifter had just become a father to quadruplets and truly, almost, in a slight way, hated to bug the bastard. However, he also knew if Jenna couldn't reach them, she would try to get into contact with the one she called her bestie. Yeah, like Damien, just thinking that way had him gagging. One day she'd look at him and his brother as her besties. Fuck, he was becoming a giant pussy thinking that way. Next, he'd schedule them regular mani and pedi sessions together.

When the link didn't immediately link him with Kellen, his fists clenched at his sides. He felt a pain behind his eyes as he strained harder. "Motherfucker, why would he do that to us. It's like he's crippled us here while our woman could be." He swallowed unable to continue with the words.

Damien waved his hand around the room, putting everything back to the way it had been when they walked in. They could erase the damage, but not the memory of watching her frightened face or the words that came out of the man, no the beings mouth. "He called us his little brothers. That would mean our father had him with another woman. Clearly, he's walking around during the day, so he's not a full vamp. Is he like us?"

Lucas thought back to the very beginning, rewinding it in his mind then allowing the scene to unfold in slow motion. The man looked almost identical to their father, down to his towering height, to the obsidian eyes. Damien and he had blue eyes thanks to their mother, but not him. Their father only had blue eyes when he became a wolf/hybrid and that was if he wasn't angry. His memory latched onto the nails the other man had flashed, the sharp points looked as if he purposely made them sharper, longer. "He wants to appear sinister. Everything he did was to scare Jennaveve. If he wanted to hurt our dad, killing her would hurt him, but it wouldn't truly devastate him. What is his end game?"

"I don't give a flying fuck what his end game is, I'm going to end his game," Damien promised.

He met Damien's stare, nodding. "If he's hurt one hair on her head, he's a dead man, brother or not."

"I'm going to bleed him for taking her and scaring her, brother or not, that's non-negotiable." Damien crossed his arms over his chest.

Lucas put his hands on his hips. "You looking for me to argue, cause newsflash, it ain't happening."

Damien put his hand out, waiting for Lucas to take it. "Jennaveve is ours to protect, ours to love, ours to get back, no matter the cost."

Lucas gripped his brother's palm, each one shifting until a nail elongated, slicing into the others palm, sealing the vow. "We will do whatever it takes to bring her back to us safely. Damned to all who stand in our way." Magic crackled between them as they both made the blood oath.

Coming 2017

About Elle Boon

Elle Boon lives in Middle-Merica as she likes to say...with her husband, two kids, and a black lab who is more like a small pony. She'd never planned to be a writer, but when life threw her a curve, she swerved with it, since she's athletically challenged. She's known for saying "Bless Your Heart" and dropping lots of F-bombs, but she loves where this new journey has taken her.

She writes what she loves to read, and that is romance, whether it's erotic, Navy SEALs, or paranormal, as long as there is a happily ever after. Her biggest hope is that after readers have read one of her stories, they fall in love with her characters as much as she did. She loves creating new worlds, and has more stories just waiting to be written. Elle believes in happily ever afters, and can guarantee you will always get one with her stories.

Connect with Elle online, she loves to hear from you:

http://www.elleboon.com/

https://www.facebook.com/elle.boon

https://www.facebook.com/Elle-Boon-Author-1429718517289545/

https://twitter.com/ElleBoon1

https://www.facebook.com/groups/RacyReads/

https://www.facebook.com/groups/188924878146358/

https://www.facebook.com/groups/1405756769719931/

https://www.facebook.com/groups/wewroteyourbookboyfriends/

https://www.goodreads.com/author/show/8120085.Elle_Boon

https://www.bookbub.com/authors/elle-boon

https://www.instagram.com/elleboon/

http://www.elleboon.com/newsletter/

Other Books by Elle Boon

Erotic Ménage
Ravens of War
Selena's Men
Two For Tamara
Jaklyn's Saviors
Kira's Warriors
Shifters Romance
Mystic Wolves
Accidentally Wolf & His Perfect Wolf
Jett's Wild Wolf
Bronx's Wicked Wolf
Paranormal Romance
SmokeJumpers
FireStarter
Berserker's Rage
A SmokeJumpers Christmas
Mind Bender, Coming Soon
MC Shifters Erotic
Iron Wolves MC
Lyric's Accidental Mate
Xan's Feisty Mate
Kellen's Tempting Mate
Slater's Enchanted Mate
Dark Lovers
Bodhi's Synful Mate
Turo's Fated Mate
Contemporary Romance
Miami Nights
Miami Inferno

Rescuing Miami, Dallas Fire & Rescue
Standalone
Wild and Dirty, Wild Irish Series
SEAL Team Phantom Series
Delta Salvation
Delta Recon
Delta Rogue
Mission Saving Shayna, Omega Team
Protecting Teagan, Special Forces
Delta Redemption

17-18

DISCARD

CPSIA information can be obtained
at www.ICGtesting.com
Printed in the USA
LVHW011452301018
595357LV00010B/679/P

9 781978 349629